MANDRAKE MANOR

Henbane Hollow Book One

9th Publishing

Contents

For every outcast, misfit, and queer person seeking refuge - may you find comfort here.

Introduction

This book was written as a serial. Chapters were written as contained weekly episodes from October 2022 to June 2023. I'm excited to have them all together, in their original serial form, in this season one volume of Mandrake Manor.

1

In the twilight's shroud, beware the Snare,
A plant of nightshade lineage rare.
Each part toxic, handle with care,
Guard your life from Devil's Stare.

Bewitching weed, Jimson's tale,
In Jamestown's lore, soldiers did ail.
For the alkaloids, they unveil,
Spin dreams into a delirious gale.

Yet in the old, a cure it hides,
For lungs that wheeze on windy tides.
Respect its power, for danger abides,
In Devil's Snare, the witch confides.

Devil's Snare

- MAT -

Dear Mr. Mandrake,

We have been trying to contact you through your family line without success. Due to time constraints, this is our last attempt.

Your late great aunt, Melinda Mandrake, has included you in her last will and testament.

Because of aforementioned time constraints, you must complete any remaining paperwork immediately, or forfeit your inheritance, to avert any financial or earthly ruin. Please come to Jimson Law, at 600 66th Street, Chicago, IL on March 21st at 9 a.m. sharp. Please be prompt, as we will deduct any expenses used to reach you *from a fund the late Melinda has put aside.*

We've included a map to the exact location, as GPS may not recognize the address.

Respectfully,
Demetri Demonte

Mat eyed the map once again, then he glanced back at his phone's GPS. He was there, where 600 66th Street should be, parked on the side of the road, staring out toward an empty field in the middle of Chicago.

Townhouses lined the other side of the street. He held the map up and confirmed several house numbers, triangulating his position. He was in the right spot.

The clock of his old, beat-up green Kia hatchback ticked away another minute, 8:58.

"Dammit," he muttered to himself, staring into his bright green eyes in the rearview mirror and running his hands through his ginger scruff. He crumpled up the paper and tossed it behind him. Another stupid prank or ill-thought scam. This one had even made him call his mother, a thing he'd sworn off doing ever since she left him stranded in an empty home for a year to finish high school as she and her new husband moved down to Florida.

"You're not moving in with us when you're done with school, right? We don't have room for you," was the last thing his mother said before he hung up on her.

No, Mom, I'd rather live in a dumpster. He looked back toward the townhouses, wishing he could afford something like that. With the way things were going, the dumpster might be his only option.

Apparently, the great city of Chicago was jammed full of dentists, and no offices were looking for brand-new graduates. His only prospect now was a studio apartment with five roommates while he found some entry-level job to hold him over.

Mat stuck his keys in the ignition as the clock on his dashboard flipped to 9 a.m. He looked back out toward the empty field once again, and his mouth fell open. It was no longer empty.

The once empty field now had a stone path leading through a short white picket fence, past landscaped bushes and trees and up to a small one-story cottage. An entire forest surrounded the house, and trees that weren't there moments ago now towered over the townhouses, casting a shadow on his car. A sign hung above the doors to the cottage, with the words Jimson Law painted in black and gold lettering.

A Black man, the same age as Mat and dressed in a perfectly tailored gray suit, stepped out of the house and stood on the stoop. Mat's eyes widened, both from the materialization of the house and the very attractive man with a shaved head, well-maintained beard, and a smile that gleamed in the beams of sunlight filtering through the trees.

Mat fumbled out of his car and smoothed his shirt, noting that his salmon shorts and linen button-up were perhaps a little too casual for whatever he was getting himself into.

As Mat rounded the Kia, the man met him at the small waist-high gate, unlatching it as he said with a smooth baritone voice, "Mathias Mandrake for our 9 o'clock, yes?"

Oh god, he's even more attractive up close, and his eyes seem to sparkle. Really, whose eyes sparkle like that? Mat smiled awkwardly and stumbled over his words. "I. Yes, but I go by Mat. How? There was an empty park here a second ago. And a suit. Should I have worn a suit? I feel like I should be in a suit."

The man only smiled and ushered Mat through the gate. "Buildings come and go, but this one is here now, and we have an appointment. As for the suit, I like to look refined for my clients, but you'd be surprised by some of the attire my clients choose to meet me in."

Mat blushed. "What does that mean?"

"I've said too much already. I am Demetri Demonte. It's a pleasure to finally meet you, Mr. Mandrake."

Demetri stepped past Mat and held the door open, carrying with him the scent of a smoky whiskey cologne that sent Mat's mind racing.

"Um, thanks. Pleasure to meet you too? What is this all—" Mat paused, noting that the inside of the cottage was much bigger. Unexplainably bigger, with a massive foyer and rooms to either side that were easily four times larger than they were outside.

"All your questions will be answered momentarily. Would you like any coffee or tea?"

All that Mat could muster was, "How is . . . ?"

Demetri placed a hand on Mat's shoulder and ushered him forward. "No, then? Why don't we head to my office?"

He led Mat down a hall that was certainly longer than the house, turned, and led Mat down another hall just as long before opening a set of French doors.

His office was filled with books resting on deep wooden shelves that carried over to the dark mahogany desk. A pair of rich red leather chairs sat on one side of the desk, and a massive, throne-like red leather chair rested on the other.

Mat took a seat in one chair, and Demetri claimed the seat behind the desk, grabbing a stack of folders and resting them in front of him. "I want to start by apologizing for the late notice. We tried contacting you earlier, but we had to resort to other means to get your address."

"Other means?"

"Let's just say we hired a private investigator to locate you after your parents failed to give us your whereabouts."

"Mother," Mat corrected. "That asshole she's with is not my father."

"Noted. Yet, regardless, I have you here now, and we have a few things we need to go over to keep your claim on the estate before time runs out."

Mat frowned. "Estate?"

Demetri flipped open the folder. "Your great aunt has left you as the sole heir to her entire estate. Primarily, this includes a property, and all the items within, in a neighborhood called Henbane Hollow."

Mat's heart thrummed heavily in his chest and his voice strained. "Wait. What? Property? A house? I have a house?" He stared at the desk, his breath racing away.

Demetri held up a hand. "You have a claim to the house, yes. Mandrake Manor, at 13 Wormwood Way in Henbane Hollow up in Connecticut."

And there it was. "Connecticut? I don't know anyone in Connecticut. How much is it worth? Can I just sell it?"

Demetri winced and pulled out a handwritten letter from the folder's contents. "Well, no. The will has a few stipulations to prevent the inheritor from outright selling the house within a year of ownership. You may, however, decline the offer, as the will provided a list of several others in line for inheritance."

Bile filled his mouth, and his breathing slowed. "A year? Why? What condition is the house in?"

Demetri flipped through a few pages. "Well, the estate provides a stipend for repairs. Mandrake Manor is an old house. One that has been in the Mandrake family for generations."

"That doesn't answer my question."

"I have not been granted permission to enter the house, but I have been told the inside is in much better condition than the outside. From what I have seen of the estate, some major repairs are needed."

Mat leaned back in his chair and crossed his arms, nodding to the paperwork. "When do you need an answer? I'm not even out of college yet. I can't. I've got plans."

Demetri pulled another paper from the folder and smiled. "You're graduating from a college of dentistry, yes? And I hear you're having trouble with job placement, correct?"

Mat frowned. "Yes? How did you—"

"It just so happens that the town a few miles from Henbane Hollow has a dental office in need of an expansion. I could put in a good word if you'd like."

Mat let out a laugh. *This is insane. It can't be real.* "Sure, a mysterious lawyer shows up in a house that was a field and offers me a house and a job. Okay, where are the cameras?"

"No cameras, Mr. Mandrake. Henbane Hollow is a tight-knit community, and I respected Melinda for all that she did for us. For her to list you as primary heir holds some significance." Demetri rested his hands on the papers and leaned forward in his seat, his eyes locked on Mat. "So, if I need to pull some strings to get you to move in, I will."

Mat frowned. *Was that a proposition? No. Calm down, Mat. Think. Stay in Chicago, with friends but no job, or move across the country with a house, job, and potentially flirty lawyer?*

"Okay," Mat said, turning away and rubbing his arms. "If you land me a job, I'll do it."

Demetri smiled and pulled several papers from his file. "Perfect. Then before you leave today, I need some signatures, and the house is yours."

Mat skimmed through the documents, spotting things like "the owner of Mandrake Manor promises to abide by all laws, treaties, and contracts of Henbane Hollow," and "I acknowledge that no agreement, legal or metaphysical, supersedes the ownership of Mandrake Manor to proclaimed heirs."

"What is all this?" Mat asked.

"Melinda Mandrake was very thorough in her contracts. Speaking of, there is one more thing now that you have agreed to take the home. Melinda asked that the new owner move in with roommates. Two of them, to be specific. It also states that I am not to hand over the keys until you've arrived with said housemates."

Mat frowned, and his heart sank. "What? Why? I don't know if I can do that."

Demetri leaned back in his chair and smiled. "I'm sure a college man like yourself has several friends stuck in the same predicament as you who might find life in Connecticut a bit more freeing." He pulled a card from the table and slid it to Mat. "If any of them need a job, let me know. I've worked with nearly everyone in a sixty-mile radius of Henbane, and they all owe me favors."

Mat picked up the pen. "I'm really doing this," he said as he signed the first paper.

2

Old Man's Beard, an herbal balm,
For wounded palm and spirits calm.
From bark, a salve, like nature's psalm,
Heals cuts and soothes, brings injured qualm.

Blossoms white, in spring's warm light,
While moth takes flight, and borer's might,
Threaten Fringe, yet it stands, in spite,
A testament to nature's fight.

In this tree's shade, remedies are made,
By bark's aid, injuries fade.
Known as Fringetree, its fame won't jade,
A healing friend in forest glade.

Old Man's Beard

- FRANKIE -

T he sun beamed onto Frankie's face as he stretched underneath soft sheets, sheets that didn't feel like his own, on a bed significantly bigger than the one he was used to. He opened his eyes and frowned.

The taste of cheap vodka still lingered on his breath, and as he took in the various baseball posters and navy blue sheets, the previous evening started to stitch together.

Another college party, aptly named "End of the World," since he and the other seniors were nearing graduation. He'd danced for hours in a room packed with sweaty bodies and flashing red lights. Danced, ground, and then found a wall to make out with one of the frat boys. One thing led to another, and they found their way back up to the frat boy's room. A frat boy named Brad, per the heavily red-lined homework on his desk.

His phone dinged from a pile of clothes in the corner of the room. Escaping the comforts of the warm bed and the memories from the night before, he grabbed a pair of underwear he hoped was his and picked up his phone.

> *Mat [7:35 a.m.]: Frankie, pls, can we talk? I know ur still mad about the money for the apt, but something came up. Can u meet today?*

Frankie rolled his eyes and tossed the phone onto his pile of clothes. He was still mad. Mad that Mat had pretended to care about moving into an apartment with Frankie after college, and now Frankie was about to be living with three randos and footing double the rent. He didn't even want to move in with these guys, but Frankie had hoped it would be a little less trashy with Mat around.

Mat was Frankie's wingman, whether he knew it or not, introducing Frankie to the baseball team back when they were sophomores, before Mat came out. If only Mat knew what Frankie had done with about half his ex-teammates.

There was a slight knock on the door, followed by a whisper. "You decent?"

Frankie looked down at his mostly naked body, thin with a collection of tattoos only slightly masked by dark body hair in all the right places. He glanced in the full body mirror behind the door and ran his fingers through his shoulder-length black curls, a genetic gift from his gorgeous Mexican mother. "I am decent, if I do say so myself."

An All-American Midwestern with the looks you'd expect from an Illinois boy named Brad, falling into the "if you squint hard enough, he looks like Captain America" category, stepped into the room carrying a plate of scrambled eggs. He gave Frankie one look, eyes wide, and slammed the door shut. "That's not what I meant."

Frankie smiled. "Aww, you made me breakfast?"

Brad kept his head down and sat on the edge of his bed, eyeing his plate. "Uh, no. I need to get ready for practice."

Frankie leaned against the door, arching his back slightly. "Well, aren't you a gentleman?"

Brad's eyes met Frankie's, then they trailed down from Frankie's face, and he blushed. "I—I'm sorry. I'm just gonna be late if I don't. Can you please put on some clothes?"

Pushing himself off the wall, Frankie crossed the room and sidled up to Brad, gripping his thigh. "Aw, you weren't so shy last night."

Brad shrugged him off. "That was different. Look, the other guys are waking up. Do you mind if you . . . ?"

"Crawl out your window so your homophobic friends don't know that you pitch for a different team? Yeah, I know the protocol." He looked over at his phone, seeing it light up from another message. "I've made breakfast plans, anyway."

"Oh, good. Thanks." Brad let out a loud sigh and stuffed a forkful of eggs into his mouth. "I promise, if you come back, you won't have to keep doing that."

Frankie squeezed Brad's thigh once more before standing. "Oh, I'm sure I will. You're a junior, right?"

Brad nodded.

"So, if I come back, you've got another year in this hellhole to look like a good straight team player." He pulled on his pants and shook his head. "God, why can't I just find me a sexy, out sugar daddy instead of fishing in a pool of closeted underclassmen?"

Brad frowned. "Hey, I might get signed on. Then I could be your sugar daddy."

"Aw, you're sweet, albeit a little dumb," Frankie said, opening the window. He looked back at Brad and grinned. "Better keep this window unlocked. The gay fairy might come back for seconds."

"So, let me get this straight. You went to the place, but it wasn't there, but then it was, and you signed some contracts in order to get a house in a state you've never been to from a relative you didn't know you had?" Frankie said, lifting his latte with both hands and taking a sip.

Mat's head fell into his hands, and he mumbled, "Yeah, that's what happened."

"What in the Pan's Labyrinth meets Bedazzled drugs were you on? Is that why you haven't been talking to me?"

Mat rubbed his eyes with the palms of his hands. "Yeah. I wasn't on any. It just didn't make sense at the time. I can't explain it. But it's real. I know it."

Frankie shook his head. "I found us a nice apartment months ago, before everything was taken. Yeah, it's a little tight, and the other roommates are questionable at best, but it fits both of our budgets. And you want to leave that for some scam over in Connecticut?"

"It's not a scam. It can't be. But I won't know unless I find two roommates."

Frankie rolled his eyes and let his gaze wander the cafe. He couldn't handle this right now. Not when graduation was in three weeks and he still didn't know if he could pay his new roommates on time.

His eyes fell on the barista, a broad-shouldered man in a tight plaid button-up and a thick dark beard peppered with gray who stood behind the cafe counter, cleaning off the steamer.

"At least you brought me somewhere good for my morning dilf hunt," Frankie said.

Mat looked over and frowned. "Dilf hunt? What?"

"It's something new I'm trying. And it's not my fault he's cute. You can't tell me he isn't cute," Frankie said, sipping on his latte.

"Him? He's like twice your age."

Frankie caught the man's attention and smiled. "And as long as his hips still work, who cares if they've been replaced a time or two?"

Mat rolled his eyes. "What have you done with the real Frankie? I know every one of your escapades. In painstakingly granular detail. None of them contained a single person older than you."

Frankie shrugged. "Maybe I need a sugar daddy in my life. Someone whose looks are as refined as their wallets."

"And that's this guy?"

"No." Frankie rolled his eyes. "But he's a start."

"I didn't bring you here to hook up with the barista. Frankie, I'm serious, this house is real. An entire house. You. Me. And someone else. That's it. And the lawyer said he'd pull some strings if you're looking for a job."

Frankie's gaze was still on the barista. "Do you know him?"

"The lawyer? No, not really, but I believe—"

"No, the barista. You'd tell me if you knew him, right?" Frankie asked.

"Oh, my god, Frankie. Are you even listening to me?"

"Ugh, yes, *dad*. Mystery hot lawyer is the answer to both of our dreams. I got it."

"So, does that mean you'll do it? You'll move with me?"

Frankie pulled his gaze away from the man and looked at Mat. They'd been best friends since freshman year in college, nearly inseparable for three and a half years. Now, Frankie stood at a crossroads. One way led to an apartment in a city he knew and loved but with people he barely trusted. The other way was with his best friend across the country to a house he knew nothing about.

Someone cleared their throat, and Frankie looked up to see the bearded man standing next to their table, holding two lattes in his hands. "These two are on the house, gentlemen." He set the mugs down and pulled a napkin from his pocket, placing it next to Frankie's cup. On the napkin was a phone number, written in pen. He winked at Frankie before turning away without another word.

Mat reached for the napkin, but Frankie snatched it up and pocketed it, a grin spreading across his face. "Morning dilf hunt is a success. I need to do this more often."

Mat's face reddened, and he sipped his latte. "And if you screw anything up, I'll have another coffee shop I can't come back to."

"The last time wasn't me. That doesn't count," Frankie said, rolling his eyes.

"Fine. But you haven't answered. Will you move with me?"

Frankie traced a finger around the lip of his mug and sighed. "They'd better have a decent coffee shop nearby. And hot guys, or I'm out."

Mat nearly jumped out of his seat as he smiled ear to ear. "Oh, my god, yes! You are amazing. I promise I will help you drag out any and all hot guys you can handle."

"Damn right you will, and the demand is high."

"You got it. Now all we need is a third. Any ideas? And don't you dare say the barista."

Frankie looked out the window and frowned. "I might have someone in mind, and I don't think it will take much to convince them."

3

Groundwart, the Fiber Vase,
Beneath pine's canopy, takes its place.
A fungal shield, in every case,
Stays root rot's advancing pace.

In sandy soil, its threads uncoil,
From Europe to North America's soil.
To birch, and oak, and beech it clings,
In nature's choir, it silent sings.

Neither feast nor famine hinders growth,
It shields the trees from pathogen's oath.
Groundwart, unseen, in roots entwined,
In the sacred script of the intertwined.

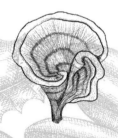

Groundwart

- AUGUST -

"Why don't we just make August the tiebreaker?" Taylor asked.

August's attention snapped back to the table and their friends. Taylor and Shawn sat around a circular outdoor table at a cafe Shawn had insisted they try. Taylor, who had a shaved head a lot like August's and wore a bright green tank top, stared at August, waiting for an answer.

August picked up their cup of cold brew and took a sip, glaring at Taylor. "Why are you pulling me into this?"

Shawn, who wore a set of massive rose-colored glasses and sported an asymmetrical bob of blue hair, shrugged. "It makes sense to me. You're like an impartial judge, since you're not coming."

There it was. The little knife jabbed into August's side. All August's friends had decided within the last month of college to up and move to Los Angeles to pursue the Hollywood dream. August, on the other hand, wasn't interested. "Fine, what do you want?"

Taylor played with the food in front of them. "So the apartment we found only has space for three bedrooms, but there are five of us. We don't want to start any drama right off the bat, but if you pick—"

"You can all blame me?"

"Exactly," Shawn said.

"Well, gee, thanks."

"You could always come with us," Taylor said. "Then it's just deciding who rooms with who."

August shook their head. "Absolutely not. I grew up there, and I have no interest in going back."

Shawn sighed. "But you'd land a job so quick. With your writing, you'd be a showrunner in no time."

August took another sip of coffee. This wasn't the first time they'd heard this pitch. Maybe if they hadn't seen decades of their father trying and failing to land anything that could consistently put food on the table, then they'd consider it an option. "It's not the life I want."

Taylor looked past August and frowned. "And here is? Do you even have anything lined up?"

August shrugged. "I don't know. Not really? I've got my RA application for the summer still pending. I figured that would hold me over while I apply for jobs."

"And you'd rather that than LA?" Shawn asked.

"Yep. LA would mean writing screenplays and working for other people. I know me. I know I'd fall right into the same chase my dad did. At least here I'm far enough away that I can pick up a job and work on the novel between breaks without thinking it has to be a screenplay."

Shawn stretched their arms overhead and said, "Whatever, less competition for me then. But you didn't answer who should be roomed together."

August finished their cold brew and crossed their arms. "The real question is, who shouldn't be roomed with anyone? We all know Cory snores like he's a chainsaw. Why would you subject anyone else to that when they don't have to? Unless one of you two will sleep in the same room as him."

Taylor laughed and nodded. "Point taken. I'll need more than a wall to drown out that sound."

Shawn groaned. "See? This is why we need you."

August's phone buzzed in their pocket. "Still not going to happen."

"I'm just saying," Shawn said. "If things don't work out here, you'll have a space at the apartment."

"I'll bring my earbuds," August said, pulling out their phone.

They tapped on their screen, and a message popped up.

> *Frankie [10:24 a.m.]: Hey, did you hear back about RA? Got an opening for a place, super cheap. Interested?*

They cleared their throat. "Or I might have a place of my own sooner than I thought."

August stared at the bathroom graffiti inside the dingy gas station known as Gobb's Gas and Grocery, wondering who in their right mind would call any of these numbers for a "good time." Maybe Frankie, if he was desperate enough.

They stepped out of the stall, averting their eyes as a large old man zipped himself up at the urinals and scurried out of the bathroom without even a glance at the sink.

Gross.

August let the water run for a few seconds, clearing out the brown color, and cupped water in their hands, letting the ice-cold water wake them up as they rubbed their face. They ran a hand through their short buzz cut and stared at themself in the mirror.

Their eyes shone a light color of gray in this light, and they pulled out a dangling silver earring from their pocket and stuck it in their ear, trying their best not to look at the grime and potential mold caked up on the sink.

Had they made a mistake leaving Chicago?

The RA position fell through anyway, but here they were, headed to this mysterious Mandrake Manor. Who knew if it was even real? And now they were stuck in the middle of nowhere.

No. August shook their head. Frankie said it was a gamble, but they had to trust the process. Connecticut was the complete opposite of LA, both physically and metaphorically, everything August wanted. And if the manor really was free to live in, then August could actually manage a part-time job while working on their novel. It would be a dream come true.

They finished up in the bathroom and found the man who'd passed them in the bathroom sitting behind the counter. He wore overalls with an embroidered *Gobb* across the chest. Before leaving, they stopped and grabbed a granola bar, luckily not expired in a place like this, and stopped at the checkout.

"This all?" the man croaked.

He looked up at August, his nose protruding out at a sharp point, and his neck, jaw, and mouth much wider than August felt they should be.

For a moment, August swore they saw the man's skin shimmer a shade of green, but when they blinked, it was back to normal.

"Yes. Well. No. We're trying to get to Henbane Hollow, but our car died. Have you heard of it?"

The man grabbed their granola bar and scanned it, shaking his head. "I've heard of it. Why the hell is someone like you going there?"

August frowned. "Someone like me? What does that mean?"

He looked up at them with dull green eyes and shrugged. "Not what you think. You're about four hours out if you take fifteen south and get back on eighty. That'll be three even." He held out his hand.

They wanted to press him for more, but the look on his face told them he was done with questions.

August paid and headed outside, finding Frankie and Mat leaning against the aptly named Green Machine packed with all three of their essentials. The three of them had rolled it an eighth of a mile to this gas station once the engine stalled on them.

"Any news?" August asked as they popped open the back passenger door and sat down.

Frankie looked over at Mat, wide-eyed, and shook his head.

"Hello? Hello?" Mat said, looking at his phone and groaning. "Great. It's dead."

"Well, they weren't much of a help anyway," Frankie said.

"How is it that no towing company is open after five? Are we supposed to just sleep in this car until sunrise?"

August peeled open their granola bar. "I remember driving by a motel about a half hour ago."

Frankie nodded. "That's the closest one." He ran a hand through his hair. "I'm sorry. I shouldn't have told you to take this shortcut. If we'd just stuck to the main roads, we'd probably be somewhere nice for the night."

Mat looked up at the sky and sighed. "No, it doesn't matter how we ended up here. We're here now."

August smiled at that. Had this happened to any of their friends, one of them would have found someone else to blame. Maybe they didn't make the wrong decision. "Is there anyone else we can call?"

Frankie snapped his fingers. "What about that cute lawyer?"

"How can he help? Subpoena the car dealership?" Mat said.

"Well, wait," August started. "When you were gushing over him, you said he knew everyone in the area. We've got to be, what, three, maybe four hours out? He might know someone who could help."

Mat nodded and stared at his phone. "Well, I'm out of juice." He fished a card out of his pocket and held it up. "Either of you want to call?"

August held out their hand and spoke before Frankie had the chance. "I got it."

As they typed in the number, they noticed how weathered the card was.

The phone rang for a solid minute before a smooth, deep voice spoke on the other end. "Hello? This is Jimson Law, Demetri Demonte speaking."

"Uh," August started. "Hi, this is August, Mat's roommate for Mandrake Manor."

"Ah, August. Pleasure to finally hear your voice. Have you three made it to Henbane alright? I know the directions can be a bit tricky."

August turned away as both Frankie and Mat waved their arms for August to get to the point. "Actually. We're stuck. About three or four hours away at a gas station. I guess the engine couldn't take a fifteen-hour drive like we thought."

"Ah, how unfortunate. So I presume I'm your last resort?"

"Yeah, actually. Mat's phone died, and all the towing companies are closed."

"Unfortunate indeed," Demetri said.

August waited for him to say more, yet he remained quiet. They turned and looked at Frankie and Mat and frowned. "So, do you think you could help us?"

They heard a strange buzzing on the other end of the line, followed by Demetri speaking in an even lower voice, "I may call on you for a favor in the future. Do you accept those terms?"

August frowned. What the hell did that mean? They turned back to Frankie and Mat, realizing they'd already dove into the deep end by coming in the first place. "Yes, I can do that."

Demetri's voice returned to his normal, deep baritone. "Excellent, then it is settled. Which gas station are you stuck at?"

August looked up at the sign. "Gobb's Gas and Grocery."

"Ah, well, that makes it easy, then. I'm in the next town over running some errands. I can pick you three up, and I'll find someone to pick up Mat's car first thing tomorrow morning and bring it over to Gobb's Garage."

"Gobb's Garage? Are you serious? There's another place called Gobb?"

Demetri chuckled. "They're related. Good people too, once you push past the brash exterior."

"Well, keep me clear of the other one. I asked about Henbane, and this one didn't seem to think I belonged there."

"Ah," Demetri said. "The Gobbs are a bit . . . protective of the people in Henbane Hollow. I'm sure once he learns where you're moving, his tune will change."

August paused. "Why's that?"

"You'll see. Anyway, I should be there in about twenty minutes. See you soon," Demetri said before hanging up.

4

Henbane, herb of mystery's lore,
Narcotic power, danger's core.
In ointments old, for skin's relief,
Yet, misuse yields a deadly grief.

Ancient brews of nightshade's kin,
In drunken sleep, life grows thin.
In prophecy, oracles' choice,
Yet holds a deadly, slumbering voice.

Brewer's herb, in beers of old,
In rites and rituals, spirits bold.
Witches' tool, in darkness danced,
Beware the fall to Henbane's trance.

Henbane

- MAT -

"Are you sure you know where we're going?" Mat asked Demetri after the third time he turned the car around.

Three hours earlier, Demetri had pulled into the gas station in a black Cadillac, like a knight in shining armor. Mat thought the man couldn't be any more handsome than in his full suit, but low and behold, a rolled sleeve button-up and a pair of jeans that fit in all the right places somehow made him look better.

In no time, they were back on the road after Demetri helped pull their luggage out of the Green Machine and into his SUV. And, as Mat was dazed by the man and his damn smoky whiskey intoxicating cologne, Frankie and August took the back seats, leaving Mat to fend for himself up front.

"No, we're not lost," Demetri said, gripping the steering wheel and squinting into the dark woods. "Sometimes the entrance gets away from me. It can be finicky like that."

A hand jutted between Mat and Demetri, pointing forward. "Wait, was that there before?" August asked.

Mat followed August's finger to a small gravel driveway to the right of the county road up ahead.

"Good eye," Demetri said. "I promise it'll be easier to find once it gets used to you."

"Don't you mean once we get used to it?" Frankie asked.

Demetri shook his head. "No. You'll see. All in due time."

Mat frowned. "What kind of neighborhood is this hard to find? Should we be worried?"

Frankie checked his phone. "At least there's service, but this is giving me some serious *Get Out* vibes."

They turned onto the gravel road, and Mat held on to his seat belt as he jostled around in his seat.

"It's not that bad, I promise," Demetri said.

Leaves and branches brushed against the SUV as they drove up a small hill. Gravel turned back into solid pavement as they broke free from the brush.

In front of them was a massive black iron gate adorned with brass filigree and the letters HH. On either side was a tall stone wall that trailed off into the woods with burning iron lanterns spaced out every few yards.

Mat didn't know what he'd expected when he'd heard names like Mandrake Manor or Henbane Hollow, but he didn't imagine a gated community that looked more like some ancient castle entrance in the middle of the woods. He looked behind him, noting that the paved road continued around a bend in the woods, and the graveled path they'd been on was completely gone.

He frowned. "Wait. Where's the . . . ?"

"Holy shit," Frankie said.

Demetri pulled the car up to the gate and rolled down his window, waving at an attendant standing in a booth next to the gates.

"Hold on, we have security too?" August said.

Demetri looked into his rearview and smiled. "Henbane Hollow is one of the oldest communities that came over from Europe. We've always had a guard at the entrance. It helps keep the peace. We don't want anyone just strolling into the neighborhood."

The guard shambled out of the booth, one leg dragging behind him and his mouth stretched open at an odd angle. He looked more like some kind of zombie as he approached the fence, baring a pair of bright yellow teeth.

"Uh, is he okay?" Mat asked.

"Yes," Demetri said, his next words loud enough for the guard to hear. "Gary just likes to make a dramatic entrance."

The guard raised an eyebrow and stood up straight. "Dramatic? Come on, when do I get to pull the gates open for new guests?"

"Just hurry up. They've been on the road for hours and would probably like to settle in for the night."

"Alright, alright," he said as he peered into the SUV. "Well, come back when you've rested for the full Gary experience."

He swung open the gates and waved the SUV through. As they drove past, Mat caught Gary's gaze and swore the man's gaunt face had turned into a pitted and torn mass of flesh with one missing eye, but when he blinked, the man was back to normal, waving them off.

Before he could ask, the sight of Henbane Hollow drew him in. Old black lampposts lit up the street, trailing up perfectly flat cobblestone sidewalks and manicured lawns. Nearly all the homes past the entrance were typical cookie-cutter suburban homes with beige siding and large French windows. But after Demetri took a turn onto Snakeroot Street, the typical suburbia was intermixed with strange houses and plots of land.

Some were cottage homes that looked like they were pulled right out of a storybook, some looked like they had been carved out of a massive tree, and others were just a plot of land with a cave entrance or a well into unknown depths.

After another turn onto Belladonna Boulevard, Mat couldn't contain himself. "Well, some of these houses are—"

"Different," August said.

Demetri nodded. "That they are. Many homes are generations old, passed down through family lines tracing back to the first settlers from Europe." He let out a sigh and said, "But as you saw with the other homes, we are in the middle of a community revitalization."

Frankie peered out his window and mumbled, "That explains the Stepford houses. I hope whoever is heading that up knows that if every house looked the same, in a gated community in the forest, that they would check all the boxes for me to get the hell out."

"I'll take it up with the HOA. You three are in luck, though. The manor has been unscathed thus far," Demetri said. "The late Ms. Mandrake was very adamant about keeping her estate as it was."

They turned onto another road, Wormwood Way, and spotted another gate at the end of the road. This one was smaller but mimicked the same black iron gate and brass filigree that the entrance to Henbane Hollow had. Instead of Hs, there were two brass Ms intertwined with each other.

The headlights to Demetri's car beamed past the gates and onto a path overgrown with bushes and unkempt landscaping. Mat followed the path up to two illuminated lamp posts that shone on a tall, three-story Victorian home overrun by ivy.

Demetri stopped the car in front of the gates. "And here is Mandrake Manor."

The more he stared at the house, the more things Mat found. A greenhouse attached to one side of the house, boarded up floor-to-ceiling windows, and a wrap-around porch with a swing. "Holy shit," Mat said.

"And this. This is ours?" Frankie asked.

Demetri nodded. "Everything inside this fence is yours."

August leaned forward in their seat. "Is it safe?"

"Yeah," Frankie added. "It's not haunted, right?"

Mat nodded. The property might have once looked astonishing in its prime, but now, even in the dark, Mat saw time had passed. The green paint on the house flaked away, windows were boarded up, and nature seemed more inclined to reclaim the house the longer Mat spent looking at it.

Demetri rested his hands on the steering wheel. "From the assessments by my inspectors, the house is safe. A few repairs will spruce this place right back up."

Mat chewed his lip. "I don't know if we can do all this. I'm not a repair guy."

"Well, luckily I know a few people who could help," Demetri said. He frowned and adjusted his rearview mirror as headlights appeared behind them. "But I guess that will have to wait. Looks like the welcoming committee is here."

A white SUV pulled up next to them, and Demetri killed the engine. He stepped out of his car as a pale woman with long black hair, bold red lipstick, and a white pantsuit stepped out of the SUV. Mat, Frankie, and August followed.

"Demetri," the woman said. "What a pleasure seeing you here. Have you been treating our new neighbors well?"

"Obviously, seeing that they are my clients."

Clients, Mat winced. Even though he barely knew Demetri, he wished for the day he'd be more than a client. He leaned close to Demetri and asked, "Who is this?"

The woman raised her eyebrows. "Oh, how rude of Demetri to not have introduced me. I'm Helena Henbane, chair of Henbane Hollow's homeowners' association."

Mat held out his hand. "Nice to meet you. I'm Mat, this is Frankie, and that's—"

Helena hefted a large tote bag into Mat's extended hand. He nearly toppled over as she cut him off. "Mathias Mandrake, what a pleasure it is to finally meet you. Your late aunt and I were such good friends, and I hope to continue that relationship with you. Here is everything you need."

"Everything I need?" Mat asked.

Helena gasped and glared at Demetri. "You mean you didn't tell them?"

"Tell us what?" Frankie asked.

"Why would I tell them? It's your initiative," Demetri said.

Helena's gaze fell on Mat, and she pointed a finger at the tote bag. "You'll find all the rules and regulations for Henbane Hollow within the binder in that welcome bag. There are also some flyers from local businesses, committees, and events in the neighborhood. Feel free to sign up for anything and return them to me."

Mat frowned. "Wait. Rules and regulations?"

Helena nodded. "We can't have our homes looking like some abandoned ghost town, can we? You'll find a guide in there on what we expect of you, especially for homes that do not partake in the revitalization project."

"You mean you want this manor turned into some suburban house?" August asked.

Helena glared at August, eyeing them up and down before returning her gaze to Mat. "Mandrake Manor will need to comply with the rules. However, regarding the revitalization project, Melinda and I came to an agreement that she could not fulfill."

"An agreement? I never saw an agreement," Demetri said, crossing his arms.

Helena rolled her eyes. "Mandrake Manor may keep its original structure but must comply with the aesthetic of the neighborhood." She looked out toward the manor. "I say this to save you time and money. As you consider repairs, refer to the guidelines and regulations to ensure the HOA won't fine you."

Mat held up the tote, eyeing the massive binder within. "Great."

Helena checked her watch and tutted her tongue. "Ah, I'm late for the board meeting. We're voting on increasing the penalty for overgrowth on visible walkways." She looked back at Mandrake Manor and smiled. "Better get someone out here soon. I wouldn't want you to rack up fines during your first week here."

5

Mandrake, root of ancient lore,
Human-like in shape and core.
In potions mixed, brings dreams of flight,
Yet too much courts eternal night.

Hallucinogen, once sought by sage,
In love and madness, takes the stage.
A potent brew for heart's delight,
Yet beware the deathly bite.

Alraune, all-rune, wisdom's claim,
In olden tales, bears many a name.
Brings luck and love, so witches tell,
Yet plucking it rings death's quiet knell.

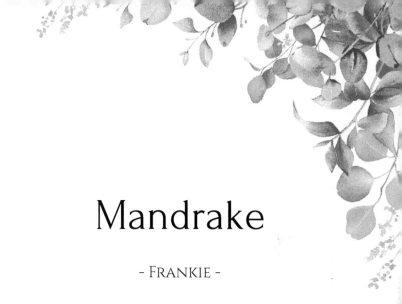

Mandrake

- FRANKIE -

Frankie pulled out his phone as Helena Henbane's white SUV pulled away. Seven more notifications popped up on his screen from a certain dating app, and he smirked as he flipped through their profiles. Maybe the options in the middle of nowhere weren't as slim as he'd thought.

"I hope she doesn't expect me to read this whole binder," Mat said, lifting the tote bag and eyeing the artistic aerial rendition of Henbane Hollow.

Demetri popped open the trunk to his SUV. "If you have questions about it, let me know. I know that thing like the back of my hand, since many people, including myself, aren't fans of what the HOA is trying to do." He fished around in his pocket and held up a ring of keys. "There are two other sets that I'll send you tomorrow. Most of the keys are marked. Like this one is for the gate, this one will unlock your front door, this one does the greenhouse, shed, cellar, and so on."

Frankie let out a laugh as he stared at the ring of at least thirty keys. "Who needs that many keys?"

Demetri shrugged. "The Mandrakes kept most of their dealings to themselves. There are plenty of nooks and crannies where you might come across a locked door."

August shoved Frankie's shoulder and said to Demetri, "He's just being an ass. Ignore him."

"Hey, rude," Frankie said, rubbing his shoulder. "I'm just saying, if I need to carry around a big ass ring of keys, then I might need to change my wardrobe."

Mat took the keys and tossed them up in the air. "Play nice." He pulled the first box out of the SUV and asked Demetri, "Did you want to come—"

"No," Demetri said as he shot up his hand. "That's alright. You all need to settle in. I can help you bring stuff to the porch, though."

Frankie raised an eyebrow. "Why can't you just—"

"It's bad luck!" Demetri said. He paused and cleared his throat. "Around here, you don't invite anyone over on your first night. You also don't just invite anyone over without getting to know them first. It's a silly custom."

August shrugged and brushed past him to the boxes. "Alright, whatever floats your boat, dude."

Mat paused and kicked his feet. "Oh. Um, okay. Maybe another time, then?"

Frankie patted Mat's shoulder and whispered. "It's okay, lover boy. That just means more wine for the rest of us." His phone dinged again as he picked up a box.

Mat smirked. "Well, it sounds like you aren't completely out of options up here."

"That's true," Frankie said. "But you know what that means?"

"What?" August asked as they all started toward the gate.

Frankie puffed out his chest. "It means, what better way to spend our first night in a new place than a game of sip and swipe?"

Mat set his box down at his feet and fumbled with the gate lock.

"Sip and swipe?" Demetri asked.

August groaned. "It's a game catty queers play back in Chicago when they have nothing better to do."

Frankie bumped shoulders with August. "Aw, come on. Don't you want to get to know some of your rainbow neighbors from their taste in photos before actually meeting them? You can learn a lot from what profile picture they share. Like, for example, the classic bare chest pic." He shot a grin at Demetri.

Demetri's eyes widened. "I . . . Uh . . . How's that lock coming along?"

Metal clinked, and the gates to Mandrake Manor swung open. "Got it," Mat said.

Demetri brushed past him, tripping over an overgrown fern on his way up to the porch. He set down his box and raced back to his car to grab more.

Frankie watched him pass by and said, "Well, someone's in a rush."

"Yeah, because you keep scaring him off," Mat hissed.

"Me?" Frankie said as they reached the porch. "He's the one that doesn't want to come inside." His eyes trailed to the front door, which was flaked forest green with a brass handle and a stained-glass window that depicted several colorful flowers.

Demetri raced by them and set down the third and final box from the SUV. "That should be the last of it. I'll swing by tomorrow with the keys and the contact details for someone who can help with the repairs."

Mat set his box down and held out his hand. "Thank you. For everything. I-I, uh, I hope to see you tomorrow?"

Demetri grabbed Mat's hand with both of his. "Thank you for taking the risk and coming to Henbane Hollow. I think the three of you will settle in just fine. Have a good night, Mr. Mandrake."

Demetri turned and passed through the gate, leaving Mat in a daze, staring at him as he left.

Frankie rolled his eyes. "Okay, I know he's your Ryan Gosling and all, but can we get into the fucking house already?"

Mat shook his head. "Let me have my moment."

August set their box down on the porch and tested the porch swing. It groaned underneath them but held, creaking back and forth. "I could sit here all day."

Frankie leaned up against the house and watched the red taillights trail off into the night. "Okay little Miss Allie Hamilton, you good?"

Mat turned around and headed to the door. "Yeah, whatever."

He set down his box and held up his keys. After flipping through a handful, he stopped on one key that fit into the lock.

It turned, and the door groaned open. A gust of wind trailed in from behind them, as if the house took in a long-awaited breath.

"Well, that was weird," August said, pushing themself up off the swing and toward the door.

Mat slowly stepped inside and peered into the dark before flipping a switch.

The house came to life as a crystal fixture bounced light onto the stained-glass door. Cobwebs lined the ceiling, and a fine coating of dust layered the floor.

Frankie frowned. "How long has your great aunt been dead?"

Mat shrugged. "I never asked. I assumed recently."

Frankie took a step forward, but his foot stopped at the entrance to the house. His intent to enter the house seemed to slip away, and he stood still.

"Uh, you going in?" August asked, stepping up beside him.

Their feet stopped right where Frankie's were, and both of them stood at the entrance to Mandrake Manor, completely dazed.

Mat turned and looked at them. "What the fuck are you two doing? Get in here."

Frankie blinked a few times as a tingling sensation washed over him. He stepped forward, over the threshold, and breathed in the stale air.

August followed suit and scratched their head. "Well, that was weird."

Nearly every inch of the walls was covered in portraits of people who looked vaguely like Mat, or paintings of strange places with high cliffs and stormy skies. Where it wasn't peeling away, the dark green wallpaper behind those portraits was busy with images of plants of every color intertwining between each other. Although a heavy coating of dust lay on the floor, he could see the dark red wood floor in the footprints that Mat had kicked up.

"I hope the rest of the house looks like this," Frankie said. He stepped into the room to the left and felt the wall, flipping on a switch as his eyes fell on a massive dining room table with high-backed chairs and a glass cabinet filled with china. The wallpaper in this room still had a green tone to it, but the plants showcased were red. A large chandelier rested above the table, draped in strands of crystal and bands of black iron that held up a circle of candles with flickering LED lights.

"Two for two, I'm sold," August said, setting down their box on the table.

All three of them finished carrying in the boxes, setting them down on the table and closing the front door.

Frankie pulled out a bottle of wine from one of his boxes and waved it in the air. "How about we pour ourselves a glass and have a little tour of the house?"

Mat eyed the boxes and frowned. "The movers won't be here until tomorrow. I don't have our glasses."

Frankie rolled his eyes and gestured to the cabinets. In his best "elderly museum curator with an English accent," he said, "Mr. Mandrake, if you look to my left, you'll see that the Manor comes fully stocked with their own glasses."

"But those have to be expensive," Mat said.

"Mr. Mandrake, need I remind you that this house, and everything within its walls, is ours?" Frankie said.

August stepped behind Frankie and pulled open the cabinet, grabbing three wine glasses and blowing out the dust before carefully setting them on the table. "It's not like we're having a party. I think we can manage three wine glasses."

Mat sighed and nodded. "Fine. Did either of you bring a corkscrew?"

Frankie eyed his bottle. "Well, shit. No."

A loud clang sounded somewhere deep in the house, and they all jumped.

"What the hell was that?" Mat said.

August's face paled. "Do you think someone else is in here? Should we check?"

"It's Mat's house. He should check," Frankie said.

"Fuck you," Mat said. "That's how people die in horror movies."

Frankie looked at his bottle of wine and sighed. "Well, the wine isn't going to uncork itself." He pulled out his phone. "We go together."

August nodded. "Yeah, that way the killer can't pick us off one by one."

Frankie glared at August. "Killer? Really?" Another clang sounded, and Frankie shuddered. "Fuck, I hate this."

The three of them stepped back into the hallway. Frankie flashed his light into the other room, which appeared to be a spacious living room with a fireplace. "Oh, my god, a fireplace," he said.

Mat poked him at his side. "Later. Keep going."

"Fine, Dad," Frankie said.

They continued down the hall, and another clang sounded. In tandem, both August and Mat screamed and Frankie dropped his phone into the sea of dust.

"Shut the fuck up," Frankie whispered, brushing the flakes of unknown substance off his phone.

Mat and August looked at each other and laughed.

"That looks disgusting," Mat said.

"I hate you both," Frankie said.

They passed through a large room with a staircase that hugged the wall as it spiraled up to the second floor. Another massive chandelier that mimicked the one in the dining room hung in the center of the room. They pressed on, passing through another arch and stepping into a kitchen.

Frankie flashed his light to the walls and found a switch as Mat and August walked by him. Small hexagonal white tiles covered the floor, and larger tiles functioned as a backsplash beneath tall white and black cabinets.

"That's weird," Mat said, running a finger along the while marbled countertop.

"What?" Frankie asked.

"There's no dust in here. Everything looks clean, too," Mat said.

August nodded to something behind Frankie. "Yeah, and did you see what's laying out?"

Frankie turned, and on an otherwise empty countertop, lay a corkscrew. He swiped it up off the counter and held it up. "Well, shall we make a toast?"

6

In ancient times, vetch found, wild and free,
Among the grains, a food source yet to be.
Untamed it grew, in folklore, a mystery,
Wandering, roaming, a silent history.

"False start" in crops, a seed not sown,
In fertile ground, its path unknown.
Wild it thrives, its power shown,
In its freedom, its truth is known.

It wanders still, in wild lands wide,
Vicia peregrina, nature's guide.
Untamed, untethered, it takes its stride,
A symbol of resilience, with time it's tied.

Wandering Vetch

- AUGUST -

"So, who wants to get murdered in the basement first?" August asked, sipping on their glass of Pinot Grigio.

"Oh, hell no," Frankie said, topping off his glass and setting the bottle on the dining room table. "I already sacrificed myself on the way to the kitchen."

Mat tilted his head from side to side. "Maybe that part of the tour can wait until the morning?"

August let out a yawn. "Well, can we get this tour on the road? I'm ready for the part where we find our rooms and crash."

Frankie picked up his glass and started into the hall. "Come now, the official Tour de Mandrake Manor has begun."

He led them into the living room and flipped the switch. The room was massive, with a boarded-up window nook, a large claw foot sofa, and two matching love seats with torn upholstery atop a blue Persian rug. The walls were covered in the same peeling wallpaper, this time with an emphasis on blue flowers. Opposite the window nook was a deep red wooden mantle fireplace with a black iron and brass filigree that matched the gates.

Mat spun around the room. "Oh, my god. Can you imagine winter here? I could just sit here and watch the fireplace." He plopped down onto the couch, dredging up a pile of dust that set him off into a fit of sneezes.

Frankie bounced his heels on the carpet. "I could have a date in front of the fire. We feed each other grapes, then bang one out."

August scoffed. "Really? Just right here, in the middle of the room?"

Frankie shrugged. "It's one of those comfy kinds of rugs. Do you think Melinda ever . . . ?"

"No. Stop talking now," Mat said, pushing himself off the sofa.

August shook their head and crossed the room, passing through an archway leading into another room. They flipped on the switch and found a room filled with floor-to-ceiling shelves of books on the right and shelves filled with jars on the left. Cobwebs covered both of them, but the rest of the room appeared relatively clean.

A pair of red leather, squashy sofas sat closest to them, followed by a large table with a stack of books, papers, dried plants, and a large mortar and pestle.

"Guys, you've got to see this," August said, gulping down their wine.

They ran their fingers along the books, spotting familiar classics intermixed with books on botany, chemistry, and some unfamiliar titles by authors like d'Aban, Molitar, and Boulton. They could spend the rest of their life in this room and still only knock out half the books here.

August stood along the back wall, eyeing the certificates that held up the yellow flower wallpaper as Frankie stepped in.

"Holy shit," he said.

"I think we found your, uh—" Mat paused, looking up to the ceiling. "Not a man cave. What would you call the 'they' equivalent?"

August turned around and grinned. "Goblin's lair seems befitting."

Frankie laughed and picked up a jar. Turning it over, he said, "Did you see these? This one's labeled Dittany of Crete. There's also Mugwort, Hawthorn thorns, and Belladonna. What the hell was your aunt into?"

Mat picked up the papers on the desk and flipped them over. "Apparently, some weird shit. 'Tea to improve one's sight.'"

Frankie spun open a jar and sniffed. He gagged and carefully returned it back to the shelf. "I mean, a creepy Victorian house in the middle of some ancient neighborhood. My bet's on an evil witch."

August shook their head and pointed to the wall of certificates. "Seeing as she had multiple degrees in biochemistry and botany, I'd guess scientist or herbalist over some evil witch."

Frankie held up another jar. "This one says 'eye of newt.' I don't know what school she went to, but these are definitely just mustard seeds. She was probably one of those new age hippie green witches."

"Well, I guess we have a stock of herbs for the apocalypse. Just maybe steer clear of any deadly ones," Mat said.

"Well, you're no fun," Frankie said.

August came to the door at the back of the room and peered through the glass. It was warm to the touch, and the light streaming in from the library fell onto a stack of empty pots. "I think I found the greenhouse."

They opened the door, and a flood of heat blew past them, carrying the scent of dirt and flowers. Frankie raced over and flipped the light switch. A set of rope lights came to life in the greenhouse, winding up banisters and into hanging trellises.

Mat followed as they all stepped out onto a brick patio encased in a glass greenhouse that spanned two stories high. Rows of waist high flower beds filled the space to the left, curving around the house, while workbenches, a small fountain, and an outside patio filled the space behind the library.

Frankie ran a hand along a metal spiraling staircase that led up to a second-floor balcony. "If this leads up to a bedroom, then dibs."

August eyed a large thermometer hanging near the workbench. "Does that say eighty? How the hell is this place still so warm?"

Frankie walked between the raised beds, running his fingers along leaves and flowers that were in full bloom. "Half of these aren't even in season." He stopped at a row of plants near the other end of the greenhouse. "And these are fully ripe vegetables. That doesn't make any sense."

August squinted, following the hoses attached to the raised beds back to the house. "Looks like your aunt put the watering on a timer."

"Okay, so we just have a fully stocked greenhouse ready for us? That's weird, right? Who's going to take care of these?" Mat asked.

Frankie perked up. "I am. Remember those few semesters in undergrad that I wanted to be a botanist?"

August raised an eyebrow. "Really? Why?"

Frankie shrugged. "The TA was cute, and I stayed late with him in the greenhouse after hours a lot."

Mat nodded. "Of course you did."

Frankie turned away from them and faced the raised bed in the back corner. "What can I say? I had a green thumb and could make things nearly triple in size."

August leaned up against the first row of flowerbeds. "Thanks for the visual. You think we could sell some of these? You could have a whole Mandrake Greenhouse business."

"Maybe after we read that stupid HOA book," Mat said. "I can almost guarantee there's something in there about small businesses."

Frankie turned around and faced them with an arm full of squash, tomatoes, and potatoes. "Well, we have half our groceries right here. I hope you're ready for Frankie's garden skillet tomorrow morning."

Mat yawned. "Oh, tomorrow sounds nice."

August finished their glass of wine and held it up. "Refill, then upstairs?"

Frankie shuffled the vegetables awkwardly in his hands and reached for his wine glass, which was resting at the edge of the raised bed.

"Um, no!" Mat shouted, racing forward. "I've got that glass, Farmer Joe."

They emptied the bottle of wine and started up the stairs.

They headed right, stopping at a door on their left. If August was correct, this room would lead out to the balcony inside the greenhouse.

"I think we all know whose room this is going to be," they said as they opened the door.

Inside was a large, high-ceilinged room with cream-colored crown molding and pink floral walls. A four-poster bed rested next to the door, with the same color pink duvet and cream-colored pillows. On the other side of the room, a pair of stained-glass doors led out to a balcony.

Frankie pushed past August, his eyes wide. "If either of you attempt to take this room from me. I. Will. Murder. You."

August shook their head. "I didn't know you liked pink so much."

Frankie picked up a silk robe that rested on a white dresser and put it on. In a terribly accented transatlantic female voice, he said, "My dear August, you don't know the half of me."

Mat backed up into the hallway. "Well, come on Miss Frankie, one room down, two to go."

August and Frankie followed, stepping into the room across the hall.

Above the kitchen was a room with a small fireplace, more bookcases, and a small writing desk. It was much bigger than the pink room, with long draping curtains, a dark brown color palette, and peeling wallpaper filled with mushrooms.

"Now this is a man cave," August said.

"You want it?" Mat asked.

August pulled out the chair from the writing desk and pulled open the curtain overlooking the backyard. "I absolutely do."

Frankie set down his glass and pulled open the closet door. "Oh, my god," he said before vanishing into its depths.

A few seconds later, he emerged with a massive fluffy brown robe.

"What the hell is that?" August asked.

He threw the robe at August and said, "That is your new house robe, really puts together the whole cave gremlin look you're going for."

August put an arm through the robe, feeling the smooth silk brush against their skin. "Well, fuck you, but damn, this is comfy."

Frankie held up his glass and pointed to the door. "We have rooms for the mistress and the themstriss of the house. Now we just need a room for my sugar daddy."

"No, you're not calling me that," Mat said.

"Sweet cakes?" Frankie asked, spanking Mat on the ass.

"If the mistress of the house wants me to lock them out of their room, then the mistress can continue," Mat said.

"Do you really trust him sleeping somewhere like the living room? Remember what he said about that rug?" August said.

Frankie laughed. "Hey, you leave my Persian lover alone."

Mat chugged the last of his wine. "Please make it stop."

They backtracked to the stairwell, passing by a mint-tiled bathroom, and journeyed to the front of the house. Inside, the room was a bold green with depictions of Monstera leaves and other large green plants on the peeling walls. There was a window nook with a small daybed, a fireplace, and an enormous bed. Across the room was both a bathroom and a walk-in closet.

Frankie brushed past Mat, a massive smile on his face. "Okay, admit it, this house is incredible. There is a bit of sprucing, patching, and whatever else to do, but who the hell cares?"

"Yeah," August agreed. "I was a little iffy before, but I can't wait to fix this place up."

Mat smiled. "Well thanks. I don't know what I expected, but it wasn't this."

He stifled a yawn that spread to Frankie and August.

August finished their wine and said, "Raincheck on the sip and swipe?"

Frankie locked arms with August and headed out Mat's bedroom door. "I'm still taking a peek before I go to bed, but fine."

As the two of them left Mat's room, August paused and turned to the unexplored door next to the stairwell. They frowned. "I don't remember seeing that."

"Where do you think that goes?" Frankie asked.

"I don't know, attic maybe?" August said. They crossed the room and tested the handle. There was no visible lock, but no matter how hard they tried, it wouldn't turn. "I think it's locked."

"I guess Mat the key-wrangler will have to unlock it for us tomorrow," Frankie said, continuing down the hall. "Night, Boo."

"Night," August said, their eyes trained on the door. Something about it felt off, something they couldn't quite put their finger on.

After another moment, they turned away and headed down the hall toward their room. A chill passed through them, and when they turned, the locked door was no longer there.

They turned to grab Frankie, but his door was already closed.

Another chill passed through them, followed by the sounds of creaking floorboards.

"Nope," August said, turning around and racing to their room. Moments later, they found solace in their covers.

7

In Sumer scripts and Greece, willow's lore,
Pain's balm, dysentery's cure, wisdom of yore.
Its bark hides Aspirin's kin, a salicylic store,
Eases woes, the Ebers Papyrus bore.

Basket weaver, weir builder, tamer of flame,
From Native hands, willow stands, utility its fame.
In Babylon, they pondered on, cuneiform's game,
Willow's seed may, indeed, fertility reclaim.

Cricket bat, fishing net, willow's gifts spread wide,
Yet its roots, in pursuit, destruction can't hide.
From art to war, willow's core, stories it narrates,
An ode to the tree, its history reverberates.

Willow

- MAT -

Light streamed in through the boarded windows and landed squarely in Mat's eyes. He winced and rolled over, snuggling back into the fluffy down feather comforter and taking in a deep breath. Stale air filled his nostrils, and his mind cleared.

The evening stitched itself back together—Demetri dropping them off, the tour of the house, and his ultimate crash into bed. Into the same bed his great aunt probably slept in. He didn't think to change out the sheets. And now, the thought of her dying in this bed surfaced as his mind betrayed his willful ignorance.

He wriggled and flung himself out of bed, shivering in his dark green boxer briefs, shaking off the idea that he'd just slept in a dead woman's bed.

In the morning light, his room was absolutely dreary. Not only were the boards covering the windows even more obvious, but there were ceiling stains he hadn't seen the night before, along with some cracks in the walls where the wallpaper had peeled.

He shut his eyes and took in a breath. "It's going to be fine. We just need time."

He crossed the room and stepped into the attached bathroom. The floor was tiled a mint green, same as the hallway bathroom, and there was a walk-in shower with a large overhead spray attachment.

Perhaps not every room was in a dire state, Mat thought as he approached the sink. He turned the handles for both hot and cold, but while the cold spun open, the hot simply broke off in his hand. "Of course the hot one would break."

Brown sludge oozed out from the faucet. "Really? Come on," he said as he hit the sink.

Pipes in the walls groaned and shook, and the sludge coming out of the faucet thinned before turning completely clear.

After the sniff test resulted in a light rusty smell, he splashed cold water onto his face and found a change of clothes in his bag.

Out in the hall, August stood wrapped in their furry brown robe, inspecting the wall beside the stairwell.

"How'd you sleep?" Mat asked.

August shrugged, their eyes still locked on the wall. "Fine, I guess. Had a few weird dreams. Then the whole 'did someone die here' thought went through my head."

"Same," Mat laughed. He looked at the wall August was inspecting, noting that it was just a plain, uninteresting wall. "You, okay? Why are you petting the wall?"

"There was a door here last night. Frankie and I both saw it, but it disappeared."

Mat frowned and knocked on the wall. "Well, it doesn't look like there are any hidden doors. Sounds pretty solid. You sure you weren't dreaming?"

"I swear I saw it," August said.

Mat's phone dinged. He turned on the screen and saw a text from Demetri.

> *Demetri [9:37 a.m.]: Can't make it out today, but there is a handyperson working next door at Mr. Jotunn's. Stop by and tell him I sent you.*

"Well," Mat said to August. "Don't break the wall down until we have someone look at it."

August tested their weight against the wall and sighed. "Fine. Frankie should be done making breakfast, anyway."

They went downstairs and into the kitchen, where Frankie hovered over the stove in his pink silk robe.

He turned around, and as Mat had expected, he wore nothing but a pair of bright yellow briefs under his robe. "Morning my lovelies." He pulled two mugs from the cupboard and poured out coffee that had been steeping in a French press. "Breakfast is almost done."

Mat gripped his mug and took a sip. It was still warm but too bitter after steeping for longer than he would have liked.

Frankie grabbed three plates and scooped out portions from the skillet. Whatever he'd made looked almost like a pie, with layers of crispy potatoes at the bottom, softened squash, peppers, and broccoli in the middle, topped off with caramelized onions and seasoning.

"Breakfast is served, bitches," Frankie said, pushing the plates toward August and Mat on the kitchen island.

They all dug in, and Mat couldn't help but smile as he thought of many days like this in the future, among his friends. He took another swig of coffee and said, "What, no mimosas?"

"Took you long enough to ask," Frankie said. "I can pick up a few things while I'm out."

August frowned. "While you're out?"

Frankie looked at the clock. "That hot lawyer helped me land a job at a vet clinic by some guy named Dr. Lupin. They're having an adoption event going on at noon, and the doc messaged me, asking if I could offer a hand."

"You? Working on a Saturday? Wait, how are you getting there? We don't have a car," Mat said.

"Well, it just so happens that Dr. Lupin lives in Henbane Hollow. He's picking me up."

Mat leaned back and crossed his arms. "I never thought I'd see the day. You, working on a weekend."

Frankie shrugged. "What better way to start my dilf hunting than a pet adoption? I mean, if they're looking to adopt, then I can just slide in and offer myself as tribute."

"So, you'll take the place of a poor puppy in need of a home?" August asked.

"You're damn right I will," Frankie said.

Mat finished his plate and walked over to the sink. "Well, don't forget the orange juice when you stop by before you move out to go live with your new sugar daddy."

Frankie gasped and placed a hand on his chest. "I would never abandon my first true sugar daddy. You're stuck with me, bitch."

"Damn," August said, "I already imagined turning your room into an art loft. I thought a delightful shade of black might do it well."

"Don't you dare touch my room," Frankie said, swiping August's plate from under them.

August snagged the last bite with their fork and stuck out their tongue.

After they cleaned up, Mat started toward the front of the house. "Well, if I don't see you off, good luck on your first day."

"Where are you going?" August asked.

"Demetri told me there is a handyperson working next door. Want to come with? Meet the neighbors?" Mat asked.

August stretched and shook their head. "I need to get some words in this morning, or I'll be cranky."

"Suit yourself," Mat said. He waved to Frankie. "Text me when you get there so I know you aren't in a ditch somewhere."

"Okay, sugar daddy," Frankie said.

Mat rolled his eyes and headed out the front door, passing by the porch with holes in it he had missed last night, and wading through the overgrown plants until he reached the gates. Mandrake Manor was at the end of a cul-de-sac. To his left, there was another smaller Victorian-style home with similar overgrowth and black peeling paint on the outside. Somehow, it looked even more abandoned than Mandrake Manor did. To his right was the home he was looking for.

The house was a two-story home in the middle of construction. Half the walls were covered in a bright blue tarp, while the rest were covered in dull beige siding. This was clearly one home undergoing the suburbanification, with an average shape, a two-car garage, a cement driveway, perfectly manicured lawn, and a white picket fence that clashed with the iron gates of Mandrake Manor. The only thing that stood out of place was a gnarled weeping willow in the middle of the lawn, its long branches brushing along the tops of the grass.

The sound of a table saw pulled him out of his thoughts, and he spotted a man standing inside a two-car garage. He was completely shirtless, showing off his tan, freckles, and muscles for the whole world to see. He hefted several beams of wood over his shoulder like they were nothing and started out of the garage.

Mat took a step back. He couldn't have a conversation with this man. He couldn't—

"Hey," the man called as he spotted Mat. His bright blue eyes and chestnut hair glinted in the sun. "I haven't seen you around here."

Mat's tongue stuck to the roof of his mouth. He contemplated running away, looking like he was some thirsty idiot gawking at the handyperson. *How the hell does Frankie do this?*

"Uh, hi," Mat said.

"Were you looking for Mr. Jotunn?" the man asked. "I can go get him for you."

Mat shook his head. "No, uh. I was actually looking for you."

The man smiled and turned around, finding a place to set down his boards.

Mat tried not to look. He really did. But he looked. And, damn, it was worth it.

The man turned and jogged up to Mat. Again, Mat tried not to look, but the man did a full-on Baywatch run right at him, for free.

He smiled and stuck out a hand covered in sweat and sawdust. "Name's Jacob."

Mat shook his hand, noting the calluses and rough skin. "I'm, uh, I'm Mat."

Jacob's eyes lit up. "Hold on. Are you the new Mandrake?"

Mat nodded. "I am. Demetri said you could help with some repairs."

Jacob looked back at the garage and rested his hands on his hips. "If Demetri sent you, then yeah, I definitely have an opening in my schedule."

"Really?" Mat asked. "That would be great. Helena cornered us last night. You know Helena, right? HOA person? Anyway, she doesn't seem like the most lenient of people."

"Oh, I know Helena, don't worry. She is definitely someone you don't want to mess with." Jacob grinned as he rocked back on his heels and scratched his chest. "I've got a few more weeks with Mr. Jotunn, but I could stop by tomorrow and assess the damage. I could probably knock out a few things on my off days."

Mat ran his hand through his hair. "Uh, if that's okay, then yeah. That would be great. I really just want to keep Helena away. I know it needs a lot of work."

Jacob reached into his pocket and pulled out a business card. "Well, don't tell anyone, but I've always wanted to get my hands on Mandrake Manor. It's . . . special."

Mat looked down at the card, noting the image of a spear piercing through the name Borowy Construction. "Well, feel free to come over and put your hands wherever you'd like." As the words came out of his mouth, uncontrollably, like word vomit, his cheeks burned hot. "That's not—I didn't."

Jacob smiled. "It was nice meeting you, Mat. I'll see you tomorrow."

Mat turned without another word, or another chance for his idiot mouth to say something else he'd regret.

8

Silvery Lupine, Western native, stands tall,
Toxic bean, confusion's call, stomach's fall.
Yet sustenance for butterflies, in skies so blue,
From forests to grasslands, its beauty true.

Lupine's secrets, sagebrush lore,
With alkaloids its seeds store.
But in hands that know, it turns benign,
Roman meals, a memory divine.

Yet caution, too, must have its voice,
In peanut's shadow, Lupine's choice.
Beware the fungus, Diaporthe's snare,
Grazers nibble with utmost care.

Silvery Lupine

- FRANKIE -

"**O**kay, but I'm fucking gorgeous," Frankie said as he pulled his hair up into a man bun. He stared at himself in the mirror, posing in colorful striped pants, a tight white tank top, and a denim vest. He put on a pair of expensive D&G sunglasses that he definitely did not steal from his bestie Liz back in Chicago and picked up his phone as it buzzed.

Dr. Lupin [10:38 a.m.]: Hey, I'm outside.

His next message was a plain smiley face. Frankie frowned. He knew Dr. Lupin was older, but a plain old smiley? Who the hell does that? Serial killers and boomers?

He quickly blended in some concealer and gave himself another once over before heading downstairs.

"I look hot as fuck and no one is here to see me off?" he shouted as he stood in the empty hall.

August's voice echoed from the back of the house. "You always look stunning."

"Yeah, but now I look stunning in denim and stripes, and you'll never know," he said as he stepped outside. He nearly ran into Mat as he raced up the walkway, his face red.

"Everything alright?" Frankie asked.

Mat brushed past him, reaching for the door. "I—no, everything isn't alright. I am annoyed at how many hot people are in this damn neighborhood. Now, if you'll excuse me, I need a cold shower or something."

Frankie turned around and walked backwards down the path. "But are the hot people going to come here and help around the house?"

"If didn't scare him off, then he's coming over tomorrow," Mat said, reaching for the door.

"Did someone get dickmatized?"

"Geez, Frankie. No. I just. Who the hell doesn't wear a shirt when they're working?".

Frankie stopped backing up and looked out the door. "Oh, maybe I should be late for work."

"No. Don't you fucking dare go over there," Mat glared.

"Whatever. We'll talk about it over dinner," Frankie said, turning back around and looking at the little silver Prius parked out front. "Wish me luck, bitch."

"Good luck, bitch," Mat grinned, skulking away into the house.

Frankie shook past through the gate.

He'd thought the man would match the Prius, that Dr. Lupin would be some skinny professor-looking guy with a silver beard who blasted NPR over the radio. As he got closer, he realized how wrong he was.

The man's shoulder was pressed up against the window, and as Frankie walked around the car, he noted that Dr. Lupin's arms were at least as thick as Frankie's thighs. He wore a sleeveless, baggy gray hoodie, which Frankie would need to talk to him about. He was also missing a beard, but the silvery scruff and peppered hair tied back in a bun was an acceptable replacement. Frankie looked down at the road before his eyes traced over the man's biceps for a bit too long as he walked around the car.

He popped open the door, and death metal played over the speakers. Definitely not NPR.

"Hi, Dr. Lupin?" Frankie asked.

The man turned down the radio and held out a gigantic hand. "Yep, but call me Remmy. Frankie, right?" His voice was deep and gravelly.

Frankie's damn knees wobbled as he slipped into the car and took his hand, which was warm and soft. How the hell was this man so attractive? Remmy gave a gentle squeeze, and Frankie wondered how he could restrain himself from outright crushing Frankie's hand.

"Nice. Nice to meet you," Frankie squeaked as his throat became suddenly dry. Several scents assaulted him at once as he closed the door. A mix of wet dog and musky man sweat hit his nose first, quickly covered by a sweet pine cologne that was working hard but failing. Regardless of the mix of scents, and that Remmy was definitely not his type, Frankie couldn't clear his damn head of all the things he'd love to do with this man.

Remmy pulled away from the cul-de-sac and out onto Belladonna Boulevard. "How are you liking Mandrake Manor?"

Frankie blinked and looked down at his feet. "It's not terrible. We did just move in, so ask me in a few weeks."

Remmy nodded. "Fair. Well, let me know if you need any help. I'm not the best, but I don't mind getting my hands dirty."

Frankie swallowed down a remark he was certain he'd regret. "I, uh, I haven't looked up the animal hospital. How far is it from here?"

"A couple miles. If you want to carpool to work, I'm happy driving. I could use the extra motivation to leave the office on time."

Frankie smirked and leaned back in his seat. "Well, in that case, I'll happily use you for rides."

Remmy laughed, "Well, I'm not your personal chauffeur, but a few bucks a week should cover it."

"Oh, deal. I was gonna get a bike and everything, but trust me, that wouldn't have ended well," Frankie said.

They pulled up to the gates, and Gary waved from the booth. During the day, he looked even worse. His skin wasn't just pale but one shade away from gray, and the wisps of hair peeking out from his cap looked brittle. Remmy waved back and muttered under his breath, "I swear this guy loves taking his sweet time."

"I mean, the poor guy looks sickly, don't you think? Like he's gonna croak any second."

Remmy bit his lip and muttered, "You don't know the half of it."

They drove through the gates and started down the road. Frankie peered out the side window, squinting along the tree line. "Demetri drove us through the woods somewhere over here."

"He got you guys lost, didn't he?" Remmy grinned.

"We turned around three times before we cut through the woods."

Remmy came to a stoplight and turned onto the county highway, passing by the spot they'd turned around twice the night before.

Frankie frowned, swiveling his head back and forth. "Wait, this road wasn't here before."

Remmy shrugged. "It's here now."

"How can it be 'here now', but not here yesterday?"

"Some say Henbane Hollow is one of those weird places where the surrounding roads change. I've never had a problem finding it, but I know people who've been here for years and still struggle to get in and out."

"That doesn't make any sense," Frankie said.

"You'll see. Give it a few weeks, and you'll start seeing a lot of things that don't make sense."

The highway crested over a hill, and a small coastal town came into view. German-style homes, intermixed with Victorian homes, peeked over trees along with churches and white-bricked apartment buildings. Frankie focused on a road that trailed closer to the coast and through a small downtown before reaching a harbor with anchored sailboats. It looked like every small coastal town in a Hallmark movie. A cookie cutter copy of a romance that Frankie could picture himself in.

"Well, here's Greenwych," Remmy said. "It's not all that special, but you can get just about everything you need downtown. Although, if you're looking for a bar, pick Ficus' over Juniper's unless you want something rowdy."

They coasted down the hill, passing through neighborhoods and closing in on downtown. "I don't know. Rowdy might be fun."

"Of course, a city boy like you would say that." Remmy grinned.

"Hey! You've got to let loose once in a while, right?"

"Oh, I know. I may or may not have been kicked out of Juniper's a few times."

They drove past a small two-story black brick building with a purple neon sign that spelled out Juniper's. It looked quaint, and a lot like a bar Frankie would have found off the beaten path in Chicago. He bit his lip, then said, "Well, maybe you can take me sometime. A guy like you is bound to make sure nothing gets too . . . rowdy."

Remmy nodded. "Yeah, I could probably convince some of the vet techs to come out for drinks."

Frankie's heart sank, realizing Remmy didn't pick up on his hint. "Yeah, I can bring my roommates too. I'm sure they'd like to meet some locals."

Remmy slowed his car and parked across the street from a one-story white building with the words "Greenwych Animal Hospital" above the door. In the parking lot were a set of tents and a little fence resting on an AstroTurf mat, filled with several puppies.

"What," Frankie started, "no funny business name?"

Remmy killed the engine and shook his head. "I wanted to go with Ruff and Scruff, but the techs told me that might bring in the wrong crowd."

Frankie rolled his eyes. "You did not."

"I did. Went so far as buying the LLC before I realized," Remmy said, popping open the door.

Frankie unbuckled and stepped out of the car. "Well, next time, run it by someone before—"

Remmy pulled off his gray hoodie, and Frankie's eyes bulged out of his head. The man had muscles that shouldn't be legal, and he wore a mint green shirt that was a few sizes too small. The distorted words "Happy Tails Adoption Fair Volunteer" were stretched across his massive chest, and a tuft of silver chest hair spilled out from his collar.

He pulled at his shirt and looked up at Frankie. "The techs keep ordering me the wrong size."

"I—I wonder why," Frankie said.

Remmy sighed and placed his hands on his hips. He looked like a damn statue. "I don't think they know that I know what they're doing. Maybe next year you can order the shirts. If you stick around."

Frankie's thoughts trailed off, imagining a day next year when he might just completely "forget" to order this man a shirt at all. "Yeah, maybe. If I stick around."

Remmy started toward the clinic and waved Frankie to follow. "Well, time to meet everyone and get you a shirt of your own."

9

Eyebright, kin to snapdragon's clan,
Soothes sore eyes since time began.
Parasitic in its roots, it thrives,
On life of others, it derives.

Assigned to Leo in olden lore,
Claimed to make the brain restore.
A morning tonic, or in ale,
It brightens sight without fail.

For blepharitis, a poultice best,
Reduces swelling, clears the rest.
In colds and fevers, it's applied,
Eyebright's power, far and wide.

Eyebright

- AUGUST -

"You always look stunning," August said as they heard Frankie heading out the door.

August stood in the library, watching the sunlight beam onto the bookshelves. Smiling, they pulled out their laptop and found a space on the red leather sofa. They turned on their computer and stared at the blank screen.

It had been weeks since they last wrote. With all the chaos happening around them, August kept pushing it off and was just waiting for the right time for the muse to strike. Surprisingly enough, the muse never did. But now that they were in a whole new house, away from the rest of the world and without the internet until someone came to install it, there was no perfect time like the present.

The front doors slammed shut, and August heard footsteps stomping up the stairs. Mat, most likely. Another distraction if they let it be one.

August blinked a few times and stared back at the blank page with the title *Former Inhabitant* scrawled across the top. Was it a problem that they couldn't even remember what this story was about? The previous chapter ended with a clockwork robot escaping from their maker's workshop, but all the life and enjoyment of the story had been completely sucked out. It was touted as a perfect story by their professor, who believed literary fiction was the only valid path for an author. So here August was, writing what could have been a steam-punk thriller, but was now confined to *Walden* with a commentary on artificial intelligence.

Scratch.

The sound pulled August out of their thoughts as they looked around the library. As expected, the place was empty, but the sense of something just at the corner of August's sight lingered longer than they wanted.

August looked back at their manuscript, wishing anything could distract them and give them reason to walk away.

Thud.

August jumped, spotting the book that fell from the shelves. They frowned, turning their head left and right before saying, "Hello?"

No answer.

They set the laptop aside and crossed the room, finding the book on the floor, flipped open to a page with a strange symbol on one side and a chapter titled, *Revealing the Unseen: A Guide to Perception*.

They frowned and picked up the book, flipping through the pages.

It was filled with strange new age nonsense, from meditating to charting out astrological events to have prophetic dreams. August laughed and muttered, "This wasn't the distraction I meant."

They started to close the book when a line caught their eye. *Some highly perceptive people may see glimpses of things that others can't. These people would have many names, but all share the gift of the Sight.*

August recalled the door upstairs. They swore it was there. They felt the doorknob in their hand. Then it was gone. An empty wall near the stairs.

"What are you doing?" a voice called from behind August.

They jumped, nearly dropping the book as they turned and saw Mat in the doorway. "You scared the shit out of me."

Mat smirked. "I'm bored. Find anything interesting?"

August looked over at their computer. "No. And I should be working."

"Aw, come on, it's a Saturday," Mat said, crossing the room and looking down at the book in August's hands.

"It fell from the shelf."

"More witchy nonsense?" Mat asked.

August nodded. "Looks like it. Too bad none of it's real."

A cool gust of air blew in from the hall, sweeping along the shelves while picking up dust before blowing past them and onto the table in the center of the room. A single sheet of paper swept up and slowly glided down onto August's laptop.

August's heart beat in their chest as they looked at Mat and then back at the paper.

"That was weird," Mat said.

"Uh, yeah," August said, handing Mat the book as they carefully crossed the room and picked up the paper.

It was the recipe for making tea that they had read the night before. "Tea to improve one's Sight." August frowned, realizing now that the word "Sight" was capitalized on the paper, just like it was in the book.

"You're not thinking of making that, are you?" Mat said.

August looked down at the list of ingredients. "Cinnamon, eyebright, jasmine, mugwort, and so on. I mean, why not?"

"Why not? Uh, I could think of a few reasons. What if you poison yourself?"

August looked up from the paper. "You said you were bored, didn't you?"

Mat nodded. "I did, but—"

"Come on," August said, turning to the wall of herbs. "Help me find the ingredients. We're making tea." They pulled down a jar marked "Eyebright" and set it on the table.

One by one, Mat and August collected the ingredients and poured them into a small stone bowl that rested on the desk.

"Now what?" Mat asked.

August squinted at the paper. "Now it says we have to get naked and dance around the mixture three times while chanting."

"You're joking."

"Obviously. It's a recipe for tea, not some sacrificial ritual. We just brew the leaves," August said, rolling their eyes. They picked up the bowl and traveled to the kitchen, finding a kettle and heating it over the stove.

"Maybe after this we do something normal like walk around the neighborhood? You know, anything but making some weird tea from a wall of jarred herbs via some paper you happened across," Mat said.

August pulled two mugs and a tea strainer from the cupboards. "I mean, if you want to be boring, yeah, why not?"

Steam rolled out from the kettle, and Mat let in a breath. "At least it smells good."

He was right, August thought. The tea was strong with floral notes of jasmine mixed with a rich herby smell. They pulled the kettle off the stove and poured it through the strainer.

After passing Mat his mug, August held up their own. "Well, here goes nothing," they said, before taking a massive gulp.

Their senses felt as if a semi hit them. Cinnamon cleared their sinuses in an instant, followed by a clean note of jasmine. The other herbs seemed to settle deep in their throat, tasting earthy and bitter while sending warmth through their whole body.

Mat followed suit and gulped down his tea. The face he gave was the same as theirs, a shock that slowly morphed into confusion. He blinked and frowned as he looked around the kitchen. "Now what?"

A light buzzing formed at the base of August's spine and traveled up to the top of their head. Shadows and lights flickered at the corners of their eyes, and the room brightened. They looked around and froze when they spotted the plants on the floral wallpaper in the hallway.

The plants on the wallpaper moved, as if blown by some unseen wind. "Uh, well, I think that walk you want to take might be a little fun now."

Mat followed August's line of sight and spotted the wallpaper. He crossed the room and placed a hand on it before turning to August. "Um, are we? Are we high?"

August picked up the paper and ran a finger along the herbs listed. "We shouldn't be. I mean, I don't feel high. Nothing on this list should do that."

Mat nodded. "I don't feel high either, but that buzzing feeling isn't normal."

August crossed the room and traced a finger along one of the vine plants on the wallpaper. It coiled around the space where their finger was and blossomed a small blue flower. "Definitely not normal."

"Frankie would love this," Mat said, running a hand along the wall and stopping at the stairwell.

The buzzing in August's head grew. A tug in their chest pulled them toward the stairs. Faint green wisps of glowing smoke lifted off the wallpaper and trailed up the steps, calling for August to follow.

They started up the stairs when Mat grabbed their hand. "This is sketchy as hell. Are you sure we should be—"

"What's the worst that could happen?" August said, pulling their hand free.

The buzzing in August's head intensified with each step until they reached the top of the stairs. It released in an instant as their eyes settled on a very familiar door.

"Holy shit. You believe me now?" August asked, pointing at the door.

Mat stopped at the top of the stairs and swallowed hard. "What the hell?"

"I told you what Frankie and I saw was real."

Mat pushed past August and ran a hand against the door. It was plain and white with a dark iron knob and keyhole. Nothing special about it, but definitely not something easily overlooked. "Yeah. But how?"

August walked up beside Mat and tested the knob. *Locked.* "Who knows? Do you have the keys on you?"

Mat nodded and pulled the ring of keys from his pocket.

August swiped them from his hand and flipped through the set. Their fingers buzzed while holding one particular black iron key with a forged M soldered onto the bow. "This is the one."

Mat stepped away from the door and gestured to August. "Well, you want to do the honors?"

August slipped the key into the lock and turned. There was a click, and they turned the knob.

The door creaked open, and a gust of stale air billowed down onto them. Inside, stacks of boxes and trinkets lined the sides of the steps, including several porcelain dolls, all looking down at them.

August stepped back, their eyes locked on the creepy dolls. "You can go first."

Mat frowned. "Really? You and Frankie are the worst."

August got behind Mat and pushed. "He trained me well with all those horror movies. I'm not dying first."

10

Gromwell, in purple it stands tall,
Cultivated since times of Nara's call.
Its roots hold antiviral might,
A potent balm in the moon's soft light.

To unleash its dye, an art unfolds,
Through patient months, its tale is told.
Dipped and dried, a ritual learned,
In alchemist's fire, the color yearned.

Roots of purple, murasaki's fame,
In forest's heart, it stakes its claim.
Historic dye, potent brew,
Gromwell's legacy, forever true.

Gromwell

- MAT -

Mat stared at the dozens of porcelain doll eyes watching him from the steps that led up to the attic. A few of them blinked back at him—he was certain of it—just before he turned back to August and glared. "I hate it. I'm not going up there. I'd rather burn the place down."

"Too bad," August said. "I want to know what's up there, and I like my room too much for you to burn it down."

"Then you go first," Mat said.

August took a step closer to the stairwell, blocking Mat in. "No."

Mat rolled his eyes and grabbed onto the handrail. "I hate you."

"Love you too," August said, gently pushing Mat forward.

He maneuvered carefully between boxes and dolls, the steps creaking after every step. After averting his eyes from the eighteenth black-haired porcelain demon child replica, he said. "If you even think of putting one of these in my room when I'm asleep, I'll—"

"Good idea," August cut him off. "I'll wait until you least expect it. Then one day, you'll come out of the shower, and *BAM*, little haunted Bethany will be staring at you."

"Then little haunted Bethany will get yeeted out the window, and you'll be paying for the repairs." Mat broke free from the stairs and onto the attic floor, walking right into a massive cobweb. He yelped and thrashed his hands around. "Fuck this! Fuck this!"

August picked out a clump of cobweb from Mat's hair and let it fall gently onto the dusty floorboards. "At least there wasn't a spider in it."

Mat shivered, imaginary spiders tickling up his arms and legs. "Why the hell would you say that?"

"I mean. It isn't a spiderweb. I figured that was a good thing." August shrugged, flipping open the lid of a box. They laughed, picking up an old, tattered book. "Well, more reading for me, I guess."

Mat surveyed the attic, noting the insurmountable stacks of cardboard boxes and draped furniture that covered nearly every inch of the massive open attic. Light streamed in from large windows on all sides of the house, illuminating a space that was four times larger than his studio apartment back in Chicago. "You know, if we cleaned this space out, it could be a whole other hangout spot."

August traveled deeper into the attic and pulled on one drape, revealing a squashy, burnt orange sofa. They plopped down and closed their eyes, relaxing. "It could be a whole game room. We just need a table and a TV, and we'd be set."

Mat looked up at the exposed ceiling, noting the water stains and blotches of dark wood. "I hope that's not mold. Great. Well, we have another thing for Jacob to look at."

"Jacob?" August asked.

Mat's face flushed red, picturing the shirtless man who was bound to still be working next door. "Handyperson. He's coming over tomorrow to scope out the place."

August smirked. "And I take it he's hot? Judging by your face and all."

"What? No!"

August rolled their eyes. "Okay, sure."

Mat turned and pulled on another drape. "Fine, maybe he is, but—AH!" The drape slipped off, revealing the creepiest mannequin Mat had ever seen, with bright painted-on makeup that even a murderous clown would run away from. It fell forward, knocking Mat to the floor.

"You okay?" August asked, jumping to their feet.

"Dolls and fucking mannequins. Why couldn't my aunt collect normal things?" Mat asked, pushing the mannequin off him and dropping the drape over it. He shivered. "That is the first thing we burn."

August laughed and flipped open another box, pulling out a long silky dress. It was a simple emerald green dress with a slit on the side. "Well, don't get burn-happy just yet. Some of these are definitely worth something."

Scritch.

A noise, followed by shuffling, sounded behind Mat, on the other side of the attic.

They both jumped, and Mat swiveled his head around, his eyes locking onto a stack of boxes still wobbling. "What the hell was that?"

August came up to his side and shook their head. "I don't know. Go check it out."

Mat glared at August. "Really? Again?"

August nodded. "It's your house. And I'll proudly say I'm a chicken."

Mat grabbed August's hand and pulled them along. "Well, I'm not dying alone."

They stepped forward, and a box to their right fell to the ground. They jumped, and Mat squeezed tight onto August's hand.

"You don't think it's ghosts, do you?" August whispered.

"Ghosts, really? You and Frankie really need to stop watching those documentaries."

The boxes ahead of them wobbled again, and Mat did everything he could to suppress the idea that the ghost of his aunt was up here, rummaging through her things.

"I mean. It could be rats," August said.

Mat groaned and turned around, looking August in the eye. "Now rats? What is wrong with you? Now all I'm going to think about are rats crawling in my bed."

August looked down. "Sorry, I can't help it. I blabber when I'm nervous."

The shuffling sounded behind Mat, followed by another box falling. He turned and pulled August forward. "Well, these would have to be some beefy rats to do this."

A beam of light obscured the path ahead of them, right onto a box that had spilled its contents on the floor. He caught movement just beyond the flecks of luminescent dust. He squinted and spotted a pair of beady eyes staring back at him.

"What the hell is that?" August asked.

Mat took another step forward, and two tiny black hands stretched out into the rays of light, slowly grabbing a silvery locket in the collection of fallen objects. The creature stepped into the light, revealing distinct black fur markings around its eyes.

"It's a fucking raccoon," Mat said, letting out a loud sigh. He lifted his hands overhead and shouted, "Get the fuck out of here!"

The raccoon wrapped its hands around the locket, eyes locked with Mat, before waddling backward on its hind legs. It made a sound, almost like a laugh, before racing along the side of the attic.

Mat hopped over the box and raced after it.

They circled the attic, knocking over a large trunk with a loud thump, before reaching the window leading out to the backyard.

The raccoon stopped at the window, which had been pushed open by the overgrowth of vines, and stared back at Mat with its beady eyes and bared teeth, locket still in hand.

"Come here, you stupid trash panda," Mat said as he took a step forward, swinging his hand, uncertain what he'd actually do if he caught the creature. Luckily, he didn't have to worry, as the raccoon slipped out the window, vanishing into the overgrowth.

Mat pulled some vines loose and swung the window shut, latching it in place. "Well, fuck that raccoon, I guess."

"Do you think it stole anything else?" August asked.

Mat knelt down next to a trunk that the raccoon knocked over. "How would we know?"

August scratched the top of their head and said, "Hopefully there aren't any babies."

Matt turned around and looked at them. "You're fucking kidding me. Why would you bring that up?"

August shrugged. "I told you. I can't help it."

Mat shook his head and turned back to the trunk. It looked ancient, and one of the straps holding it shut had even frayed away in Mat's hand. He undid the other strap and carefully lifted the lid.

A powerful scent of perfume and herbs assaulted his senses as he spotted bundles of dried herbs and incense sticks lining the side of the case along with an assortment of crystals and stones. "Well, this is some witchy shit, for sure."

August looked over Mat's shoulder. "Should we be messing with it, then? What if it's cursed?"

"Says the one who made the drugged-up tea," Mat said as he eyed a green velvet cloth in the center of the trunk, embossed in gold filigree. He ran a finger over it, feeling something solid underneath before a strange vibration jolted up his fingertips, and he jumped.

"See? I told you! Put it back," August said.

"Then it's too late for me anyway," Mat said, carefully pulling off the cloth and revealing a book with a weathered green cover and an M scrawled among gold filigree. His hands brushed over the cover, and the strange vibration was replaced with a warmth and thrum beneath his fingers. He pulled it out of the trunk, noting a second book beneath it titled *Gromwell Grimoirium.*

His focus, however, was on the book in his hands. He flipped open the cover and read the passage out loud.

"Mandrake kin, claim thy rites.

Help those in need,

Protect those who ask,

And mend all that breaks.

Do no harm, lest you wish justice by threefold law."

August let out a huff. "Okay, maybe you shouldn't read weird things like that out loud?"

Mat flipped to the next page, which was titled, *Coven of Three: A Mandrake's First Rite.*

"Seriously, put it back," August said.

Mat couldn't look away from the page. Something called to him, like a parent calling out for their child. "We should do this."

"What?" August asked. "No."

Mat stood up, book in hand, skimming over the first page. "No. We totally should. Frankie would get a kick out of it." He laughed and looked up at August. "What? It'll be a bonding experience. New home, glass of wine, and a weird ritual. I mean, can you think of a better housewarming party?"

August looked down at the book and slowly nodded. "Yeah, sure, why not read from the book in the creepy attic?"

Mat smiled. "I like your attitude. Help me find some candles."

11

Dogwood, vibrant in woodland shade,
Hardwood for tools, and toothbrush made.
A quinine mimic, fever's bane,
In forest and field, its healing reign.

Flesh of the bark, steeped in water's heat,
Civil War soldiers drank for respite sweet.
A poultice for wounds, the leaves provide,
In nature's pharmacy, secrets reside.

Cornelian-cherries, bright gems of the wild,
In syrups and preserves, they're compiled.
The sturdy dogwood, healer so tall,
Its medicinal gifts are offered to all.

Dogwood

- FRANKIE -

"Hello?" Frankie called as he stepped into the foyer. He flipped on the light switch as the last remains of sunlight dipped under the horizon. "Where are my beautiful lovelies? I have a surprise for you."

"Maybe they went out?" Remmy called from the porch.

Frankie turned on his heel and settled his eyes back on the massive, broad-shouldered man standing on the other side of the doorway with a bundle of groceries in one hand and a leash in the other. "If you knew them, you'd know they wouldn't go out without me. Wait there. I'll find them."

Frankie peeked into the dining room, then the living room, and found nothing. He traveled deeper into the house, flipping on the lights to the kitchen. Again, nothing, except a tea kettle and two mugs resting on the island.

Muffled voices sounded from the next room over. He scoffed and muttered, "If they aren't pouring me a glass of wine . . ."

He stepped into the half library, half apothecary, and found the two of them huddled over a book, jars in hand. He crept up close to them, spotting the word "Rites" on a book laid out on the table.

"What are you two looking at?" he whispered.

They both jumped, eyes wide, and August dropped their jar of herbs. It shattered on the floor, and a pungent, woody smell filled the air.

"Frankie, what the hell?" August groaned, stomping out of the room and returning with a broom and dustpan.

"Sorry," Frankie said, kneeling down and picking up the fallen herbs. "Neither of you answered me when I called. I have a surprise for you. You're never gonna guess—"

"We found something," Mat cut him off. "Remember how we thought my great aunt was a—"

"Witch?" Frankie said.

Mat nodded.

"Okay, that's cool, but I've got something I need to show you two. Come on." Frankie said, standing and setting the herbs on the table.

"What are you wearing?" Mat asked, looking at Frankie's slightly oversized T-shirt for the first time.

Frankie pulled on his mint green *Happy Tails Adoption Fair Volunteer* T-shirt and said, "What? Is mint green not my color?"

"No," August laughed. "But is it anyone's color?"

"Well, Rude One and Rude Two, it is my color now, so deal with it. Alright, shut up and follow me," Frankie said, turning around and heading back to the front of the house.

"But," Mat started.

"No buts. Unless we're talking butts, then maybe I'll listen," Frankie said.

He led the both of them into the hall and blocked the view to the front door as he turned around. "Okay. So I got the groceries you wanted. But I also got this." Frankie stepped out of the way.

Mat and August frowned.

"You brought us a burly man to carry our groceries?" Mat asked.

"I mean, at least you picked a good one," August whispered. "But I can't imagine you brought him to share."

"No, you dorks. That's Remmy, my boss," Frankie said. He turned and faced the front door. "Where's Sir Snickerdoodle?"

Remmy held up a frayed leash, his eyes wide. "It broke the second he tried to get inside. I tried to follow, but you didn't invite me in."

"Who's Sir Snickerdoodle?" Mat asked.

At that moment, a dog with a mottled gray, black, white, and brown coat came trotting out of the dining room and into the living room, its nose trained to the floor.

"You got a dog?" August asked.

Frankie turned and smiled. "We got a dog."

"What? Why? Who's going to take care of it?" Mat asked.

"Who is going to take care of *him*," Frankie said. "His name is Sir Snickerdoodle, Dude for short."

"And who is going to take care of . . . Dude?" Mat asked.

Frankie trailed after the dog. "Remmy, can you come help me catch him? I don't want him getting into anything just yet."

Remmy took a deep breath, closed his eyes, and stepped into the house. He blinked a few times, staring back at the threshold. He set down the groceries beside the door before following Frankie into the living room.

They cornered Sir Snickerdoodle, who stared up at Frankie with bright blue eyes. "Okay Dude, just let me grab onto that collar of yours and—"

Sir Snickerdoodle lifted his leg, eyes locked on Frankie, readying to relieve himself all over the wall.

"You'd better not!" Frankie called out.

Right then, the floor creaked and a segment of wallpaper came rolling off the wall, landing right on Sir Snickerdoodle.

He yelped and raced to cower between Frankie's legs, which allowed Frankie the chance to tie his frayed leash back together before the dog tried to drag him outside.

"Okay, so again, why do we have a dog?" Mat asked from the porch as he, August, and Remmy stared down at Frankie.

Frankie shrugged. "Because no one wanted to adopt him, and Remmy said the poor guy hadn't been adopted for two years now."

"I would have taken him myself," Remmy cut in, "but I already have a collection of geriatric dogs, and the HOA said I can't have any more. Dude here has been at the doggie doctor since he came in from a discarded litter."

Frankie looked up at Mat with wide eyes. "See, the poor guy needs a home."

"He is pretty cute," August said, hopping off the porch and sticking out a hand for Dude to smell.

"It would do me a huge favor," Remmy added. "He gets all the attention at the vet, but he needs a home where he can retire and relax."

"We can fence in the backyard, and he'd have plenty of space to run around," Frankie said. "Please, can we keep him?"

Mat crossed his arms. "Fine. But you're cleaning up after him. Got it?"

Frankie nodded. "Got it."

Remmy grabbed Mat's shoulder with his gigantic hands and squeezed. "Thank you! You don't know how happy that makes me."

Mat's face reddened as he looked at Remmy, then he stepped back. "It's not a problem, uh, sir."

Remmy hopped off the porch and scratched the top of Dude's head. "You can grab a new leash on Monday. Call me if you need anything."

Frankie smirked. "I will, don't worry."

Remmy stretched, his massive chest really testing the stitching strength of his shirt. "Well, if I don't feed my pack soon, they might tear apart the couch again. Pick you up Monday morning, 7:30?"

Frankie nodded. "I might be a bit of a grouch, but don't take it personally."

Remmy held out a hand and smiled. "Thanks for coming out today."

Really, a handshake? Frankie paused for a second, then held out his hand. Remmy gripped tight, and all Frankie could think about was what else those hands could be doing. "It—It was my pleasure."

Remmy waved to Mat and August before passing through the gate and heading to his car.

Frankie fanned his face as he brought Dude up to Mat and August. "That man has my nethers all in a bunch."

August frowned. "He's your boss."

Frankie held up a hand. "Yeah, yeah, we'll keep it professional or whatever."

"Sure you will," Mat said.

"I mean, did you see him? Of course I won't," Frankie said.

August knelt down and petted Dude. "Well, hi Mr. Dude."

Dude wagged his tail and nearly knocked August over as he licked their face.

Mat joined August and scratched behind Dude's ears before looking up at Frankie. "So, my aunt . . ."

Frankie grinned. "Did she hide sacrifices in the basement?"

"We haven't checked the basement," August said.

Mat groaned. "If there is a body in the basement, one of you is dealing with it. No, it's the book. Come on, I want to show you."

They closed the front door and scooped up the groceries before Frankie let Sir Snickerdoodle loose. He eyed the walls warily, tail between his legs as he sniffed. Then his ears perked up, and he gave the wall a lick before racing off to collect all the smells he could.

In the library, Mat and August hovered around the old book, surrounded by a collection of herbs.

"Okay, so what is it?" Frankie asked.

August picked up a white candle. "It's a spell from Mat's great aunt Melinda's spell book."

"We found it in the attic," Mat said.

Frankie frowned. "That door. The one that was there and then it wasn't?"

August nodded. "There is an enormous space up there. Tons of boxes. And this." August pointed to the book.

Frankie stepped up to the book, reading the top of the page, which read, "Coven of Three: A Mandrake's First Rite." He flipped through a few pages, reading titles like "Strengthening the Wards," "A Spell to Conceal What Must be Kept Hidden," and "Signs of Lycanthropy."

Mat stepped beside Frankie. "I mean, it's obviously bullshit. But I figured you'd get a kick out of a little housewarming ritual."

Frankie flipped back to the first page, reading over the preparation for the spell. "I mean, it calls for wine and a circle of candles. Drunk witchy stuff is my jam. When are we getting our witch on?"

"Now," August said, striking a match and lighting a candle.

12

Mugwort, ancient herb of lore and might,
Guardian of roads, in the moon's pale light.
Thujone-rich, caution we heed,
Neurotoxic in excess, with abortive seed.

In medicine and cuisine, it does partake,
Digestive aid, respiratory respite does it make.
Anthelminthic power, expels the worm,
And for the insomniac, sleep it does affirm.

A magical protector in Middle Ages past,
Against fatigue and evil spirits it was cast.
In sandals of Roman soldiers, it found a place,
Guarding feet from weariness, cramps to erase.

Mugwort

- AUGUST -

"Don't worry, Frankie. We'll make sure not to fuck up your sex rug," August said as they pushed the couch out of the way.

After some discussion, the three of them came to the conclusion that the living room had the most space to create a ring of candles for the three of them to sit in, like Melinda Mandrake's spell book said.

Frankie picked up a candle from the box he'd brought in and turned it over. "I mean, a little hot wax would hardly ruin the sex rug," he said, positioning the candles.

Mat groaned. "It's not a sex rug. It will never be a sex rug. Stop fantasizing about having sex on the rug." He placed the book in the center of the rug and double-checked the collection of herbs inside the small stone bowl.

August laughed. "Well, if you didn't think Frankie was going to have sex on the rug, telling him not to have sex on the rug will definitely make sure he's going to have sex on this rug."

"August is correct," Frankie said as he grabbed an armful of candles and pushed the box over to Mat. "Okay, party pooper, help me with these candles before you chicken out."

"I'm not going to chicken out," Mat said, his voice shaking.

August dimmed the lights as Mat and Frankie lit the candles. When both of them paused to look at August, August shrugged. "What? It sets the mood."

"This is feeling more and more like a teenage sleepover where someone brings over a Ouija board and someone else ends up crying," Mat mumbled.

"Are you having second thoughts, my sweet boy?" Frankie asked, patting Mat on the shoulder.

"No. Not if you two still want to do this," he said.

Frankie leaned back. "And unlike a Ouija board sleepover, we have a bona fide spell book, wine, and we're grown-ass adults. So if I see a tear coming out of those eyes, I'm going to slap you. Okay, Rose?"

Mat lit the last candle and sat back. "Whatever you say, Blanche."

"Does that make me Sophia or Dorothy?" August asked, popping open the bottle of wine.

"Dorothy," Mat said.

"Wait. Blanche?" Frankie asked, his hand on his chest. "Of all of them, you call me Blanche?"

August carried over the glasses and stepped into the candle circle. "I mean, 'Join the Navy, see the world, sleep with Blanche Devereaux.' Seems like you are two peas in a pod."

Frankie took a drink of his wine and looked down at the book. "Enough chitchat. Are we doing this or what?"

Mat picked up the book and ran a finger down the page. "Alright, we did the circle, and it looks like we have everything. Mandrake, belladonna, garlic, mugwort, lavender, graveyard dirt, salt—"

"Graveyard dirt?" Frankie asked. "What the hell is graveyard dirt?"

"Well, I'd imagine it's dirt. From a graveyard," August said, picking up the bowl of herbs and pointing out the clump of dirt at the bottom of the bowl.

Frankie rolled his eyes. "Thank you for that marvelous definition."

August took a drink of their wine. "Any time."

"Okay," Frankie said, peering over Mat's shoulder. "So, what's next?"

Mat pulled a black candle from the box. "Once we start, we go around in a circle, all saying our parts. I got the black candle, so one of you gets the green, and the other gets the blue one. Then we'll pass the book around, say a few lines, and pour wax from our candles and wine from our cups into the bowl."

Frankie looked at August. "Green or blue, which one do you want?"

August shrugged and shut their eyes, reaching into the box. Their hand wrapped around one candle. It felt warm, and when they opened their eyes, they found they were holding the blue one. "Blue, I guess."

Frankie grabbed the remaining candle, and all three of them lit their wicks.

"Alright, I guess I'll go first," Mat said, clearing his throat and looking at the book. "Our lady of the underground, goddess of depths unseen and realms, we call on you. We invite you into the circle and offer a promise to guide those who are lost."

He tilted his candle and the hot wax dripped onto the herbs, then took a sip of his wine before pouring a small bit into the bowl.

"That's it?" Frankie asked.

A stream of cold air blew in from the fireplace, and the candles flickered.

"Isn't the flue closed?" August asked.

Mat shook his head. "You told me I can't chicken out. So, I don't want to know. Either let me believe it was a weird coincidence or we are stopping right now."

Frankie grabbed the book from Mat and held up his candle. "We are definitely not stopping." He looked down at the pages and said, "Our man of the mountain, god of earth and purveyor of life, we call on you. We invite you into the circle and offer a promise to protect those who need it most."

As Frankie tilted his candle and dripped hot wax onto the herbs, the entire house creaked and the floorboards rattled.

Mat stood up, his eyes darting around. "Okay, fuck that! I'm chickening out."

The floorboards stopped instantly, and the house grew silent, as if holding in a breath. August grabbed Mat's hand before he stepped out of the circle. "No, don't." They weren't sure why they were so adamant, but everything in their body pleaded for Mat to stay. "We've got to finish it."

"But—"

"No," Frankie said, pushing the book over to August. "No buts. Sit down."

August pulled the book over and held up their candle to see the words, words which seemed to shift and change as they read them. "Our majesty of the skies above, watcher of history and seer of things to come, we call on you. We invite you into the circle and offer a promise to heal those who come for help."

The curtains slid open, and the boards on the windows fell from the window frames. Moonlight beamed into the room, bouncing a bright silvery light onto the floor.

Unseen wind swirled around them, and the house groaned as if taking in a long awaited breath. Candles flickered and floorboards shook.

"Okay, that's it. Spell done. We did it. Let's fucking go," Mat said.

August shook their head. "There's one more line. We're supposed to say it together."

Mat threw up his hands. "Am I the only sane person here? There is a literal wind tunnel and floorboards shaking."

Frankie smirked. "So, then maybe the magic is real, and we should finish it instead of leaving the circle, which it says not to do."

August held up the book. "It says, right at the bottom, in big letters, 'Do Not Stop Midway Through The Spell.'"

"Ugh, fine," Mat said, sitting back down in the circle.

"Repeat after me. Both of you," August said. All three tipped their candles into the bowl. The flames caught the mixture of herbs, and a stream of fire blazed. "Being. Known by many names. God, goddess, and all things between. Being of three, being of one, Hecate to many, chaos to none. We call on you, hear our plea, as we pledge our rite of three. We are your guides. We are your protectors. We are your healers."

The fire within the stone bowl grew bright, flashed, and was out in an instant. Then the circle of candles extinguished, and the three of them sat in the dark.

Mat stood up and cleared his throat, breaking the silence. He then stepped out of the circle and flipped on the light switch. "I didn't like that," he mumbled as he knelt down and picked up the candles.

"Well, few people can say they did a spell for a housewarming party. So you have that going for you now," Frankie said as both he and August helped Mat carry the candles back to the library.

"Ha, ha," Mat said. "But now what? Was that real?"

August shrugged. "Maybe?"

"Well, I don't know if I want it to be real. Did we just pledge ourselves to some elder god? Are we going to get eaten?" Mat asked.

Frankie held up his hands. "Slow your roll there, big boy. You're sounding like August."

Mat held onto the book and sighed. "I—I think I just need to go to bed."

"I can look over that," August said, pointing to the book. "See if there is anything else in there."

"No," Mat said, holding the book up to his chest. "No more spell books right now."

"How are we going to know if some raging elder god is after us?" August asked. "We need to look over the book."

Mat shook his head. "No. I don't know what that was in there, but I don't want more of it. We can look at it later. Maybe. But right now, it's going with me. And I'm going to bed."

"But—" August started.

"No," Frankie cut them off. "Mat's right, we all just need to cool our jets. It's late. Let's go to bed and worry about it tomorrow."

August held their tongue. "Fine. But we should look it over sooner rather than later."

Mat nodded. "I won't look at it without you."

13

Maroon stems tell of Amaranth's might,
Aztec staple, full of health's insight.
Grains rich in minerals, protein's delight,
But beware, high oxalate, a shadow in the light.

Versatile seed, in meals takes flight,
Popped or ground, a culinary delight.
A gluten-free trove, for diets just right,
Yet oxalate's presence cautions each bite.

Ancient and resilient, in harshest of site,
A crop for survival, in the darkest of night.
Yet, in the bounty that is our right,
Let not forget, its potential plight.

Amaranth

- MAT -

Mat's dreams melted away, and he felt the weight of the blankets on top of him. His eyelids were no longer holding in the darkness, but a bold red from the morning sun.

He stretched, blinked, and his voice caught in his throat.

Hovering above him, inches from his face, was that of a withered old woman with gray hair draping down on either side of Mat's head.

Mat lay there, frozen, as cloudy eyes stared at him, and the withered old woman opened a mouth full of yellowed teeth. She let out a sigh, which left behind a putrid scent of rot.

She spoke in a low whisper, which rattled at Mat's chest. "I died right here, in this bed."

Mat squeezed his eyes shut, repeating the word, "No," over and over until the word hit his lips and he shouted it.

He could still smell the woman above him, and she laughed.

Thunderous footsteps sounded all around him, rattling and racing toward him as he kept shouting, wishing it would all be over.

The door slammed open, and Frankie yelled, "Hey! Are you alright? Mat?"

The woman's laughter melted away, followed by a faint whisper, "I always wanted—"

"Hey! Earth to Mat! You okay?" Frankie asked.

Following behind him was the clack of nails as Dude came rushing in and jumped on top of Mat's bed, spinning in a circle while he barked.

Mat carefully opened one eye, then a wet tongue barraged him as Dude slobbered all over his face. The ghostly woman was no longer there. He pushed Dude off him, offering belly rubs as he looked over at Frankie, sporting the silken pink robe and fuzzy slippers. "Yeah, I'm fine. I think," Mat said, sitting up and looking around the room. "Just a bad dream."

Frankie crossed the room and pulled open Mat's curtains, letting in more bright morning light. "Well, get your ass out of bed and have some coffee, then. Breakfast is almost ready."

Mat finished his last swig of coffee and took a bite of his tomato, basil, and feta frittata. "Oh, my god, Frankie. You're cooking for us every morning, right?"

"No," Frankie said, pointing a spatula at Mat. "Weekends? Maybe. But you'll be lucky if you get coffee from me during the week."

August took one bite of their food then damn near shoveled the whole thing in their mouth. "I could help you prep, if you want. And I know a few mean muffin recipes to hold us off if needed."

They looked down at their side, where Sir Snickerdoodle sat like a proper boy, head cocked to one side as his eyes locked onto August's fork.

Mat looked down at his plate and scratched his head. "Well . . . I know how to make—"

"Honey, this isn't a competition. No one wants to try your moldy burned cheese toasty," Frankie said.

"Hey," Mat frowned. "That was one time."

Frankie rolled his eyes and topped off his coffee. "And yet, that one time made me question my love for cheese for a week."

"That was not my fault. How was I supposed to know the cheese went bad?"

"Oh, I don't know. Maybe the fact that half of it was green?" Frankie teased.

"Well, my appetite is gone," August said, staring at their forkful of food. They had grabbed a second helping but handed it over to Dude, who daintily pulled the frittata off the fork.

A knock sounded from the front of the house, and they all turned to look. Dude stood up and wagged his tail lazily.

"Which one of your suitors could that be?" Frankie asked.

"My suitors? The way you were fawning over your new boss, I'm surprised you didn't try to keep him over for the night," Mat said.

"Oh, I want to," Frankie said. "But something says I need to take it slow. Woo him a little before I show him the rug."

"You, wooing?" August asked. "I can't wait to see what that looks like."

Frankie crossed his arms. "I'll have you know I can play the long game. Just you wait. That man will be eating out of my hand before you know it."

Mat pushed himself up out of his seat. "Well, don't either of you rush to get the door or anything."

"If it's Remmy, be sure to tell him to run," August called after Mat.

Mat waved them off and walked to the front of the house, joined by Dude, who happily trotted by his side. As he grabbed onto the door and pulled it open, his eye caught the mirror positioned next to the door.

There she was again, standing just behind his reflection, the old woman with long gray hair and yellowed teeth. From this angle, she looked a lot like his mother, except the resting bitch face was warmer, even on a ghostly apparition that scared the shit out of him.

Her mouth opened, and she rested a hand on his shoulder. "Mathias," she whispered.

"Uh, hello? You there?" A voice called to him.

Mat blinked a few times, and the apparition in the mirror vanished.

He turned and looked in the doorway, where a man in a tight plaid shirt and light brown scruff hunched over, petting a thrilled Dude.

"Yeah, sorry. I thought I saw something," Mat said. "Jacob, right?"

"Yep, that's me. I said I'd come by today and assess the house. Is this a good time?"

Mat struggled to find words. On top of that, his mouth was dry, and he could hear the comebacks that Frankie would have if he knew. "Uh, yeah. Now's good. Come in, we're just finishing breakfast."

Jacob stepped inside and looked around the house while leaving one hand dangling to scratch Dude's head. "I did a quick sweep outside. There are a few repairs to the siding, and the roof needs some work." He bounced up and down on the floor and ran a hand along the wall, pushing some of the wallpaper back into place. "Feels pretty sound. Despite that, I want to make sure the house is still safe to be in before doing any patchwork."

"Why, hello there," Frankie said as he left the kitchen. He held up a second mug of coffee and handed it over. "I'm Frankie, and this is August. You must be the handyperson Mat was telling us about."

Jacob took the mug and smiled. "That I am. Please, let me know if there is anything you want me to inspect."

Frankie started up the stairs and turned around. "Don't worry, I'm sure I can find plenty of things for you to . . . inspect." Frankie snapped his fingers, and Dude's ears perked up. "Come on, Sir Snickerdoodle. Let's leave this man to his work."

Dude did as he was told, bounding up the stairs behind Frankie.

Mat rolled his eyes. "Sorry about that. Frankie is chipper this morning."

Jacob finished his mug of coffee in one last gulp. "Not a problem. Especially since I got a free coffee out of it."

"Well," Mat said, "Where should we start?"

"Basement. That will tell me what I need to know about the foundation, then we can work our way up."

Mat shivered at the thought of going down into a creepy basement. Especially now. "Uh, great. Yeah. Funny, we haven't been down there yet."

Jacob smiled. A stupid, dimpled smile that made Mat want to slap him. Seriously, how could this man be so damn attractive? Mat turned and led him toward the kitchen.

Jacob ran a finger along the kitchen countertop and whistled. "Well, this looks newer than the rest of the house. That should save you a lot. I'll do a check on the plumbing, but I wouldn't touch this space if I were you."

Mat grabbed the basement door and pulled it open. Immediately, a chill blew past him, and the sensation of icy fingers wrapped around his neck for a second. "Great," he mumbled. "So, I was right on the creepy basement part."

Jacob laughed and peered down into the depths before finding a switch and flipping it on.

As expected, wooden stairs that looked as if they might fall apart any second trailed off into the dark, and a handrail was missing altogether. "You don't have to go with me if you don't want to. I've been in plenty of worse places than this."

His damn smile. Why did he have to have such a beautiful damn smile? "No. I should see the space for myself. Since, you know, I own the house and all."

"Fair enough," Jacob said, leading the way down into the dark and stale air.

Small basement windows, frosted over in grime, streamed in light from outside. Exposed rock lined the walls of the open basement. Not quite the finished space that Mat had been hoping for, and definitely one step away from being a cave someone would get murdered in.

Not three feet away from the steps were three wooden shelves filled with wine bottles. Mat grabbed one and wiped away the dust, squinting as he read *Lenox Madeira, bottled 1798*. "Holy shit," he said.

Jacob glanced over at Mat, "Melinda was big into wine. At least, that's what my parents said. She had these elaborate house parties where everyone did wine tastings."

Mat let out a laugh. "Well, sounds like those parties should start back up. Frankie would love something like that."

Jacob walked around the basement, knocking and squeezing the support beams, testing the above flooring, and shining a flashlight onto the wood. After a few minutes, he rested his hands on his hips.

"This house has good bones. Fantastic bones. No signs of rot or infestation, and the wood looks to be original. It's dry enough down here that I don't think you need to worry."

"Well, that's a relief." Mat said, running his eyes along the walls.

"Enormous relief," Jacob nodded. "Did you want to—"

His voice faded away as Mat's vision tunneled directly behind Jacob, right to the apparition of the woman standing directly behind him. Her mouth was open wide, and she held up a bony hand.

Jacob leaned into view, waving a hand, "—out? Uh, Mat?"

Mat shook his head, and the apparition disappeared. "What was that? You want to go out? Uh, yeah, I'd love that."

Jacob's face reddened. "I asked if you wanted to head out. As in, head back upstairs?"

Mat gasped and turned around, blood pumping in his ears. "Oh, fuck. I'm—I'm sorry."

"Well," Jacob said. "I'm not saying no."

Mat looked back at Jacob. "Wait, what?"

Jacob shrugged. "How does next Friday sound? On me. I know a great little restaurant."

"Uh, what? I mean. Yes. Yes, I'd love that."

"Great, then it's a date," Jacob said, his stupid dimples showing.

Another chill ran through Mat, and he shivered. "Okay, can we get out of this creepy ass basement?"

14

In deceptive bloom, the Caladenia lies,
Mimicking insects, its crafty disguise.
Its pollination trick, a horticulturist defies,
Shared with fungus, its survival allies.

Its tubers scarce, in hunger's eyes,
An emergency feast under open skies.
Yet grueling to grow, it oft denies,
To the untrained hand, its yield never ties.

Caladenia, the Spider Orchid, a beauty that belies,
An emergency morsel, nature's surprise.
Yet caution in cultivation, for its yield oft lies,
In symbiosis with fungus, its true strength lies.

Caladenia

- FRANKIE -

Frankie chugged his last bit of coffee and eyed the carafe. He looked outside, noting that the morning sun hadn't even peaked over the horizon. *Who the hell gets up at this hour?* "Should I leave any for August?" He asked Mat.

Mat sipped on his coffee and scratched Dude's head. He wore a finely pressed pale blue button-up and tan slacks that screamed department store corporate indoctrination starter set. Definitely not the attire Frankie would catch himself dead in. Even now, heading into a vet's office, he wore his embroidered jeans and oversized bright-ass yellow geometric knit sweater.

"I wouldn't. Who knows when they'll get up," Mat said, gazing into his mug.

"Fair point, lucky little shit." Frankie pulled himself off his seat and grabbed a thermos, topping off the rest of the coffee. "You ready for your first day, Dr. Mandrake?"

Mat looked over his shoulder for a moment, his face paling before he blinked and looked at Frankie. "Yeah. Anything that will get me out of this house."

Frankie looked over to the empty corner in the kitchen and frowned. "What, first day jitters got you seeing things?"

"You could say something like that. I can't wait for this week to be over. Dr. Denton wants me doing paperwork the first week until she's ready to hand new clients to me."

"Riveting. I'm sure you can handle it, sweetie. My life will be paperwork and puppy breath for the next six months, anyway." Frankie's phone dinged in his pocket, a message from Remmy. "My ride's here. Are you sure you don't need one?"

"Yep," Mat said. "Demetri said he'd pick me up and take me over to get the Green Machine later today."

Frankie grabbed his coffee and planted a kiss on Mat's cheek. "Have a lovely day at work." He then snapped his fingers and said, "Come on, Dude, let's go to work."

Dude perked up from Mat's side and trotted behind Frankie, tongue hanging out.

Frankie opened the front door, and the potent scent of smoky whiskey hit him before he noticed the tall Black man standing in the doorway. "Uh, Demetri, hi."

Demetri smiled, a grin that made Frankie weak in the knees. He spoke in a low baritone, "Hey. I tried calling. Is Mat up?"

"Of course you did," Frankie said before turning around and shouting. "Take your phone off silent, doofus. Your ride's here."

Frankie heard a jingle coming from Demetri, and when he turned, the man was holding out two rings filled with keys. "I come bearing gifts for you and August."

"Aw, you shouldn't have," Frankie said, grabbing them from Demetri. A twinge of electricity surged up Frankie's arm and throughout his body, and he looked down at the two sets of keys. The sets were identical, except for a little charm. Both were a shiny copper, but one was in the shape of a Monstera leaf, while the other was an eye.

He placed the ring of keys with an eye on one of the coat hooks near the door and tossed his own set up in the air. "Thanks."

Demetri stared at Frankie, his eyebrow raised. "Any time."

A familiar tiny car pulled up to the front of the house behind Demetri's black sedan, and Frankie shouldered past Demetri, snapping his fingers for Dude to follow. "Well, my ride's here. You two have fun."

Demetri smiled. "Tell Remmy I said hi."

"Excuse me," the old woman holding her toy poodle in her arms in front of the check-in counter said. "I have been standing here for five minutes. Are you going to check me in?"

Frankie blinked a few times, pulling his eyes away from Remmy, who was outside at the moment, fawning over a giant mastiff who had outright refused to enter the vet's office. "Uh, yeah, sorry about that. What was your name again?"

"Appleton, A-P-P."

"Penelope Appleton, got it. And this is Henry?" Frankie asked, nodding to the poodle.

The poodle huffed and glared at Frankie with the same Karen energy that Mrs. Appleton had.

"Yes," the woman said. "Henry here got into something last night and hasn't been acting himself. I called ahead so I could drop him off."

At that moment, the little dog looked up, and a thick tongue slithered out of his mouth like a tentacle and licked the woman under her chin. Frankie leaned back in his chair, eying the now innocent, doe-eyed Henry. "Oh. I see. Well, uh, have a seat and we'll get you all checked in."

Mrs. Appleton frowned, then slowly shuffled away to the waiting room.

"Actually," a voice boomed from behind Frankie. He turned and saw the head vet tech, Denise, a short Black woman with thick, red-rimmed glasses. She smiled at Mrs. Appleton. "Frankie here will take Henry into room two and prep him for Dr. Lupin."

Frankie frowned, eyeing Henry, whose eyes blinked out of sync, and whispered, "What, why me?"

Denise picked up a chart from the table and flipped over the papers, muttering, "Because you are a vet tech in training, and you want a good recommendation from me."

Frankie sat up from his chair and beamed at Mrs. Appleton. "Alright, I'll take Henry and get him all checked in."

She looked at Denise and smiled before handing Henry over. "Be nice to the poor boy. He gets nervous around strangers."

A wet tentacle lolled out from Henry's mouth and wrapped around Frankie's wrist. He did everything he could to not throw the dog as far away from him as possible. "He's—" Frankie swallowed. "He's in excellent hands."

Frankie carried Henry quickly into room two, wincing at the strong smell of bleach, and set Henry down on the scale. A normal tongue hung from his mouth as he panted and stared up at Frankie.

"Alright, what the hell are you?" Frankie asked.

The dog's eyes flashed pitch black for a moment as Henry tilted his head from side to side, then huffed.

Frankie's heart beat heavily in his chest, and his fingertips numbed as every sane voice in his head told him to run. "Show yourself, weird tentacle thing."

As the words left his lips, a ripple of electricity ran down his back and the scent of dirt filled the room.

The dog sniffed the air and yawned heavily, then the coiled white fur retracted, leaving behind a rather hideous hairless dog.

"What the fuck?" Frankie said, backing up.

The hairless dog transformed again, losing its rigid shape as the surrounding light contorted and shifted into a mass of dark shadows. Blackened tentacles stretched in all directions.

Frankie couldn't help but scream as Henry tripled in size, shadows and darkness overtaking the scale and spilling out onto the counter.

The door burst open, and Dr. Lupin raced into the room. He looked at Frankie, then at the blob formerly known as Henry. "Are you alright?"

"Uh, no, there's a fucking shadow monster," Frankie said, pointing.

Dr. Lupin paused, sniffing the air, and his eyes widened. He slammed the door shut, his back to Frankie.

"Well, thanks for saving everyone else from the *Thing*, but I'm about to jump out the window," Frankie said, fumbling with the lock on the way-to-small window.

Remmy's back muscles bulged, tearing his lab coat, and a tuft of white hair curled out from his lab coat collar. "Frankie, I'm going to need you to be cool with something really quick, okay?"

Shadow Henry lifted a tentacle toward Remmy, and a patchy white-haired hand batted it away.

"Uh, what the fuck is going on?" Frankie said.

Remmy turned, and his dark eyes were now a bright yellow. His nose was now flat, with slits on either side, and his scruff was filled with patchy white fur. A mouth full of sharp teeth spoke, "Please, don't scream."

Frankie felt the blood drain from his face. "I—I think I'm beyond screaming. What. The. Fuck?"

Remmy sniffed the air again and looked at Frankie. "What spell did you cast?"

Frankie blinked and stared at the blob of darkness. "What?"

Remmy groaned, his lower jaw protruding more from his face. His shirt ripped completely free, along with his lab coat, as he became a massive half-man, half-wolf. "You said or did something. You need to undo it. Reverse whatever spell you did. Before . . ."

Remmy fell onto all fours, his body shrinking and reshaping into a patchy white wolf that bared his teeth right at Frankie.

Frankie shut his eyes and fell into the corner of the room. "Oh fuck. Uh, undo whatever the fuck I said. Please? Whatever witchy thing out there is listening."

The earthy air vanished, and the scent of bleach and sanitizer filled the air once again.

Frankie opened his eyes, spotting the toy poodle sitting happily on the scale, and a very naked Remmy on all fours.

Remmy stood up, wrapping himself around the waist with his tattered lab coat.

Frankie pushed himself up off the floor and eyed the scars on Remmy's chest. Frankie bit his lip. "There are usually drinks involved before something like this happens."

"Well, I'm sorry to break it to you, but I'm not usual." Remmy blushed.

"What? Hot werewolf guys aren't common around here? Shocker," Frankie said, rubbing the back of his neck.

Remmy shook his head and laughed, looking down at the heap of clothes. "Maybe, but I've got the whole trans werewolf thing all to myself."

Frankie eyed Remmy, tracing his body before shrugging. "You're probably all the same. A bunch of smelly frat bros."

"Yep, you caught me. Smelly frat bro, right here."

Frankie laughed, then looked over at the innocent-looking shadow monster who sat happily on the scale, wagging his tail. "So, the fuck is that?"

"A pooka," Remmy said, sticking out a hand to let Henry sniff it before scratching him behind the ears. "Pretty sure it ate the old Henry."

"Um, what?"

"As long as Mrs. Appleton feeds it, it should be fine," Remmy said.

"Sure. So . . . question. Shouldn't we be worried?"

Remmy shook his head. "It knows you can command it. The thing is pretty smart, so it shouldn't do anything too drastic."

"Great," Frankie pointed a finger at the new Henry. "Well, you'd better behave or I will get you, my pretty."

A faint earthen scent rose in the air, followed by the smell of roses, then vanished. Henry simply stared, blinking out of sync.

"So," Remmy started. "Mind getting me some clothes? I have an extra pair in my office."

Frankie raised an eyebrow. "Depends. Do you want to grab a drink after work?"

15

The Little Owl Eyes, in African lands,
Blooms in stripes, as beauty demands.
Yet beware the odor it commands,
A carrion call to fly-filled bands.

Beware its sap, the milkweed's hands,
Latex deadly, as poison expands.
Ingested it's lethal, it reprimands,
Causes eye and skin turmoil, as danger stands.

Yet in its venom, medicine's plans,
Cardiac glycosides in its strands.
A paradox of harm and healing bands,
In the Little Owl Eyes, nature's commands.

Little Owl Eyes

- AUGUST -

August sat at their desk, furiously typing away at the keyboard as the words traveled across the screen.

Ping.

They turned away, peering out into the darkened sky, frowning as they tried to remember when the storm had rolled in. They looked back at their screen, and the words that had previously filled the page were all gone, and the dreaded white screen stared back at them.

Ding.

Something bounced off August's head and clattered to the ground. They looked up, saw nothing, and looked down at the ground, spotting something small and brown laying on the floor.

Ting.

Another fell, bouncing off the desk and clattering to the ground. Then another, and another. August grabbed one of the little circular objects and turned it over. It was a dark brown coffee bean. Before they could process it anymore, an outright downpour of coffee beans fell from the ceiling, covering the floor in an instant.

August tried to stand, but the floor beneath them shifted, and they sank waist deep in a pit of coffee. They kept sinking, fear billowing up in their chest as they swung their arms about. But their efforts were futile, and their head submerged entirely, darkness engulfing them.

Then, a warm hand wrapped around theirs. They squeezed tight, and the mysterious stranger pulled them up out of the dark.

The world shifted, and they stood on a road in the middle of the woods. In front of them was a red wooden bridge, and just beyond that stood the most beautiful person August had ever seen. Their skin glowed like moonlight, and their long, curly brown hair and silky dress swayed in the wind.

The person at the other end of the bridge smiled and waved, and a burst of blue butterflies rose around August.

"Hey," a low voice called to August on their left.

They turned and found a massive deer staring back at them from the treeline. Gigantic moss-covered antlers grew out from its head like tree branches. And on those antlers, staring at August with wide, yellow eyes, were a collection of tiny owls.

"Hey," the deer said in a rough New York accent. "I'm talkin' to you. Watch where you're walkin'."

A horn sounded, and August turned just in time to see a pair of bright lights rushing into them.

August sat up in bed, covered in sweat. They blinked a few times, their room slowly coming back into vision. They looked at the clock, well past 10 a.m., and groaned. Another morning of writing, nearly gone.

They yanked off their covers and trudged over to the thick curtains, revealing the blinding morning light that forced them to wince and recoil like some kind of gremlin. "Oh look, another glorious morning," they mumbled, pulling on their robe and heading off to the bathroom.

After forming some semblance of humanity and heading downstairs, they didn't even notice they weren't alone in the house until they ran right into Jacob, literally.

August stumbled, nearly falling on top of the poor man, who was crouched over one second and flung onto his side the next. The first thought that crossed August's mind, for only a second, was the hilarity that they both wore the same red plaid shirt, and of course, Jacob clearly looked way better in it.

"Oh, shit! I'm sorry," August shouted, racing to help Jacob get back up on his feet. "What are you—Why are you here?"

Jacob rubbed his arm and winced. "Mat left me a key. I came to grab some wallpaper samples before I ran into town."

August stared blankly at him, then at the square of wallpaper missing from the wall. "Gotcha," they said, scratching their head. "Well, sorry. I'll be sure to watch out for Crouching Jacob, Hidden Handyman next time."

They started toward the kitchen when Jacob cleared his throat. "Hope you don't want any coffee."

"Uh, why?" August asked, turning around.

"Mat offered me some. I, well, uh. I spilled the carafe." He looked away the moment August's stare transformed into a glare.

August let out a breath and pinched the bridge of their nose. "And that was the last of the coffee, wasn't it?"

Jacob's eyes widened, a look that resembled that of a lost puppy. "I was going to pick some up while I was in town. But, now that you're up, want to hitch a ride? There's a nice coffee shop there."

August weighed their options. Either spend the day in glorious solitude, but cursed with caffeine irritability, or interact with more humans and risk actually talking to some of them. The former seemed to be the best option, although that damn puppy dog face of Jacob's was making it difficult.

"It has a fun name too, if you ask me. The Owlet Cafe," Jacob said, grinning.

Owlet, just like the little owls that had rested on those deer's antlers. *Was that a sign?*

"Sure," August said before thinking too hard on it. "I could use a change of scene."

Jacob smiled. "Great, meet me in my car in ten minutes?"

August nearly broke a sweat climbing into Jacob's truck. The damn man had one of those massive pickups that seemed to mock those who were vertically challenged.

"Sorry," Jacob said. "I go off-roading out in the woods a lot."

"Don't tell me you harvest your own wood or something," August said.

"Nope. You're looking at a part time junior park ranger," he said, smiling ear to ear.

August eyed the maps, binoculars, and radios in the truck and nodded. "Somehow, that doesn't surprise me. Handyperson by day, ranger by night. A real vigilante for all."

"Hey, someone's gotta do it," Jacob said, turning out of Henbane Hollow. "And I wouldn't give it up either."

August gripped their messenger bag, their attention drawn to the road. Their stomach coiled, and sweat formed on their hands. Trees loomed over the road, and up ahead, a bridge. Not just any bridge, but the same red bridge they saw in their dream.

They looked off to the treeline, expecting to see the same ancient deer peeking out from the treeline, but saw nothing. "Hey, can you slow down up here?"

He touched the brakes, squinting ahead. "Why? Do you see something?"

"No, I just—"

Tires screeched as a small doe leaped out from the woods right in front of the truck. The seatbelt in August's chair tightened against them, and they shut their eyes.

The truck jerked to a halt, and August expected to see a heap of bloody carnage when they opened their eyes. Instead, they caught the tail end of the doe vanishing off into the woods.

Jacob laughed and started across the bridge, eyes ahead. "Good eye. One second slower and who knows what would have happened."

"Yeah," August muttered, wiping their hands on their pants. "Good thing I saw it coming."

Jacob slowed in front of a black building with the drawing of a colorful owlet overtaking half the building and the white letters "The Owlet Cafe" at the top of it.

"It might be an hour or so. Are you good if I just leave you here?" Jacob asked.

August nodded, patting their messenger bag. "Good ol' Agatha will keep me busy. As long as she doesn't crash."

After free climbing out of the truck and landing safely on the ground, August opened the doors to the cafe and was greeted with the smell of rich, freshly roasted coffee and buttery pastries. The inside was a mix of white paint and illustrations of multicolored owls enjoying cups of coffee or getting into various forms of mischief.

Their mouth watered as they drifted up to the front counter and eyed the menu. As expected, every drink was owl themed, from the Nightjar Roast to the Earl Grey Owl, Snowy Owl Frappihoono, and the Tawny Toffee Owlatte.

"Be with you in one second," a voice called from the back.

"No rush." August peered into the bakery display, eyeing a particular loaf of spiced pumpkin bread with a light snow of powdered sugar and an imprint of an owl in a cup of coffee.

"Alright, what can I get for you?" the voice said on the other side of the display case.

August looked up, following the trail of long curly brown hair up to a round face and a bright smile. August's stomach fluttered, and a cold sweat formed on their brow. *It was them. The person they saw in their dream.* "Uh. What?"

The person behind the counter smiled. "First time here?"

"Yeah, how could you tell?"

"Must be my wild intuition. I'm Ragana, she/her, by the way. The youngest shop owner here in Greenwych, if I say so myself." She posed, one hand on her hip.

August blushed. "Uh, nice to meet you. I'm August, they/them. What, uh? What do you recommend?"

Ragana looked them up and down and smiled. "Let me guess. You're a novelist, aren't you, August?"

August looked down at their messenger bag, frowning. "I am. How did you—"

"Another one of my intuitions, let's say." Ragana smiled before looking down at the display case. "Well, if you ask me, any self-respecting novelist who comes into my cafe would need some Christmas Boobook Bread and a nice Cinnamon Screech Owlatte."

August bit their lip. Their eyes met Ragana's. "Owlatte it is," August said, handing over some cash. "Owl just be over here."

Ragana smirked. "Well, aren't you a hoot?"

16

Beneath the spines of the Toothache Tree,
A salve for pain, nature's remedy.
Chew the bark, feel the relief's decree,
An analgesic cure, our ancestors' legacy.

Yet heed this, friend, of its strength take heed,
Numbness ensues, from its use, indeed.
Tongue, teeth, and gums, the sensations recede,
In the folklorist's tale, we find this creed.

Housing swallowtails and beetles with glee,
Under its shadow, life's vast spree.
Birds find nourishment, in joy, they flee,
In the Toothache Tree, life's rhythm proceeds.

Toothache Tree

- MAT -

"Rinse, please," Dr. Denton said.

The words passed over Mat, whose focus was cast on the wispy ghost standing in the corner of Room One at the dentist's office.

Dr. Denton leaned back in her seat and snapped her fingers. "Earth to Dr. Mandrake. You there?"

"What?" he said. The ethereal woman, who had been popping in and out of his life for the past week, vanished again. His attention was drawn back to the woman in the white coat with a pair of thick black-rimmed glasses that caused her to look more like a praying mantis than a doctor.

She pointed a gloved hand to his side, at the two tubes he was supposed to be in charge of. "Rinse, please."

"Right," Mat said, jumping to work and picking up the water pick and suction tube. He focused on the poor elderly woman who'd been waiting for him. She was the last patient of the week, and even though he'd proven himself more than capable of taking on his own clients, he was certain Dr. Denton was more interested in keeping him as her assistant.

He rinsed out and suctioned the debris and spittle as he caught a glance into the elderly woman's eyes. She looked at him, then shifted her gaze to the corner of the room where the ghost had been. Her eyes widened, and a slight smile formed.

Dr. Denton placed her utensils down and pulled off her gloves. "Well, that should be all, Mrs. Haag. Join me up front, and I'll finish up your paperwork and get you out of here."

"Oh, no dear," Mrs. Haag said as she sat up. She looked at the doctor and spoke in a soft, melodic tone that made Mat's eyes feel heavy. "Shouldn't you get that?"

Dr. Denton's shoulders drooped, and she seemed to lose her focus.

Mat frowned. "Get what?"

A ring sounded out in the lobby, close to, but not quite, the ringing of the phone Mat had been all too accustomed to this week. It had an ethereal tone to it, as if he might have just imagined the sound instead.

Dr. Denton stood up, half in a daze, and mumbled, "I'm sorry, I need to get that. Dr. Mandrake will help you." She left without another word.

Mat frowned, staring at Mrs. Haag. "How did you know the phone was going to—"

"You're Melinda Mandrake's relative, yes?" Mrs. Haag asked, her tone less melodic and more chipper as she leaned back in her seat.

"Uh, yeah?"

She nodded to the corner of the room. "And if you could see her, then I take it you've started your coven?"

"Coven?" Mat asked. "What are you talking about?"

Mrs. Haag rested her head back in the seat and flipped on the extendable lamp, shining the light on her face. "Great, so you don't know yet. Well, the bewitching won't last long, and I need this tooth extracted now. If you don't mind."

"Extraction? But your teeth are fine. You were just in for a cleaning."

"Not those teeth," Mrs. Haag laughed. "Poor Dr. Denton would lose her mind if she saw the other pair."

"Other pair?"

Mrs. Haag opened her mouth wide, and a set of sharp teeth extended out over her gums, covering her other set completely. They looked exactly like shark teeth, with jagged edges and all. She spoke with a slight lisp as she said, "These usually cycle through every year or so, but this one," she said as she pointed to one that was slightly off center and yellowed, "has been stuck for years and won't seem to come out."

Mat nearly fell out of his chair, his eyes dead set on the mouth full of teeth right in front of him. "What? How? What the hell is that?"

Mrs. Haag sighed. "You really don't know? You really need to read your book."

"Know what?" Mat asked.

"Henbane Hollow is a haven. And you've inherited more than just a house. The covens at Mandrake Manor have kept us safe for centuries."

"Safe from what?"

Mrs. Haag looked past him toward the front lobby. "From people like them finding out. People who fear us. People who'd do anything to ensure that their world is preserved."

Mat had so much more he wanted to ask, so much more he needed to know, but something she had said resonated. "So, I'm supposed to keep you safe, and your bewitching doesn't last long." He pulled on a pair of gloves. "So let's get this tooth looked at and get you on your way."

Her face relaxed, and she opened wide, and Mat peered into a mouth full of razor-sharp teeth.

Mat stepped inside Mandrake Manor, tossing the keys to the Green Machine on the hook and shouting, "House meeting! I'm calling a house meeting. Now!"

August groaned and spoke up from the living room. "House meeting? Why?"

Mat found August resting on the couch, their computer cracked open on their lap as they lay wrapped in a blanket, Dude resting at their feet. "Because I just extracted a tooth from an old woman with a set of big ass shark teeth, and I've been seeing a ghost all week. If that doesn't warrant a house meeting, then I don't know what does."

"Ghost?" Frankie said, coming in from the kitchen, holding a glass of something brightly colored.

"Yes, a real-life fucking ghost. I thought I was losing my mind all week, but—"

His words fell out of his mouth as he turned and came face-to-face with Remmy.

Mat's face grew hot. "Oh, uh, Dr. Lupin. I didn't know you were here. Uh."

Frankie sipped on his drink and wedged his way onto the couch beside Dude. "I invited him over for a drink. Didn't think you'd be coming home with a mental breakdown."

Mat frowned. "Oh, well, this is kind of important. I don't mean to be a buzzkill, but—"

"But what?" Frankie asked.

Mat looked at Remmy, then Frankie. "But I think there are some things we need to talk about. Things I learned today that you two need to know."

"Remmy's a werewolf," Frankie said.

"What?" Mat asked.

"Werewolf," August said. "You know, like the whole turn into a wolf on the full moon."

"I know what a werewolf is, August," Mat said, rolling his eyes.

"Maybe now wasn't the best time to tell him," Remmy said, slipping past Mat and sitting on the armrest of the couch beside Frankie.

Frankie shrugged. "But now he might calm down."

"Wait," Mat said. "So, both of you know? Are there others? I mean, other than Mrs. Haag?"

"Oh," Remmy said, smiling. "Did she finally get that tooth looked at? I offered, but she took offense to the whole vet thing."

Mat pinched his brow. "I don't know if I can handle this right now. I—What is going on?"

"We're witches," Frankie said, slapping August's knee.

"Ow, dick," August said. "Watch it, or I'll turn you into a frog or something."

Mat looked at Remmy. "And he's a werewolf?"

"Yep," Frankie said. "It's all pretty straightforward, if you ask me."

"And you're both just okay with it?" Mat asked.

August nodded. "You said you were seeing a ghost all week, right? Well, Frankie's been dealing with a demon dog—"

"Pooka," Remmy said. "Not a demon."

"Fine, a pooka pup," August corrected. "And I've had some wild dreams that came true. I'd say we are collectively losing our minds, or that little welcoming spell we did worked."

"Okay," Mat said. "Okay. Magic is real. Remmy is a werewolf. Mrs. Haag is some shark lady."

"Siren," Remmy said.

"Siren," Mat corrected. "And, uh, what else?"

August shrugged. "I'm pretty sure the house is alive."

As if in response, a draft blew past Mat and into the living room, causing the curtains to give a slight wave.

"I'm surprised Demetri didn't tell you any of this," Remmy said.

"Demetri? Does he know too?" Mat asked.

Remmy's face blushed. "I—Well, it's not my place to say."

"But you told him that Haag lady was a siren," Frankie said.

"Well, she showed him first," Remmy said. "And I don't know anything anymore. There was a time when everyone at Henbane Hollow wasn't mundane. But now . . ."

"Now? Now what?" Frankie asked.

Remmy frowned, as if the words strained to come out of his mouth. "I don't know. It's like we are losing the old ways. And the more I look, the more normal everything is becoming. Even now, talking about it feels . . . strange."

August's eyes widened, and they sat up. "Like the houses?"

"The houses? What are you talking about?" Mat asked.

"I mean, why do half the houses here look like they are pulled from some 1980s suburban neighborhood? That has to be what you are talking about, right? Is something happening here, Remmy?" August asked.

Remmy's eyes glazed over for a second, then he blinked and frowned. "I don't—What were we just talking about?" He looked at his drink and nudged Frankie. "I think you made these a little strong."

Frankie eyed Remmy for a moment, then tossed back the rest of his drink. "Well, Mandrake Coven, I think it's time we looked at that book of ours. Don't you think so?"

17

Ancient Ginkgo, standing firm and hale,
A living fossil, scribing nature's tale.
But wanderer, heed this, as the tale tells,
In its gifted seeds, a subtle danger swells.

Fabled for memory, for thought's clear streams,
Yet, consume with caution, not all is as it seems.
Nausea, palpitations, the unsettling dreams,
Tread gently 'round the seeds, beware their schemes.

Tales speak of easing dementia's decline,
And soothing bronchitis, asthma's bind.
Such blessings from Ginkgo, nature's sign,
In whispers of the wild, your tales intertwine.

Gingko

- FRANKIE -

"How do you forget where you put the book?" Frankie asked, closing the side drawer of Mat's nightstand.

"I didn't forget," Mat said, flipping open a cardboard box and rifling through it. "It's in here somewhere. I think."

Remmy leaned against the door frame and sighed.

"What?" Frankie asked, carefully picking up a pair of underwear and tossing it aside. "Do you have something to add?"

Remmy considered, then slowly stepped into the room. "Well, I'm no expert, but the book is probably mad at you for locking it away."

Mat groaned. "You're telling me the book's alive too?"

"Probably," Remmy said. "I can't know for sure, but if a book were to be alive, it would be the Mandrake spellbook, right?"

August plopped down on the chair next to the window, scratching Dude's head. "And if I were a sentient book who'd been locked away, only to be found, used once, and locked away again, I'd be upset."

Frankie looked up at the ceiling and shouted. "Hey . . . book? Ignore what mean old Mat did to you." He pushed himself up off the bed and pulled open the armoire, inspecting the dusty insides. "I didn't want to lock you up. He's the asshole."

"Hey, dick." Mat grabbed a handful of dirty socks and threw them at him. "You really think I was about to let you have free rein over a spellbook? Do you remember what happened when I gave you the keycard to the library so you could study?"

"That was one time! And your head librarian was overreacting. That fire did like no damage. There wasn't even a light crisping on the books."

August laughed to themself and rubbed their fingers behind Dude's ears. They spoke in a high-pitched baby voice. "We wouldn't let poor Frankie burn the house down, would we? I bet that book cares about us. I bet it wouldn't let us burn the house down, even if we tried."

The lights in the house dimmed and brightened for a moment, as if giving some kind of nod to what August had to say.

"I think you should apologize," Frankie said.

"What?" Mat said, shifting his gaze from Frankie to August. "Why? I shouldn't have to—"

"They have a point," Remmy said, crossing his arms. "You've opened how many drawers now and haven't found it? I'd bet if you just apologized, maybe with a little rhyme, it would show up."

"Fine," Mat said, looking up at the ceiling, thinking. He started slowly, pondering over his words. "I'm sorry, book. I'm sorry, house. I had my doubts that I . . . renounce? We didn't know what we were doing. And it freaked me out, okay?"

The four of them stood in silence, waiting for some kind of response. For a long while, there was none. The house was silent, pondering the apology.

Then, the window beside August unlatched, and they all looked as a breeze blew in, swaying the curtains. The lights glowed brighter for a moment too before settling.

"Think that means the apology was accepted?" Frankie asked as he turned back around. Then he spotted the book, resting right on top of Mat's bed as if it had been there the whole time. "Voila!" he shouted, grabbing the book and feeling a warmth spread across his fingertips. "There you are, beautiful. We missed you."

"Are you flirting with the book?" Mat asked.

"Maybe? I'll flirt with whomever I want, thank you," Frankie said.

He hopped onto Mat's bed and flipped open the book. "Let's see . . . 'Coven Spell, Wards and How to Recharge Them,' 'Types of Wards,' 'Common Magical Ailments' . . . Hey, maybe I can help you with your fur situation."

August cocked their head to the side. "Fur situation?"

Remmy blushed and looked down at the ground. "Hair loss. Started happening to my wolf's form a few months ago."

Frankie ran his finger along the section on ailments, which included everything from magical blockage to Satyr's Itch, which sounded very much like a sexually transmitted infection. "There's nothing spelled out in this thing about that specifically," Frankie finally said. "But it looks like there might be some tests we can do to see what is causing it. I think we could do them. They look easy enough."

Mat put his hands on his hips. "Shouldn't we be learning the basics before testing on living people? We'd be putting him at risk."

Frankie flipped through a few more pages and looked up. "Pretty sure that ninety percent of this book is making herbs and helping others from their otherworldly STIs. So that puts our 'learning the basics' right into practical application." Frankie flipped back a few pages. "Unless you want to have a go at this ward spell. Ingredients are blood and graveyard dirt, and you need to charge the spell, which sounds kind of hot, but maybe not something you would do on a first date."

"Fine," Mat said. "Point taken. Remmy, I hope you don't mind being the guinea pig."

Remmy shrugged. "I don't think you can make my wolf's form any worse. Why not?"

"Hopefully you don't have to eat those words," Frankie said.

A ding echoed loudly in the room, and Frankie nearly fell off the bed as he jumped.

"Was that the doorbell?" August asked.

"I didn't know we had a doorbell," Mat said, frowning.

"Seems like we do. Are you going to get that?" Frankie asked.

Mat rolled his eyes before exiting the bedroom.

Frankie picked up the book and followed behind him, flipping past a few more pages as all of them traveled down the stairs.

Before Mat reached the door, he turned and pointed at the book. "Put that away. We don't know who's here."

"Fine," Frankie said, closing the book and setting it down on the credenza beside him.

Mat pulled the door open, and a pale-faced Helena stared back. She wore her hair up in a tight bun, a plain black pantsuit, and a silvery locket around her neck. Her cold eyes met Frankie's for a moment, causing him to shiver, before she landed them on Mat.

"Uh, hi?" Mat started. "Everything alright?"

"One week," Helena said, lifting a finger.

"Sorry?" Mat said.

"When we spoke last, I thought I clarified that Mandrake Manor had accumulated several infractions." She turned and gestured behind her. "Including this overgrown walkway."

Frankie pushed himself off the credenza and walked next to Mat, looking past Helena. "But it isn't overgrown. Jacob came by and cleared all of it—"

Helena moved out of the way, and sure enough, the walkway was covered in weeds and overgrown hedges that spilled out onto the sidewalk.

"An untamed house needs more than just a simple pruning," Helena said. "Seems like Jacob Borowy is losing his touch. I have a few contacts, better contacts, if you need someone who knows a thing or two about landscaping."

"Thanks for the offer, but I think I'll stick with Jacob," Mat said, his words cold.

Frankie held onto the memory of coming home. He remembered the sidewalk was completely manicured. It had to have been. Yet, the more he thought about it, the more the overgrowth encroached on his memory. "I swear it was clear. I think. I—"

"Either way," Helena started. "You've incurred your first infraction."

"Really?" Mat asked. "But we've only been here a week. We haven't even unpacked all our boxes."

Helena flipped open a notepad and started scrawling on it. "If you'd like to dispute it, you'll need to attend the next HOA meeting. But since a member of the HOA is administering the fine firsthand, it may not be the wisest of choices to dispute at your first attended meeting."

"But you know we hired someone," August started. "We're working on fixing this place up after who knows how many years of neglect. How can you punish us after one week?"

"Rules are rules." Helena looked up. She froze for a second, her mouth slightly agape as her eyes settled on something behind Frankie for a moment. She blinked and pulled the paper from her notepad and handed it over to Mat. "Payment is due in thirty days."

"But—"

Helena looked into the house, at Remmy, and cut off Mat. "Ah, Dr. Lupin. Nice to see you. If I'd known better, I'd think you were trying to avoid me."

"The office has been busy, as always. I've been meaning to call," Remmy said.

"No need," Helena said, smiling. "We have denied your request for additional canine occupancy. We can't have you turning your home into a haven for stray dogs, not for the premium living we offer at Henbane Hollow."

Dude let out a low growl, the first time he'd done so since they had him. Frankie looked at him, noting the tail between his legs and the hackles raised on his back.

Helena cleared her throat, and Dude stopped instantly. "I hope this isn't another one of your rescues."

"Dude is ours," August said.

Helena smiled. "Ah, and have you filed the proper paperwork to own a pet in this neighborhood?"

Frankie's heart sank. "No. There's paperwork?"

"You're in an HOA, dear," Helena smirked. "There's paperwork for everything. I'd get that in before Monday morning, if I were you. I hear the fine can be fairly steep."

Mat stepped back and started closing the door on her. "It was a pleasure seeing you again, Helena, but we need to get going."

"The pleasure is all mine, Mr. Mandrake," she said as he closed the door in her face.

After a few moments of silence, August cleared their throat. "Well, fuck her."

Frankie crossed the room and picked up the book, cracking it open, and mumbled, "I wonder if there's a spell to turn her into a newt or something."

Remmy eyed the floor. "You really don't want to cross Helena. She's good at getting her way. No matter how much you try to evade her."

"Fair," Frankie said, flipping through the pages. "But if she were a newt, then we wouldn't have anything to worry about."

"We're not turning our neighbors into newts," Mat said. "We need to keep the high ground."

August shrugged. "Turning her into a newt might be an improvement."

"See?" Frankie said, grinning. "Even August agrees. So, magical case number one, help Remmy. Magical case number two, newtify Helena."

"No," Mat said. "Or do I need to reiterate why I locked the book up?"

"Oh, come on. I'm joking," Frankie said, before looking over at Remmy and smiling as he mouthed, "I'm not joking."

Remmy smirked back and shook his head. "You really are a troublemaker, aren't you?"

Frankie shut the book and took a step toward Remmy. "That's why they love me. Want another drink?"

18

Fireweed's tale begins in ashes bare,
In bomb sites and oil spills, it dares to dare.
Resilient and adaptive, it makes its stand,
Cloaking barren scars across the land.

Tender shoots and leaves, when young, may feed,
Proffering vitamins in time of need.
Yet caution, wanderer, as seasons fly,
A bitter taste, as it ages, lies.

In affliction's throes, seek its humble stem,
Upon raw cuts, it's a soothing gem.
It draws out the pus, quickens the pace,
Healing's ally in nature's embrace.

Fireweed

- AUGUST -

"**A**re you done yet?" Frankie asked, hovering behind August.

August sat on the couch in the house library and flipped through the book, finding sparse notes on dream interpretations. "No. Not until I find out more about this damn dream."

"Well, I need the book. Remmy is coming over, and I said I'd have one of those tests ready."

August ran a finger down the page, skipping past the notes on drowning, flying, and falling until their finger hovered over the word fire. Transformation, destruction, and danger were the three words next to it.

"Fuck," August said.

"That bad?" Frankie asked.

"I dreamed the cafe was on fire."

"And you're looking at the book instead of racing off to the cafe because?"

August sighed. "Because the dreams I've had aren't that straight-forward. Fire doesn't mean actual fire. I had a dream that I was drowning in coffee, and that didn't happen. This time, the cafe was in black and white, and there was a caged owl in the center of the room. I couldn't feel the heat from the fire, but it was the only thing with color, burning at the walls and ceiling."

"Still, why wouldn't you just go there?"

August turned their head and glared at Frankie. "Because some people have social anxiety, okay? And if I'm wrong, then what? I cried wolf for no reason. Ragana would think I'm some psychopath, and then—"

"Or," Frankie cut them off. "Hear me out. You go to the cafe to work and see if everything is alright. No one has to know about your dream."

"And if it is something?"

Frankie walked around the couch and plopped right next to August. "Then you call me, and we'll do a spell or something. There's a ward against fire in here somewhere."

August nodded. Frankie was right. The only way they were going to know what their dreams meant was to just go and find out. They handed the book over. "Fine, you win. I'll go."

"I think Mat is headed downtown. You might still be able to catch a ride."

August pushed themself off the couch and frowned. "Is this a ploy to get both of us out of the house so you have time alone with Remmy?"

Frankie jumped up and wrapped an arm around August, guiding them out of the room. "Uh, yeah, obviously. But also, if you dream my bedroom is burning down, you better run your ass to my room and not this book, understand?"

"Loud and clear."

"Mat!" Frankie shouted. "You still here?"

"Yeah," an echo came from upstairs. "What do you want?"

"August is coming with you. They need to go see a special someone at the cafe."

Mat appeared at the top of the stairs, his hair combed back and sporting a pair of gray suit pants and a crisp white button-down. "Do I look okay?" he asked as he descended the stairs.

The moment Frankie had a chance, his hands went straight to Mat's hair. "You are banned from doing that to your hair again." He manipulated it until it had volume and showed off the loose curls in his hair. "Much better."

"So, both of you have dates?" August asked.

Mat shrugged. "I think so? Demetri asked me out for lunch. He said there was something else I needed to sign, but—"

"But," Franke said, "he is totally asking you out on a date. Otherwise, he'd be asking you to come into the office."

Mat turned to August. "Are you okay being there for a while? I don't know how long Demetri will be."

"Once I get my computer, I can bunker down with an owlatte and crank out words. So, yeah. Both of you can have your wonderful little fairytale dates, and I'll be the gremlin at the cafe."

Frankie leaned against the wall and crossed his arms. "You know . . . You could always talk it up with Ragana. I'm sure she's dating material. Maybe the fire is your passion."

"Fire?" Mat asked.

August groaned and started up the stairs. "Ignore him. Let me grab my computer, and we can let Frankie finally break in the sex rug or something."

"Hey!" Frankie started, then laughed. "Maybe."

August looked up at the multicolored Owlet Cafe as Mat drove away, focusing on the near perfect replica of the colorless version they had seen in their dream. "Better now than never," they said, taking in a breath and heading to the doors.

At least the building hadn't actually burned down, and from the looks of it, there wasn't a hint of a fire in sight.

They stepped into the most heavenly scent of coffee, intermixed with the doughy scent of freshly baked pastries.

"So the novelist has returned," Ragana said, catching sight of August from behind the counter. She had her curly brown hair tied up in a ponytail and wore a black denim apron covered in flour. "Come to fill these walls with words?"

"Hopefully," August said, their cheeks growing hot as they approached the counter. Ragana had pulled out a tray of freshly baked cinnamon rolls and topped them with icing. August took the moment to lean over the counter, looking for signs of fire, before saying, "So, weird question, but is everything alright?"

Ragana set down the icing and frowned. "I think so? It was a bit of a late start today, but nothing noteworthy. Why do you ask?"

August shrugged and leaned back, adjusting their messenger bag. "No reason." They let out a breath, then said, "How about an owlatte? Your choice. And one of those cinnamon rolls?"

"Absolutely. These have a hint of orange in them," Ragana said.

"Great, I'll take it," August said, handing over cash before turning and finding a spot near the counter with an outlet. They stared at the center of the cafe, thinking about the table in their dream, where an owl was perched, staring at August while the building burned down around them. It made little sense. They knew it meant something, that it felt the same as the other dreams, but Ragana was fine. The cafe was fine

.

Moments later, Ragana came out with a massive roll and a latte with the milk foam designed as a small owl. "I think the Tawny Toffee Owlatte will go well with the bun. Perfect fuel to get you writing, if I say so myself. Let me know what you think."

August blinked a few times, pulling their attention back to the present, and looked up at Ragana. "Thanks," they muttered before Ragana turned and headed back behind the counter.

August had to do everything in their power to not devour the bun and the latte in seconds. The buttery caramel notes of the latte blended with the cinnamon and orange from the bun perfectly, leaving August wanting more. They opened up their computer and stared at the blank page, something in them ready to tackle their work.

Ragana was right, and time slipped away as words billowed out of them. People came and went into the cafe, a blur in August's peripheral vision. They'd come up for air every so often, seeking a bite from the bun and a sip of coffee, before diving back into their work.

Pages filled in what felt like seconds, but based on the sunlight beaming in from outside, they'd been there for hours, and the cafe was empty once again. Mat would likely be back any minute, and Ragana was busy wiping down tables.

The door to the cafe dinged, and August looked up.

It wasn't Mat, but Helena, standing in a black and white pinstripe suit, pale skin, and black hair tied back in a tight bun.

"Ragana," Helena said, staring up and down at the walls. "Love what you've done with the place."

"Helena? Hi," Ragana said back, tossing down a rag and placing her hands on her hips. "What are you doing on this side of town?"

Helena checked her nails for a moment, then said, "I came to check in on Gran. I hadn't seen her in ages, and that poor woman doesn't have much time left. Since I was in the area, why not check in on my favorite cousin?"

"Favorite cousin? Hardly," Ragana scoffed.

Helena smiled, and her eyes fell on August. "Ah, I see the new tenants of Mandrake Manor have scuttled their way over here. Which one are you, again? Francis?"

August did everything they could to remain civil, even though the empty plate in front of them would serve well as a frisbee into Helena's head. "August."

"Right, the novelist." Helena emphasized the word, as if jabbing a knife into August's heart.

Ragana tutted her tongue. "Actually, August has been here all afternoon, typing so much I was afraid their fingers might fall off."

"No surprise there. You always fostered . . . inspiring environments," Helena said, eyeing the paintings on the walls.

"What is it you want, Helena?" Ragana asked.

"The loans," Helena said. "The ones you used to buy this shop?"

"Yes, I know which loans."

Helena stepped forward, running a hand along the table beside her. "Well, they're coming due. And I have a proposition for you that might help ease some of the burden."

August grimaced. At least the cafe was empty, aside from them, but what kind of person comes in and talks like this? They looked over at Ragana and clenched their jaw.

Ragana bit her lip. "Go on."

"Your home, the one on Hemlock Way? You haven't submitted paperwork for the suburban rejuvenation project yet. If I were to get those papers, say by the end of this week, then the grant approval might include some incentives for a local business owner. Perhaps, coverage of half the loan?"

"Wait," August shouted, glaring at Helena. "You can't force her to do that. You're bribing her!"

Helena eyed August. "I can't force her. You are right. But the project is focused on local integrity, and local business owners are at the heart of it. So the HOA has worked with the town for some relief for participating business owners. All contracts and forms are available online, if you wish to dispute." She turned her gaze back to Ragana. "Just something to think about. I'd hate to see a place like this go up in flames because you stood your ground on an old home in need of renovations."

Ragana looked at August, then around the cafe, and sighed. "I'll think about it."

"Excellent," Helena said, turning and heading toward the exit. "You can mail me the forms directly. I'll put it on top of the pile for processing. Anything I can do for family. Wish you well, cousin."

The door closed, and Ragana let out a groan. "There was a reason she was the black sheep of the family."

"I'm sorry. I shouldn't have butted in. It's just. It's not right. The entire project. It's wrong," August said, closing their computer and packing their things up.

"I almost took it if you didn't speak up," Ragana said.

August paused. "Oh, well—"

"Do you want to go out? This Friday?"

"What?" August asked.

Ragana crossed the room and picked up the empty mug at August's table. "Out. On a date. You and me. This Friday, my treat."

A lump formed in August's throat. "A date. With me? Why? I mean. Yes, but why?"

Ragana shrugged. "I like you, August. Isn't that enough?"

19

Behold the Devil's Fingers, in their gory array,
A fungal spawn in two acts, an eerie ballet.
From humble egg to star-fished flare,
Four to six arms in the air, a sight rare.

Yet, wanderer, heed, despite its spectacle,
It mimics rotting flesh, an attractant effectual.
Flies it lures, to spread its spore,
Global presence it ensures, forever more.

Consume it not, though no toxin resides,
Its rotten stench, a gustatory divide.
In Devil's Fingers, nature's jest resides,
In leaf litter and mulch, it confides.

Devil's Fingers

- MAT -

Mat eyed the ghost sitting across from him as he finished his second glass of wine. It was the same ethereal woman, dressed in some tattered wispy dress. When their eyes met, he looked away, down at the menu in front of him, tracing the fancy lettering that spelled Basil & Balsamic, confirming for the hundredth time that he was in the right place.

Demetri had made the reservation, which Mat used to earn a seat right in the middle of the restaurant, for all the onlookers to see him seated alone.

When he looked up from the menu, the ghost was still staring at Mat. His frustration took the better of him, and he hissed, "What?"

The ghost mouthed a few words Mat couldn't hear.

"I can't fucking hear you," he whispered.

"Oh, I'm sorry," a voice said beside him.

Mat jumped, looking up at the older gentleman, his waiter named Phil, who sported a fine head of gray hair and a thick mustache to match.

"Sorry," Mat said. "I think the wine might be a little strong."

Phil smiled, pulling out a basket of baked breads from behind his back. "Oh look, fresh baked house bread, how convenient." He set the basket on the table and looked up toward the door. "Care for another glass with your bread?"

Mat rested his head in his hands. "What would you say is customary? Finishing three glasses of wine before calling it quits, or two?"

Phil placed his hands on his hips and let in a deep breath. "I'd probably say one glass, if you ask me. But here we are, down two, so a third wouldn't hurt."

"So, should I just go?"

Phil shook his head and grabbed Mat's shoulder, squeezing. "Not until you have some bread and a glass of water. You leave here when you've sobered up. You hear me?"

Mat picked up a roll and bit into it. It still steamed as he tore off the crunchy crust and took in the slightly sweet flavor inside. "I hear you loud and clear," Mat said, his mouth full.

By his second roll, and half a glass of water, his mind cleared, and he looked up toward the door.

A Black man, dressed in a perfectly tailored navy suit, with a line of sweat down the side of his clean-shaved face, looked back at him. Demetri's shoulders relaxed as he raced over.

"I am so sorry," he said as he pulled off his coat and rested it on the chair across from Mat. During Mat's gorging of the breads, the ghost who'd been sitting across from him vanished. Mat didn't blame her. Who'd want to watch him stuff his face like some sort of crazed gremlin after realizing how good the bread was?

"It's fine," Mat said, trying his best to suppress his thoughts as Demetri's whiskey-scented cologne wafted by. He picked up his glass of water and sipped.

Demetri sat and shook his head. "No, it's not, and I don't blame you if you're mad. I was waiting for someone to show up at the office and drop off some documents, but they stood me up." He half smirked and patted his head with a napkin. "Which is exactly what I nearly ended up doing to you."

"You did," Mat nodded. He looked up at Demetri, into his eyes. There was no malice. No ill intent. And the longer he looked, the more his insides fluttered. "But I still don't know what this is. More contract business? Is there something wrong with the house?"

Demetri's cheeks turned pink, and he grabbed his now iceless glass of water next to him. "Well, actually. I was hoping this could be like a date. If you wanted it to be, I mean."

"I see the rest of the party has finally arrived," Phil said as he approached the table. "Would you care for another wine, Mr. Mandrake? And, Mr. Demonte, is it? What would you like?"

Mat nodded, and Demetri quickly eyed the menu. "I'll have a glass of the Ferriera port, please."

"Right away, gentlemen," Phil said, backing away.

They both sat in silence, far longer than Mat would have liked.

"So," Demetri finally said, then paused.

"So," Mat replied. When Demetri winced, Mat sighed. "Sorry, I might be two wines deep already. I didn't mean for that to come off—"

"I don't blame you. Look, I'm not the best at this. And I feel like I already blew my chance, but I'd love to hear how everything has been going. The house, your job, anything."

Mat leaned back in his chair, wondering how much Demetri might know about the house. "Well, there's never a dull moment, if that is what you're asking. And now we've got Helena breathing down our necks, so that's fun."

Demetri groaned. "I'll talk to her. She's had a grudge against Melinda that she must have passed on to you. I swear she was reasonable once."

Mat shrugged. "Other than that, things have been okay. Dr. Denton is still clutching onto her patients with an iron grip, and aside from the repairs, the house has been amazing."

"Good," Demetri said, a smile spreading across his face. "I'm really glad you've stayed."

"Me too," Mat said, leaning forward in his seat, gazing into Demetri's eyes. "What about you? Seems like work has kept you busy."

"Alright, gentlemen," Phil said, reapproaching the table and setting down two glasses of wine. "Pinot for Mr. Mandrake and port for Mr. Demonte. Do you need anything—"

Silence barreled through the room, and Phil froze mid-step backward.

"What the hell?" Mat said, leaning toward Phil and waving a hand in front of the man. He didn't respond, and when Mat focused on the rest of the room, he found that everyone else had frozen too in mid-drink or bite of their food. Everyone but Demetri.

Demetri groaned and grabbed his glass of port. "I take it you've read from the book?"

"What? What is this?" Mat asked.

"My office visit, at the worst time possible."

A wisp of greenish light caught Mat's eye, and he saw the spirit of the old woman waving her hands and mouthing, "Run!"

The ground trembled, and the floor beside them gave way, tiles cracking and falling away into a sinkhole that consumed an entire table.

Mat stood and stumbled back, looking at the frozen patrons in the restaurant, wondering how he could help them.

Demetri stood and straightened his suit. "I'm sorry you have to see this. It should be over in a minute. Please, don't worry about them. They'll be fine."

Two curved horns pushed out from the hole, followed by a cross between a man and a bull, with a flat, slitted nose and a chest that was nearly double that of Remmy. Coarse black hair covered the man's bottom half and forearms. As he stepped out, cloven hooves clacked on the tile floor.

Again, Mat caught a glimpse of the ghostly woman, waving her arms, pleading for him to run. But he couldn't. His feet were leaden, and his eyes were transfixed.

"What impeccable timing," Demetri said.

The horned man smiled, his eyes falling on Mat. His voice was low, resonating throughout the room. "I couldn't pass up the opportunity to meet the new Mandrake, could I?"

Demetri sighed. "Mat, this is Damian. My brother."

"Brother?" Mat spit out. "He's your brother?"

"Half-brother," Damian replied. "He never committed to the roles."

"Do you have it or not? Mat doesn't need to hear about our family drama."

Damian looked at the two of them and grinned. "You had me believe this was a business meeting. It would seem that's not the case."

"Do you have it?" Demetri asked again.

Damian nodded. "Always straight to the point with you. I do, but I'd like to revisit the terms of our agreement."

"No. We had a deal."

Damian held up an envelope. "I was to bring you the information you asked for. And I have. However, unfortunately it is written in a cipher. One of those infernal ones I could easily solve for you once we settled a new deal."

"Fine, what do you want?" Demetri asked.

"A home. In Henbane Hollow. Where Dad can start thinking about retirement."

"No. You and Dad are not welcome here," Demetri said.

"Hm," Damian said, looking at Mat. "Then perhaps I take this one and call it settled?" He snapped his fingers.

Mat's mind clouded, and he stepped forward. A part of him wanted to protest this, but the more he stared at Damian, tracing down his cheek and to his chest, the more he wondered why he wouldn't obey. He took another step toward Damian. Toward the pit.

"Stop!" Demetri shouted.

"I don't think I will," Damian said, baring a set of pointed teeth.

"Let me in," a woman's voice whispered in Mat's mind. "Let me help."

In his clouded state, he didn't know why he wouldn't let the poor woman help. A part of him opened up, like a latch on a lockbox, something he'd kept closed for his entire life.

A stream of cold filled his body, and thoughts of an old woman, matronly and smelling of flowers and dirt, filled his mind.

He stopped in his tracks, halfway to Damian.

Damian frowned, waving his hand at Mat once more.

A woman's voice came out of Mat's mouth as he held up his hand. "You will not cull my kin, demon. Heed my words, creatures from beyond the veil, return whence you came." Mat drew a symbol in the air with a trailing green light, full of curves and winding paths.

"No!" Demetri shouted, "Wait!"

Mat couldn't wait, nor stop the woman, as she pressed his hand against the air-drawn symbol. An unseen force instantly pulled Damian back into the hole in the ground without another word. Mat heard a thud next to him and the sound of glass shattering. He turned and found Demetri on the floor, some invisible tendril wrapped around his ankle, pulling him toward the hole.

"No!" Mat shouted, pushing against the ghostly woman, reclaiming control over his body. She fell to the ground and vanished in a green mist.

Mat scrambled to grab Demetri's hand but missed.

The last thing Mat saw was the fear in Demetri's eyes as he slipped into the hole.

Then the hole blinked out of existence, and Mat sat in the middle of an unsuspecting restaurant with a broken wine glass beside him and Demetri's discarded coat hanging on the back of his chair.

20

In daisy's kin, the Milk Thistle stands,
Gift of liver aid, stretched forth in caring hands.
No solid proof, yet whispers of tradition,
Claim improved appetite, a wholesome mission.

Yet heed caution, for not all is benign,
Stomach upset and allergies, in some, align.
Toxic to cattle, sheep in fields it roam,
Beware the nitrate, a silent threat in loam.

Supplements of thistle, tainted by mycotoxin's trace,
Potential dangers lurking in its graceful face.
An enigma, Milk Thistle, in medicinal race,
A dance twixt help and harm, in nature's embrace.

Milk Thistle

- FRANKIE -

"I think you're gonna want another glass of whiskey," Frankie said, looking up from the Mandrake spellbook and grabbing his glass, finishing the contents.

Remmy had brought the bottle, a local maple whiskey, which was the right amount of sweet and smoky aftertaste.

"Why?" Remmy asked, sipping from his glass as he sat on the couch next to Dude, scratching his head.

"Because per this, you need to at least be shirtless," Frankie said.

"At least be shirtless?"

Frankie cleared his throat. "And I quote, 'The spell is best performed in the dead of night, under a new moon and stark naked. However, as long as the oils and herbs touch flesh around the heart, the spell should work.' I doubt you want to go full traditional."

Remmy finished his glass and pushed himself up off the couch. "You would be correct."

Frankie looked at his empty glass, then toward the kitchen. "So, do you want another glass or—"

Remmy started unbuttoning his shirt, and the words left Frankie's mouth as the curls of gray chest hair sprung free from beneath. Remmy pulled off his buffalo plaid red shirt, revealing his muscled chest, biceps that could crush a man, and an undefined belly that Frankie dreamt of using as a pillow.

Remmy cleared his throat. "Enjoying the view?"

Frankie jumped and looked down at the book. "Right, yes, uh. Well, I need to crush up some herbs. Sage, willow bark, mandrake seed, thistle stems, rosebuds, and juniper berries to start."

Both Frankie and Remmy turned toward the wall of jarred herbs. Frankie found the sage in an instant, followed by Remmy with the rosemary. As they continued to scan the shelves, Remmy said, "Mrs. Appleton came into the vet today."

"Oh, really?" Frankie asked as he ran a finger along the jars, finding the willow bark and mandrake seeds.

"You remember her, right?" Remmy asked, pulling the juniper berries and rosebuds from the wall and setting them on the table. All that was left was the thistle.

Both of them paused, staring at the shelves. Frankie was hoping the thistle stems would just jump out at him when he remembered who Mrs. Appleton was. "Wait. Did something happen with Henry the Second? Did he eat another dog?"

Remmy pushed aside a few herbs and grabbed a dusty jar hidden behind the jars marked dandelion root and castor bean. "Found it," he said, handing the jar over. "And no, not really. Apparently, this pooka had a pack, and they all tried to get in the house."

Frankie measured out the contents in the jar and dropped them into a mortar, mashing them together with a pestle. He looked up at Remmy, his eyes tracing the man's shoulder. "Mrs. Appleton seems like a one-dog lady. I mean, she let Henry the First get eaten."

Remmy crossed his arms. "True, but she's stuck with Henry the Second now, and all his friends want in on the action."

"Oil," Frankie said, shaking his head as he looked down at the book.

"What?" Remmy asked.

"I need oil." Frankie pointed at the book. He turned to the wall of herbs and grabbed a small bottle from the bottom shelf. "This should do," he said as he flipped open the cap. A pungent odor that was both sickly sweet and slightly sour hit his nostrils, and he winced.

Remmy closed his eyes and stifled his breathing. "You're going to put that on me, aren't you?"

Frankie dumped the oil into the mortar and mixed it around. "Yep. And what's your point with Mrs. Appleton?"

A loud sneeze came from Dude on the couch, followed by a sequence of other sneezes as he pushed himself up off the couch and trotted off into the living room, finding a spot where he could still keep eye contact with Remmy.

"The other pookas are wild animals. That's why she came in," Remmy said. "She came home to Henry surrounded by a raven, squirrel, opossum, and a skunk. She thought he'd gotten rabies or something."

Frankie picked up the mixture and took a whiff, quickly regretting his decision as the oil only smelled worse with the addition of herbs. He walked over to Remmy, standing inches away from him. "I mean, that sounds like a magical forest princess's dream." He held up the oil. "Ready?"

"No," Remmy said.

Frankie dipped his fingers into the oil and smiled. "Good, me neither." His fingers brushed along Remmy's clavicle, and butterflies fluttered in Frankie's stomach. Frankie traced along the man's chest, drawing crude symbols and markings from the book, which just entangled herbs into chest hair.

Heat billowed off Remmy, and either from the whiskey or the fumes from the oil, Frankie just wanted to curl up next to this man on the couch and watch a roaring fire.

Remmy flinched as Frankie traced over his scar. "Oh, sorry," Frankie said, stopping. "Did I . . . did it hurt?"

"No," Remmy said, holding back a smirk. "It tickled."

Frankie blushed, gently finishing the last marking as Remmy flinched and backed away. He could see where he'd put the oil, but the mass of chest hair distorted the symbols completely. "Well, part one is done. Are you ready for part two?"

Remmy looked up and took in a deep breath. "This smells so bad. I'm not doing this again."

"I'll take that as a yes." Frankie walked around and faced the book, scooping it up with one hand, avoiding touching the book with his oiled hand as he secured it in the crook of his arm and walked back over to Remmy. He paused. "So, why were you telling me about Mrs. Appleton? Are we going to have to de-scent a skunk or something? Because that's a hard pass for me."

"The pookas aren't going to leave her alone. Not since she took in Henry. So, I was thinking we could help them become more appealing pets."

Frankie raised an eyebrow and stepped back. "Woah, wait, hold on. You aren't saying we're feeding the pookas, are you?"

"We're a veterinary clinic. We have access to pets that have passed. So, yes," Remmy said.

Frankie stared at him, words failing to come out.

"What? Better than the pookas realizing it on their own and snacking on the neighbor's cat or something."

"Fair," Frankie said. "Fine. Maybe. We'll see how you feel after this."

Remmy breathed in, scrunched up his nose, and breathed out, "This stuff really stinks. Is it supposed to burn when you—"

Frankie placed a hand on Remmy's chest, his fingers slipping into his mass of chest hair. He cleared his throat and looked down at the book.

"Ailment's disguise, truth now arise,
Secrets no more, let it advise,
Reveal the source, let it be found,
With this spell, truth be unbound."

Warmth spread underneath Frankie's palm, and Remmy shivered. "Is it working?" he asked.

Frankie nodded, then continued,

"If the curse stems from a place,
Let the source reveal with grace."

Remmy shuddered, and the hair on his chest grew coarse and white. Tufts of hair sprouted from his shoulders and arms, and his eyes turned a shade of yellow.

Frankie looked at the book, then back at Remmy. "Inconclusive."

Remmy lifted his arms, looking at the patchy hair covering his body. "Inconclusive? How is this inconclusive?"

"That's not what's supposed to happen. It says nothing about fur."

Remmy sniffled and scratched his chest. "I think I'm allergic to this stuff."

"Two more, then you can wash it off, okay?" Frankie asked.

Remmy stood tall and nodded. "Fine."

"If the curse seeded from an object,
Unveil the root and let it detect."

"ACHOO!" Remmy sneezed, and tufts of fur burst out from his arms, floating down to create a circle around him.

They looked down at the ring of white fur. Frankie laughed and said, "It looks like we murdered a poodle."

"Ha ha," Remmy said, wiping his eyes. "So it's that then? Some object cursed me?"

"No, the symbols I drew are supposed to glow," Frankie said, holding up the book.

"If the curse buds from person's might,
Let the truth now shine bright."

The symbols on Remmy's chest glowed brightly for a second, then white fur covered them. Remmy clutched his stomach and fell to all fours. He sneezed, and in an instant he was a patchy white wolf having a sneezing fit in the middle of the library.

"Oh shit," Frankie said, stepping back. "Uh, turn back?"

Remmy opened his mouth, baring sharp fangs, and he squinted his eyes. He let out another sneeze, shaking his head and body. Four more sneezes hit him and tossed up the pile of fur around him.

A loud bang sounded near the front of the house, followed by a shout. "Frankie!"

Frankie looked at Remmy, who was preoccupied with shaking off the tufts of loose hair that had landed on his face. Frankie held up his hands and said, "Uh, stay?"

Remmy paused and glared up at him with golden eyes. He huffed, knocking free some more fur before sitting down next to the pile of wolf fur.

Mat shouted again, his footsteps bounding closer to Frankie. "Frankie, we need your help. Like right now, where—"

"Wolf," August said, freezing in the doorway, staring at Remmy.

Mat stared at Remmy's patchy wolf form, then at Frankie holding the book, and frowned. "Not going well?"

"No," Frankie said. "I think he's stuck."

Mat held a hand out toward Remmy. "He won't bite, right?"

Remmy backed up and squinted his eyes.

"I don't think so, but he's not a dog. So, maybe don't pet the wolf in the library without consent from the wolf," Frankie said.

"Fair," Mat said, grabbing the book from Frankie and flipping through the pages.

"I take it your date didn't go well?" Frankie asked.

August smirked and shook their head, looking down at the ground. "Sorry. It's not funny."

Mat looked up from the book and shot August a glare. "It did not. I might have accidentally sent Demetri to some underground hell or something."

"Oh, shit," Frankie said. "Wait, how do you 'accidentally' send someone to hell?"

21

Valerian, with blossoms pink or white,
Offers tranquil slumber in the night.
In ancient times, the "allheal" was praised,
For countless ailments, it supposedly razed.

Beware the danger, for not all find peace,
With other depressants, its use must cease.
Pregnant mothers, too, should steer clear,
Uncertainty and potential harm, they fear.

Yet in feline hearts, a different story unfolds,
A dance of delight, as catnip of old.
An enigma, Valerian, both healer and threat,
A testament to nature's complex silhouette.

Valerian

- AUGUST -

"So, that's the only way?" August asked, arms crossed as they paced around the library.

Frankie, sprawled on the rug with the patchy white wolf and Dude snuggled beside him, closed his eyes. "We gotta act soon if we want to help Remmy."

Mat turned the pages of the ancient spellbook one more time, then drew a deep breath. "Nope. This is our only shot at bringing Demetri back. And . . . you're the one who needs to face him."

August shook their head. "Why can't it be you or Frankie?"

Frankie chuckled quietly. "I can't even remember my dreams half the time."

Mat ran his finger along the book. "It says the spell is meant for the person who remembers their dreams the most vividly. All you do is cast the spell, find out where he is, and come back. Once we know that, we can cast the gate spell that will bring him back."

"But I don't know how to lucid dream; my dreams are so disjointed and vague, there's no way to make sense of them," August said, looking away from Mat.

Mat looked up from the book and frowned. "That's why there's a spell for it. If you make a tea with valerian, chamomile, and lavender, then recite these words to summon a dream guide, it should work."

August sighed and followed Mat into the kitchen. As August readied the water for the tea, Mat started mixing the ingredients in the pot. Pushing the book to August, Mat said, "Read this aloud while stirring the tea counterclockwise, and then drink it all."

August grabbed onto the mug of tea, dipped in a spoon, and said, "Do you think this will work?"

"We won't know until you try," Mat replied as he moved closer to August and adjusted his grip on the cup of tea.

Frankie shouted from the other room. "Ask your guide if they know anything about changing werewolves back into human form!"

August looked down at the mug and dipped the spoon in, stirring slowly.

"Chamomile, lavender, valerian root,
I summon a guide who can help my pursuit.
By lavender's scent, may I rouse,
aware of the dream, released from drowse.
Valerian's strength, I call on my guide
to transport me to realms far and wide.
Chamomile's clarity sustains my mind.
While we search for what I must find."

Mat gave a slight nod before August drank down every last drop of tea. The herbs tingled on their tongue, and a heavy weight sank onto their shoulders.

"I think. I might—"

The entire world went black, and the last thing August remembered was hearing the cup smash on the floor.

August sat on a bench in an open grass field that bordered a forest, enjoying the taste of a sweet, buttery cinnamon roll as they picked it apart with sticky fingers. The leaves on the trees shifted from greens to oranges, yellows, and reds before their eyes. Then the leaves fell off entirely, carried away by the wind, only for new leaves to grow in their place and the cycle start anew.

August watched this for hours, eating from a never-ending cinnamon roll, as the sun slowly drifted across the sky and settled in under the horizon. Shortly after, the moon rose, and the cold swept over August. Snow piled up on the surrounding ground, and the clear starry sky twinkled down.

"A novelist and a dreamer," a voice called behind them.

August turned, expecting to find someone standing behind them. Instead, all they saw was an endless winter park, sprinkled with snow-laden trees.

"Hello?" August asked, their voice echoing in the cold air.

"Up here," the voice said.

August looked up, spotting a great white owl perched in the tree nearby, its starry eyes gazing down upon them.

A distant memory hit August, of them standing in a kitchen, mixing a tea and reciting a spell. "Are you my guide?"

The owl swooped down from the tree, headed right for August. They closed their eyes and outstretched their arms, ready to accept whatever fate had in store for them, only to feel a slight gust of wind brush past them.

They cautiously opened their eyes and saw a familiar sight. Ragana stood before them in all her magnificence, wearing a gown that seemed to be sewn from the fabric of the universe, filled with stars and distant nebulas. Her face glowed with silvery and blue makeup, framed by long dark curls that draped over her shoulders.

"Ragana? But? What?"

She smiled and raised an eyebrow. "You asked for a guide, yes?"

"Yes, but—"

"I heeded your call, and I came. Would you rather it be someone else?"

"No! No, I just. I didn't." August stood, and as they did, the cinnamon bun vanished from their hands.

Ragana stepped forward, closing the space between them. "What do you seek?"

August felt the warmth coming off her body, and their mind drifted. One moment, they stood in the middle of a park, and the next they stood in the plaza of a city, surrounded by skyscrapers.

Ragana placed a hand on August's cheek. "Focus on me. Don't give in to the dream."

August placed a hand on hers, their senses clearing. "It's Demetri. He's lost, and we need to find him. The book said I needed to find him in dreams first."

Ragana nodded and lowered her hand. "Then let's find him. Take my other hand."

August complied, and warmth shot through their body. Light shone between them, and in the moments that followed, reality melted away.

"Focus on Demetri," Ragana said.

Everything shifted and changed. Entire worlds sprouted around them. One moment they were high in the sky looking upon purple mountains, the next they stood on a beach made of black sand, and then they were deep underwater standing among lost ruins.

August kept their mind on Demetri, picturing him while they stared at Ragana. Her eyes were deep and vast, like an abyss that carried them to every corner of the universe.

Heat billowed around August, and the shifting landscapes settled into a cavern.

Ragana was the first to pull her attention away, surveying the place as they stopped. "He's here," she said, her voice wavering.

August looked down, noting the rock ledge where they stood and the massive pool of lava below. "Where the hell are we?"

"Some call it that. Hell, the underworld, Helheim, Tartarus. This place has many names, but they are all the same. A gateway to the beyond, a waystation for spirits."

"And Demetri is here?" August asked.

Ragana nodded and pointed across the pool of lava to another ledge where a man in a suit lay unconscious.

August took a step forward. "We have to help him."

Ragana grabbed his shoulder and squeezed. "You can't. Not like this. If you step off the path, you will be lost forever. Demetri is safe, for now."

August stepped back and looked at Ragana. "Fine, now what?"

Ragana pulled a small knife from her pocket. "If you want to find this place again, you need to leave a piece of you behind. I'd suggest a lock of hair, but . . ." Ragana looked up at August's shaved head.

August pushed Ragana's knife away and bit their lip. The metallic taste of blood filled their mouth, and they spat on the ground. "Does that work? Is that it?"

Ragana nodded. "That's it. Time to wake, my dear novelist. Hope I see you soon, in the waking world." She lifted a hand and tapped them once on the forehead. The cavern vanished in an instant, and August fell into darkness.

August's eyes snapped open, staring up at the living room ceiling. They groaned as they sat up from the couch.

Mat was slouched in the chair beside them, rubbing his eyes, and he yawned. "Did you find him?"

August blinked and nodded. "I marked the way there."

"Good," Mat said, pushing himself up off the chair.

Mat stood and kicked Frankie's leg to wake him, who shot him a glare and said, "What?"

"August is back. We need your help with the spell."

Frankie yawned and stretched, scratching at the top of Remmy's head. "Five more minutes."

August stood up and said, "If we do this now, you can go sleep in your own bed."

Frankie raised his head and squinted at August. "Fair point. Then, once I get my beauty sleep, you're helping me get Remmy back."

"Yeah, yeah," August said.

The three of them gathered in the library, Mat grabbing a jar of salt and pouring a circle onto the floor. August grabbed candles from a box on the bottom shelf of the herbs, and Frankie found a comfortable spot on the couch and watched.

Once the salt circle was complete with candles lined around it, Mat set the book on the ground and looked at August. "Says you need like for like of what was left behind. Whatever that means."

August nodded and bit their lip, in the same spot they'd done in their dream, and spat on the floor.

"Um, the fuck?" Frankie asked.

"Well, I didn't have hair to leave behind, so it was blood." August said.

"Okay, um, cool," Frankie said, slipping off the couch.

Mat cleared his throat. "Okay, August, you sit inside the circle, hands down, focusing on the gate. Frankie, you sit outside the circle, back against August, hands up, focused on protecting the circle. It says the circle can sometimes call unwanted guests."

"Oh cool, what the hell does that mean?" Frankie yawned.

Mat shrugged, "It doesn't say. Here," He set the book down so everyone could see it. "Say this together."

The three looked down at the book and started the spell.

"A spark of hope, a burning flame,
locate the essence that we reclaim.
Lift the veil and weave the threads,
so a crossing may be tread."

They chanted the words over and over, and the air buzzed and crackled to life. Flames danced and stretched, twisting left and right, as if weaving some unseen fabric in the air.

August could feel the stone beneath them and the heat from the lava as if they were kneeling where they had spat in their dream.

Slowly, a shimmering light appeared in front of them, like some kind of semi-translucent curtain. The fabric shifted, and for a moment August could see the place underground where they had been.

"That's it," August said, keeping their hands pressed onto the floorboards.

Mat took a step forward. "If I'm not back in twenty minutes, uh, send help?"

"Sure," Frankie said, back pressed against August. "We'll do that."

August watched as Mat stepped through, vanishing behind the shimmering curtains.

22

In the stillness of caves where light dares not thread,
Sprouts Schistostega, a tapestry spread.
Tiny filaments glowing, a luminous bloom,
In dim places they capture light's gloom.

Known as goblin's gold, a treasure untrue,
Emeralds mistaken, in a greenish hue.
Its brilliance deceives in rocky clefts' hold,
The basis of tales of goblin gold told.

Its nature, intriguing, through darkness it thrives,
Glowing gently in habitats where scarce light arrives.
A testament of life in cavernous cold,
In darkness and silence, its stories unfold.

Cave Moss

- MAT -

Mat blinked a few times, his eyes adjusting to the dim light as he stepped through the gate that connected Mandrake Manor to the underworld. Orange light bounced off cave walls as his gaze traveled around the vast cavern. Heat radiated beneath him, and as he looked over the ledge of rock he stood on, he saw a massive sea of molten rock.

"Oh, fuck this," he muttered to himself. He turned around and saw August staring back at him through the gate, sitting within the circle of salt they created. "I'll be right back. Don't go anywhere."

August looked up at him, their hands still on the floor, and a bead of sweat sliding down their forehead. "I got this. Don't worry."

"Same here," Frankie shouted, waving his hand in the air as he sat against August's back, facing away from the gate.

Mat spun on his heel and peered across the cavern. He spotted a mass across the pit of lava, and when he squinted, he could make out the suit and bald head of Demetri. Butterflies fluttered in his stomach as he eyed the unconscious man.

"Demetri?" he shouted, hearing his voice echo back several times.

He didn't move, and as his voice vanished, traveling into far-off corners, he wondered what else might hear his cry.

Mat squinted, looking left, then right, as far as his eyes could see, searching for any hint of how he might get across. The orange light vanished into shadows a few dozen feet away from him on either side, bouncing off jutting rocks that highlighted a path along the cavern wall but never joined with the other side.

Then he saw something, a faint glow of green, which took the shape of a person. Nearly a football field away, Mat could make out the shape of a ghostly person stepping off the ledge, their faint glow illuminating a footbridge that stretched across the lava.

"Of course it's ghosts," Mat groaned. He looked back over at Demetri's unconscious body and whispered, "I'll be right back."

He inched along the rock ledge, hugging the side of the cavern wall as he climbed up and down.

He stepped down onto a large, flat stone, noting a much smoother path along the cavern leading up to the bridge. As for the bridge, it was everything he expected it to be. An old, one-person bridge made of rope and wood that looked like it might crumble to dust if he set foot on it.

"You're not supposed to be here. Where is your guide?" a voice called out from the bridge.

Mat squinted, and wisps of green light came together to create a portly man with a bulbous nose standing in the center of the bridge. He wore a long judge's robe which swished back and forth, and he waddled toward Mat.

"What?" Mat asked.

"I said you're not supposed to be here. No guide either? I'm gonna have to call you in."

Mat frowned. "Call me in? To who? For what?"

The man stepped off the bridge and put his hands on his hips. "Meatsacks don't belong down here without a guide. Last time one of you wandered in, they started an entire revolution looking for their dead wife. Can't have that again."

"Wait, no. I'm not here for that. I promise. I'm just trying to get to my friend. Demetri. I accidentally sent him here."

The man knelt down, using his finger to draw a symbol on the stone. "Accidental death is still death. Can't have you mucking things up. Stay put for the guardians, unless you want them to chase you down and drag you out."

Mat shook his head. "No, I just need to get across. Please."

The thought of leaving Demetri behind while he was dragged out of here ran through Mat's mind. He couldn't leave him. Wouldn't leave him.

He stepped forward, unsure what he could do to this spirit.

Cold air filled his chest, and he gasped.

"Lay off it, you old coot," a voice shouted beside Mat.

Green haze coalesced into a familiar elderly woman as she stepped past Mat and pushed the man away from the symbol he drew. She kicked at the ground, and the symbol vanished.

The man looked up and sighed. "Margaret. I should have known this was your doing."

The woman, whose name was apparently Margaret, straightened her back and crossed her arms. "Oh, shut up, Ted. Are you going to let my descendant pass, or am I going to have to push you off the bridge like I did last time?"

Ted stood up and straightened his robes, glaring up at Mat. "So he's another Mandrake, then?"

"Yes. A bit too green to be in a place like this," she turned and glared at Mat, "but I suppose this is my fault for sending his friend back here."

"Wait. Hold on. What the hell is going on?" Mat asked.

"You called me," Margaret said. "By reflex I suppose."

"What? And why can I hear you?"

Ted scoffed. "This is very irresponsible of you, Margaret. The boy clearly isn't ready."

"I might not know what's going on," Mat said, "but I'm not irresponsible. I just want to get Demetri and go."

Ted glared at Mat, much like when a parent gives that mommy-and-daddy-are-talking look.

"Regardless of his readiness," Margaret said, "he is here now, and he is fetching a guardian. Let us pass."

"Fine," Ted said. "But he must report directly to that guardian. If he runs into anyone past this bridge, I won't vouch for him. Understand?"

Margaret nodded. "Understood, you old bat."

Ted stepped to the side and looked away from the bridge.

Margaret stared at Mat, then pointed to the bridge. "Well, I can't walk across for you. Move."

Mat started on the bridge, feeling it creak and groan under him when Ted shouted at him. "Stay vigilant! Things are not always what they seem past here."

Mat turned back to nod, but the translucent man had vanished, as did Margaret.

He grabbed the two rope handrails and carefully put one foot in front of the other.

Halfway across, something wooshed overhead, bringing down a gust of hot air as he stumbled, knuckles turning white as he gripped the ropes as hard as he could. He looked around, but only saw the tip of a wing disappearing into the shadows.

His feet met rock on the other side of the bridge. Ahead of him was a cave entrance, covered in a black, shadowed mist. Something tugged in his chest, a desire to step forward and feel the shadowy mist fall over him.

Light caught the corner of his eye, and he turned, coming face to face with Margaret. "No, not there. Not yet."

"What's past there?" Mat asked, looking back at the mist.

"Death has many layers. Here, in the caverns, is one of the first. Beyond there is more danger. Not something for you. Not yet."

Mat breathed in and looked away, the pull in his chest dissipating. He traced along the cavern's side, seeing a path along the wall that would lead him to Demetri. He cleared his throat. "Demetri's this way."

Margaret nodded, and the surrounding light dimmed. "I can't stay. Stick to the wall and get back through the gate quickly."

"Wait, no," Mat said, turning to her. "I have questions. Who are you? Why can I hear you?"

She smiled. "A distant relative. Margaret Mandrake. Your awakening should have summoned the last Mandrake, but the call came to me instead."

Mat frowned at that, noting the look on her face. "Why you? Why wasn't it Melinda?"

She shrugged, her form losing shape around the edges. "I don't know. But I was deep into death, so my time up here is fleeting. Use the book in thirteen days' time. I'll have enough strength for us to speak again."

At that, Margaret vanished in a wisp of green smoke.

"Wait," Mat called, but it was too late, and she was gone.

He walked down the path to Demetri, carefully clinging to the wall when the path was only a foot's width across. At one point, he slipped, the rock he stood on breaking free and tumbling into the lava below. He dug his fingers into the rocks in front of him and scrambled onto the ledge.

He could finally see Demetri, sprawled out on the stones in front of him, still unconscious.

Mat raced over, running hands gently over him, looking for any signs of injury. Demetri seemed fine, no pools of blood or protruding bones, just a slight bruise on his forehead.

Mat rested a hand on Demetri's shoulder and gently shook. "Hey. Can you hear me?"

Demetri let in a sharp breath, then coughed. He blinked a few times before lazily turning and looking up at Mat. "Where? What happened?"

"Before or after your brother showed up?"

Demetri winced as he rolled onto his side and sat up. "I feel like a bus hit me." He looked around, his fingers running along the stone, and said, "Wait, are we?"

"If you are about to ask if we are in the land of the dead or whatever, then yes, we are," Mat said.

"But. How did you?"

"Frankie, August, and I opened a gate. It's just over—"

Mat looked across the lake of lava, at the ledge with the shimmering curtain of light, and their way home.

As he watched, the curtain seemed to waver. A candle came flying out from the entrance, soaring right into the lake of lava below. Then the entrance flashed a bright light before vanishing completely.

"Fuck," Mat said. And at that, he heard a faint whooshing overhead.

23

In the realm where the bold and wild abide,
Lies Aconitum, clothed in deadly pride.
Potent neurotoxin and heart's snare,
A mere touch, a lethal affair.

An arrow's poison, death's swift lance,
Beneath its bloom, danger does dance.
Used in warfare, hunting, and crime,
Its whispers echo through the chime.

Yet within its peril, a paradox found,
In Ayurveda and lore, its uses abound.
A double-edged blade, both cure and bane,
Such is the legend of the wolfsbane.

Wolf's Bane

- FRANKIE -

"**I**s he back yet?" Frankie asked, looking over his shoulder at the shimmering gateway into the underworld.

"He literally just left," August said. "And he needs to find a way across."

Frankie bounced up and down in his seat and groaned. "Why couldn't you get him any closer? I need to pee."

August let out a quick laugh. "Well, for one, you should have thought about that sooner. For two, I don't know. It didn't feel like I could get any closer to Demetri, and we were close enough."

Frankie looked down at the spellbook beside him, then the salt circle, then over at Remmy who was still in his white wolf form, curled up on the couch beside Dude. "I mean, Remmy could guard the circle for a second while I peed, right? I mean, what the hell is even going to come in here? Shouldn't we be more worried about what might come through the gate?"

Frankie saw a flash from the corner of his eye and the gate flickered for a moment. August leaned forward and grunted.

"What was that?" Frankie asked.

"Your yapping isn't helping," August said. "I need to focus on the gate, or else it'll collapse."

Frankie turned around and pressed his back up against August's. He stared at Remmy and Dude. "Sorry, I do really need to pee. But I can shut up. I can try to shut up, yeah."

Moments passed, and before Frankie knew it, he was bouncing again.

"Just go fucking pee!" August shouted.

"Yep. You're right, fine," Frankie said, standing up. "I'll be right back. Remmy, you got this?"

Remmy lifted his head from the couch and yawned as he pushed himself up. He hopped down from the couch and stretched before sitting down where Frankie had been.

"I'll take that as a yes," Frankie said, racing out of the room.

Frankie ran down the hall and into the bathroom across the stairs. With barely seconds to spare, he made it, shouting, "This is the best piss of my life!"

"Thanks for sharing," August shouted back.

Frankie zipped up and turned on the sink.

A scratching sound echoed down the hall. He turned off the sink and leaned an ear against the bathroom door.

The scratching sounded again, and he frowned. "You hear that?"

He stepped out of the bathroom and froze. Down the hall, creeping slowly into the house from the front door, was a massive raccoon staring right at him.

The raccoon didn't move, looking down the hall right at Frankie, little hands outstretched.

"You better fucking not," Frankie said.

In response, the raccoon bared its teeth and raced into the house, scuttling into the living room, straight for the library.

"August!" Frankie shouted, racing toward the library. "There's a fucking raccoon in the house!"

There was a loud growl as Frankie reached the doorway to the library. Before him was the raccoon, riding on top of Remmy, pulling his ears as Remmy growled and yelped.

"What the hell is going on?" August shouted, leaning forward, his eyes focused on the gate as it flickered.

"I'm on it," Frankie said, diving around Dude as he raced out into the kitchen, tail between his legs.

The raccoon steered Remmy right into the wall of herbs, and jars tumbled down off the wall, crashing onto the floor.

"Fucking stop, you little shit!" Frankie shouted, crouching down and reaching toward the raccoon, prepping to wrestle the thing. "Get your grubby little hands off my man."

"Frankie!" August shouted, the gate fluctuating.

Frankie took a step closer to Remmy while the raccoon pulled hard on the wolf's ears.

Remmy yelped and ran into the wall again, knocking loose more jars, one of which landed on the raccoon's head. The raccoon blinked a few times and loosened its grip on Remmy's ears. Remmy whipped his head left and right, and the raccoon flew off his head, soaring through the air and landing behind the couch.

"You okay?" Frankie asked Remmy, who lifted his paw and rubbed at his ears in response. "Of course you're not. I'm sorry."

Frankie turned toward the couch, expecting the furry devil to be perched on the top of the couch, ready for round two. Instead, he saw a pale white hand clutch the back of the couch and a woman with straight black hair stand, her eyes locked on Frankie.

"Uh, Helena?" Frankie said.

"What?" August said. "Helena's here?"

"Just focus on the gate. I got this," Frankie said.

Helena patted the top of her head and checked her hand, noting the small smudge of blood on her head. Her ice-cold eyes locked onto Remmy. "You hurt me."

Remmy growled and leaped at her.

Helena's eyes glowed green, and she snapped her fingers. She spoke in a flat, monotone voice. "Sit, boy."

Remmy's momentum stopped completely, and he sat in silence, as if he were some obedient dog.

Frankie stepped back, blocking Helena from August. "What do you want?" he asked.

Helena looked down at the ground, at the open book on the floor. "You three don't deserve that."

Frankie followed her gaze. "The book? What? Why?"

"It shouldn't have been you three." She held up her hands, her eyes glowing a shimmering green.

The candles flickered, and Remmy let out a whimper.

"Frankie, if I let go, I don't know if we'll get Mat—"

Helena cut August off.

"*By the power of endless night,*

I cast this curse to dim your light."

Frankie stepped back to the salt circle and picked up a candle. He aimed and chucked it at her head. "Oh fuck no, spooky bitch."

The candle flew true, aimed right at her head. He thought he was going to hit her too, when her hand streaked up and caught the candle in midair.

She eyed the still lit candle, then glared at Frankie. Before he could think to grab another candle for round two, she snapped her fingers. Her eyes glowed, and she spat at his feet.

Frankie tried to step toward her, but his muscles didn't respond. He was stuck, frozen against his will.

Helena tutted her tongue. "Even a simple holding spell works against you. Disgrace."

"Frankie," August said, "I don't think you've got this."

Helena tapped a finger on her throat. The voice that came out wasn't hers, but Frankie's. "It's fine, just focus on the gate!" she shouted.

Another wave of her hand, and she rolled her eyes. "And now your friend can't hear us," Helena said.

She walked up close to Frankie, circling around him before muttering, "I was going to put you to sleep, but I wouldn't want to separate you and your . . . *man.*" Then she smiled. "Ah, yes, that should do."

She placed both hands on his shoulders and looked into his eyes, a grin on her face.

"*Teeth will sharpen, hair will grow,*
Senses deepen, and eyes will glow.
May you run wild, with the heart of a hunter,
And may you howl at the moon like thunder."

Pain jolted up Frankie's legs, and the hold on him melted away. He fell to his knees, clutching his stomach as a wave of pain washed over him. It shot up his back, searing his nerves. He let out a scream, but instead of what he'd expect, he howled.

He felt the bones shifting in his face, and when he looked down, he saw bristly gray hair sprouting from his arms. The light from the candles brightened, and before he knew it, he didn't feel human anymore.

He breathed in, and images filled his mind. The oak flooring cast memories of the people who installed them, cut them, and the forests they grew in. They filled his mind in ways he didn't think were possible, an entirely new world put in front of him. He turned and found Remmy, who carried scents of familiarity. The world around him stopped undulating as he found safety in those eyes.

"Aw, isn't that cute? The pack is coming together," Helena said, holding up the still lit candle. "Now, what to do with the gatekeeper? Ah, yes, where were we?"

She whispered into the candle, her eyes flaring green.

"*Let sleep come and hold you tight,*

And not wake until next full moon's night."

Then she threw the candle at the back of August's head.

The candlelight twirling in the air transfixed Frankie. He stayed still, feeling the primal fear of fire overrule the urge to leap up and catch the candle in his mouth.

When the end of the candle hit August, a pulse of green energy illuminated them, and they collapsed with a thud onto the floor. The candle bounced off their head, tumbling through the gate.

The shimmering fabric that outlined the gate vanished in an instant, and Helena stepped forward. "Stay," she commanded, and Frankie wanted to do nothing else but stay where he was.

She passed by him, reaching down and scooping up the book, holding it tight to her chest as she started toward the door. "I'll leave the door open. A home is no place for wolves."

24

Evergreen sentinel, of ancient yore,
Buxus sempervirens, in lore, a store.
Hardwood in service of art and sound,
In its leaves, a bitter potion found.

Treated gout, and fever's fierce plight,
Even malaria in the lantern's light.
Yet caution lies in its potent brew,
Side effects noted, better cures we knew.

Still, in homeopathy, some persist,
In leaf tea's power, they insist.
In Turkey's grasp, a dye and a cure,
The Boxwood's legacy, complex and pure.

Boxwood

- AUGUST -

T he scent of damp earth and decaying wood hit August's nose first as they blinked, finding themself standing in the middle of a moonlit forest.

Streaks of white passed by them, followed by playful yips as two wolves bounded ahead, pouncing and nudging each other. Calm hit August, a sense of peace and happiness as they watched these two wolves play in the night.

Rustling sounded behind them, and one wolf looked right past August, baring its teeth.

Trees overhead swayed and creaked, and both wolves backed away, tails between their legs.

They ran while August stood still, watching roots rip up from the ground, the scent of earth and musk filling the air. Trees fell and decayed in an instant, creating a clearing leading up to a small neighborhood off in the distance.

Something wriggled beneath August's feet. They jumped and looked down at the earth, watching as thin blades of grass sprouted between their feet.

Trees erupted up from the ground, ignoring decades of growth to create perfect rows of trees on either side of August.

In minutes, the forest that August had stood in, the forest that sat outside Henbane Hollow, had transformed into perfectly manicured woods, complete with a massive grass field.

And the wolves August had seen, the wolves they felt some connection with, were gone.

August stared up at the ceiling of their bedroom, at the flaking paint and crown molding that led up to a small black iron chandelier in their dark wood walled room.

"What the hell?" August mumbled to themself.

They hadn't been in bed when they went to sleep. And they were just standing in a forest, weren't they?

August sat up, rubbing the sleep from their eyes as they swung their legs over the bed and pulled on their fluffy brown robe. Light streamed in from the windows, a strange pink hue of light which streamed in from both windows, even though they were on different walls.

"Mat? Frankie?" August asked.

A laugh echoed through the house, high and childlike.

"Heck, I'll even take a creepy demon child if they know what's going on," August said, then immediately regretted it as they approached the door, worried that an actual demon child might be on the other side.

But when they opened the door, there was just an empty hallway, with Frankie's bedroom door wide open on the other side of the hall.

August started down the hall, noting the array of portraits along the walls. More than there should be. Faces of strangers, mostly women, lined the walls, staring right at August.

They jumped when the first portrait fell. Before they could turn around, two more fell off the wall. Unfamiliar faces faded away from the fallen portraits, leaving behind blank canvases on the floor.

Then the dark green wallpaper, filled with images of flowers and vines, peeled away from the wall, exposing a bland beige wall and wooden paneling on the bottom half of the wall.

August turned and ran, racing toward the stairs.

"Mat? Frankie? The walls are fucked up," August shouted.

The more they ran, the farther the stairs seemed to be. The hall stretched and contorted, more and more portraits filling the walls as the hall behind them continued to peel and knock the portraits free.

The hallway ahead of them seemed to stretch into infinity. No matter how much they ran, they couldn't see the end.

A voice whispered in their ear, faint, "Wake up."

August stopped and turned around, the mass of wallpaper and portraits overtaking them.

August stood in the bathroom, adjusting their tie, feeling the fabric of their blazer stretch across their shoulders. When they looked into the mirror, they almost didn't recognize themself. Slicked-back hair that reminded them of some asshole businessman had replaced their shaved head. They pressed their hand against their crunchy head, feeling the thick gel that held their hair in place.

"What is going on?" August asked, leaning in and taking in their new look.

Their eyes traveled to the rest of the bathroom, noting that a brass-framed sliding glass door was in place of the bathtub, the walls were lined with off-white tile instead of mint green, and a vanity of honey-colored oak replaced the sink that had been there before.

August ran their hand along the off-white marbled countertop. "Is this . . . real?"

Then the voice came again. "Wake up." This time, it was louder and more familiar.

"Ragana?" August asked.

The bathroom faded away as the floor beneath them gave out and gravity took hold, pulling them into nothingness.

August snapped awake, seated at a small honey oak table with a lace runner. It was the dining room of Mandrake Manor, but everything that made it a Victorian home was stripped away, replaced with beige walls and the same boring light-colored wood.

They looked down at their hands, noting they were out of a suit and now in a polo and khakis with a sweater loosely tied around their shoulders.

"You look tired," a voice said.

August looked up and saw Ragana, dressed in a form-fitting dress and apron with her brown hair draped over her shoulders in large curls.

She carried a large pot which steamed as she put it down on the center of the table. It was a dark brown stew filled with carrots, potatoes, and chunks of meat. The scent of rosemary and thyme filled August's nose, and their mouth watered.

"Ragana, what's going on?" August asked.

Ragana shot them a wide-eyed glance, which trailed to the door.

A groan sounded in the house, as if the foundation itself was about to snap.

She shook her head and smiled, then leaned in and kissed August's cheek. Before August could say anything, Ragana turned around and pulled bowls from the cupboard. "Nothing, dear. You just got back home from work at the office. Remember?"

Her voice was unfamiliar, too sing-songy and fake from the few times August has spoken with her.

"No," August said. "I don't. I remember I was . . . I was . . ." The thoughts completely slipped away from August. Faint images of a hallway, a forest, and a cave filled with orange light flashed across their mind, quickly snuffed out as Ragana placed the bowl of stew in front of them.

"Zombie?" Ragana asked, her hands folded in front of her like some strange picture of a housewife.

August looked up and frowned. "What?"

"A zombie, dear. Your favorite drink? Remember?"

"Oh, uh, right. Sure?" August said.

Ragana nodded and turned, heading back to the kitchen while August stared down at their food.

"Uh, Ragana, what's going on?"

Ragana shouted down the hallway. "Work must really be taking a toll on you. Have those boys at work been harassing you to finish your project? What were their names again? Frank and Matty?"

The names rang a bell, but August couldn't put a face to them. "Yeah, that must be it," they said.

Ragana returned from the kitchen, holding a peach-colored cocktail with a cherry on top. She smiled and handed August the glass, looking down at their bowl of stew. "You haven't touched your food. What's wrong with it?"

"Nothing. Nothing," August said, setting down the cup. "It's just. I'm confused, I think. Where did you say I worked?"

Ragana bit her lip, locking eyes with August before trailing her gaze to the window.

August followed her gaze, peering out the window and seeing an overgrown hedge. At first, it seemed like any other overgrown hedge, but the longer August stared, the more they realized the hedge was growing at a rapid rate. It sprouted toward the window and tapped on the glass.

The window moved of its own accord, sliding up and slamming down on the ends of the hedge as if they were someone's fingers, and then the curtain slid down, hiding the sight altogether.

"What the fuck was that?" August asked.

The table trembled, and the floorboards rippled.

Ragana took in a deep breath and stared at August, slowly shaking her head. "It was nothing, dear." She picked up her spoon and ate a mouthful of stew. "Eat up before it gets cold."

August's heart raced. "Ragana, what's going on? Where's Mat and Frankie?" they asked, their voice shaky.

"I don't know, dear," Ragana said, looking around anxiously. "Please, eat your soup. Unless you're really awake."

"Awake?" August looked around the room, frowning. "I'm pretty sure this is another one of my . . ."

Ragana jumped forward in her seat, waving her arms and holding a finger to her lips.

The house groaned again, this time more like an angry growl that shook the walls.

August glanced down the hall, noting the beige walls overtook the halls on the first floor as well, and that the intricate staircase was now as boring and carpeted as they expect to see in any house.

"Is it the house?" August asked.

At that, the table trembled, and the chair underneath August tipped backward, throwing August to the floor.

Ragana raced over to him and grabbed his arm, her false housewife facade completely gone. "Thank the gods. Come on."

"What's happening?" August shouted as the groans grew louder and louder.

"The house is bewitched," she said, pulling them up.

They raced to the front door, getting tossed in the hallway. The door transformed in front of them, growing several locks that snapped shut as they reached it.

August twisted one lock, and another appeared.

"Stand back," Ragana said, pulling August away from the door.

Before August's eyes, Ragana grew twice her size. Fur sprouted from her skin. In an instant, a massive bear stood beside August.

The bear raced forward and slammed into the door, turning it into splinters in an instant.

August raced out the door, falling onto the grass as the floorboards of the porch made one last attempt at grabbing them.

Ragana, back in her human form, collapsed next to him, breathing heavily. Between breaths, she said, "The house wouldn't let you go. I had. I had to stay. Only way you'd wake up."

August looked up at the house, no longer a Victorian mansion but a house like any other with a sloped roof and beige siding. Had it not tried to kill the both of them, it might have even looked inviting.

Memories flooded back into August's mind. They turned and looked at Ragana. "Helena did this. She turned Frankie into a wolf. And Mat's stuck in the underworld. I've got to save them. I . . ."

Ragana pushed herself up and held out a hand. "We need to get out of here first. Before Helena comes back. My place."

25

Pomegranate, Punica granatum, your story we tell,
In dishes, and cures, your influence fell.
Ripe with ellagitannins, a bitter-sweet song,
In your crimson seeds, nutrition strong.

From the heart of the Middle East, your secrets flowed,
In syrup, molasses, and seeds bestowed.
Yet caution, fair fruit, in promise you bear,
Punicic acid in your core, consumers beware.

In ancient lore, you held death's dark key,
Yet promised prosperity, fertility's decree.
From the cradle of civilization to modern plight,
Your story, pomegranate, a paradox bright.

Pomegranate

- MAT -

"Shit. What do we do now?" Mat asked, watching the remains of the candle as it sank into the lava below.

Demetri pushed himself up off the rocky ground, stabilizing himself along the wall, and looked across the cavern. "I hope they're okay."

"You hope they're okay?" Mat looked back at Demetri and frowned. "I mean, I do too, but we don't have a way back."

Demetri brushed off his suit and gestured to himself. "Uh, hello, I was born here."

Mat let out a long sigh. "Right. Right. So, how do we get out of here?"

Demetri shrugged. "I dunno."

"What?" Mat shouted. "You just said—"

"I know, but we'll figure it out. There are a few ways, I think, but we need to stop somewhere first." Demetri started down the rocky path toward the bridge.

"Stop where? Not the bridge guy. He was an asshole."

Demetri laughed. "Ted? He's not an asshole, just a stickler for rules. And no, not that way."

Mat followed behind Demetri as they made their way back to the bridge. He brushed off his pants and straightened his shirt before noticing that Demetri was looking right at the gate.

Mat followed his gaze, looking into the mass of swirling shadows. "You aren't planning on going through there, right?"

"I was," Demetri said. "Why?"

"Margaret told me not to."

"Margaret?"

"She's a relative. A ghost."

"Ah," Demetri smiled. "She's right, you shouldn't, if you are alone." He held out a hand. "But those rules don't apply when you're with me."

Mat looked at the gate and shivered. He could feel a pull from it, a desire to fall in and get lost. Could he trust Demetri to know what he was doing? He was born here, after all. And that smile on his face, the slight dimple on his cheek . . .

"Okay," Mat said. He wrapped his hand around Demetri's, feeling a warmth as Demetri squeezed tight.

Demetri smiled and pulled Mat over to the gate. "Just walk through. It might feel weird, but don't let go." He stepped through, vanishing behind the darkness.

Mat let Demetri pull him, and the darkness engulfed him.

Cold was the first sensation, pouring down on him like a waterfall, begging him to give up and let the cold bore into him. If Demetri hadn't held onto his hand, if Mat hadn't felt the warmth in his palm, he wondered if he'd stop and stand under that waterfall forever. But Demetri pulled, and Mat stepped out into a place filled with gray light.

Mat let go of Demetri and lifted a hand, shielding his eyes as he blinked and they adjusted to an overcast sky. "What the hell?"

He found they were not at the mouth of a cavern but at the top of a hill overlooking forests and mountains covered in dense tendrils of fog in all directions.

Mat frowned, eyeing a gate filled with white swirling mist outlined by a black stone frame at the top of the hill.

"Not quite hell. Some people call this place limbo." Demetri took in a deep breath and closed his eyes. "I always loved the smell. My parents kept our summer home here because of the air."

"Is that where you're taking us?"

Demetri nodded. "Yep. My brother and I used to mark all the weird ways to the surface and stash the notes there. It's been a while, but I'm hoping they're still there."

"The brother that remodeled the restaurant during our date?" Mat asked, remembering the man with the horns crawling out from the hole in the ground.

"The one and only Damien," Demetri said. "About the date—"

"Don't worry about it," Mat said. "I think I ruined it anyway with the whole sending you here."

Demetri smirked. "And yet you came here and found me. So . . ."

"So?" Mat asked.

Demetri bit his lip and looked at Mat. "So, this could be a continuation of that date. I don't think you ruined it. And if you don't think I ruined it, then who's saying the date's over?"

Mat felt the heat rise in his neck. "Oh. Oh! Sure. I mean, strolling through some sort of spooky woods after traveling through some death gate is a little weird, but yeah."

"Sorry," Demetri said, kicking at the ground. "That was stupid."

"No, it's not. That's not what I meant." Mat stepped closer to Demetri. "It would definitely make a strong impression."

Demetri smiled. "Perfect, then it's a date." He turned around and started down the hill, waving Mat along. "Follow me. I promise this won't be boring."

Mat rubbed his hands together and chased after Demetri. "Do I get the special tour? What's first?"

"Ha ha. Just stay close. This place can get a little weird."

A flash of light caught Mat's eye, and he looked to his left. A bright blue tree shimmered, leaves moving gently in the breeze. "Like that?" he asked, gawking at the tree. Then, as if on cue, the blue leaves fell off and flapped in the wind. What Mat had thought were leaves were, in fact, hundreds of butterflies resting on one tree.

"At night they glow, moving from tree to tree, leading you deeper into the woods," Demetri said.

"Woah."

Demetri wrapped an arm around Mat's shoulder and guided him through the trees. "Come on, I promise there is more ahead."

Mat couldn't keep the smile off his face as they traveled further into the woods. Not only from Demetri, whose arm lay heavy on his shoulder, but from the oddities and beauties that lined their path.

They stopped at a patch of brightly colored flowers and watched as they grew nearly five feet tall in front of their eyes. Then they walked around a pond with a frog the size of a large dog resting in the middle, croaking out the most intricate song Mat had ever heard.

"Cool, isn't it?" Demetri asked as they passed by a copse of crystalline trees. "My parents let my brother and I roam around here when we were growing up. I remember I once found a pond filled with rainbow pearls. Never found it again."

Mat ran a finger along one of the quartz-like branches on the tree. "How do these exist?"

"My mom said this place reflects imaginations and desires from the living." He knelt down and touched the ground. "It used to be my favorite place."

"And now?" Mat asked.

Demetri looked at Mat. "And now I have a life up there. One that's hopefully worth going back to."

"Hopefully," Mat said, biting his lip. He stared at Demetri's lips, tracing them with his eyes. He imagined how nice they would feel against his. How nice his facial hair might feel. "Look, I—"

Demetri closed the space between them and planted a kiss on Mat's lips.

It was everything Mat wanted it to be. He pushed back, rubbing against Demetri's scruff. The crystal trees around them turned into a crimson red before fading to pink.

Demetri lowered his head and stepped back. "Sorry."

"Don't. I've been wanting to do that."

Mat watched Demetri bite his lip and look away, and wondered if Demetri's cheeks were as hot as his.

"Come on," Demetri said. "The house is this way."

They continued on in silence, Mat's head reeling as they passed by more strange sights bubbling up around them.

Eventually, they stood at the edge of a clearing which opened up onto an enormous lake.

A home, made of wood as dark as night, stood at the edge of the waters. Large windows peaked on both sides of the house, and a wrap-around porch led out into the water. Wooden ravens rested on the corners of the house like gargoyles peering out into the woods.

The roof was steep and high, covered in black shingles except for a glass peak that stood higher than the treetops.

"Mom and Dad would let us play up there," Demetri said, pointing to the peak. "We could see all the way to the mountains up there."

They walked down a stone path lined by shoulder-high shrubs covered in ripe red pomegranates and stepped onto the porch. Demetri grabbed the silver handle of the large black oak with silver inlays and pushed it open, holding the door for Mat.

"What, no locks?" Mat asked.

"Nope. Most people can't get past the ravens."

Mat shivered, imagining what might have happened if he went here without Demetri. He quickly stepped inside, which was even more gorgeous than the outside. White marble with black veins covered the floor, and a slate fireplace stood next to a wall of windows that overlooked the lake.

Beside the fireplace was a figure, standing with their back turned to Mat.

"I wondered when you two would show up." He turned, and Mat recognized the face in an instant. An older, and now hornless, version of Demetri.

"Damien?" Demetri asked.

"Brother," Damien said, slowly sauntering toward them, eyes on Mat.

Mat looked down at Damien's feet, knowing all too well what would happen if he let Damien catch his gaze.

"So you know what I'm here for?" Demetri asked.

Damien reached into his pocket and pulled out a small yellowed piece of paper. "Yes. Yes, I do."

26

Elder tree, Sambucus, your lore runs deep,
In healing and magic, secrets you keep.
Flowers and berries, remedies yield,
Yet uncooked parts, a poison shield.

Rich in vitamin C, your berries of might,
Can aid the weary, lend the sick light.
But heed the warning, for your power's twofold,
Toxicity lurks in your folds, bold.

In folklore and myth, you're wisdom's old tree,
A symbol of change, fertility, glee.
Guardian elder, of stories untold,
In your branches, life's mysteries unfold.

Elder

-Frankie-

Frankie crouched down low to the ground, creeping through the brush as he locked his eyes on a bunny chewing on a patch of clover. He could almost taste the meat in his mouth, the sharp iron taste on his tongue.

He frowned, stepping back away from the thicket of trees. This wasn't right. Where was he?

"Wolves!" a grayish bird screeched above him, chirping loudly as it flew between trees.

Frankie turned back to his pack, which was the farthest thing from a pack of wolves. A beagle with droopy ears rested her head in the dirt while a small golden retriever puppy kept trying to climb on top of him. An Australian Shepherd sat still, eyes on Frankie.

The only other wolf Frankie could see was a patchy white one with large tufts of fur missing. Frankie cocked his head to the side, his thoughts clearing. *Other wolf.*

He noted the beagle, retriever, collie, and Shepherd, but there wasn't another wolf. Just Remmy.

He looked down, glimpsing two enormous paws holding him up.

"Woah, what the fuck?" Frankie tried to say. Instead of words, he hopped backward and yipped.

The beagle lifted her head and huffed, "Language."

Memories flooded back into Frankie. He'd been in Mandrake Manor with Remmy. Then he was on the street. Then the woods. Dogs found them. Remmy's dogs. And Dude.

"What happened?" Frankie asked.

Remmy lowered his ears and cautiously stepped forward. "Are you back with us?"

Frankie blinked. "Back? I. I think so. How long was I—"

"A few days," Remmy said, lifting his head and sniffing.

"Days?!" Frankie shouted, looking around the woods. "Where are we? August! We need to get back."

"Back home?" Dude said, sitting up, his tongue lolling from his mouth. "Back to treats? Back to pets? And naps? I like naps."

Remmy let out a low growl, eying Dude before stepping closer to Frankie. "We can't. Not yet."

"Why not?" Frankie asked. "They need our help. We can't just leave them."

"And how do you plan on helping them as a wolf?"

Frankie yipped and paced around the tree. "Fine. But what option do I have? You can't turn me back. Maybe August can. I'm sure there's something in the book."

"Helena took it, remember?"

Frankie huffed, his fear overwhelming him. Before he could stop himself, he let out a howl. It rang in his ears, a desperate plea and surge of emotion that carried on the wind.

Remmy joined in, filling in calming notes that resonated with Frankie's.

Then the dogs joined in, not quite at the caliber of a wolf's howl, but comforting nonetheless.

Frankie's mind slowed, and the song left his throat as he slumped down into the dirt. "What do we do?"

"There might be someone in Henbane Hollow who could help. As long as they . . ."

Remmy trailed off, lifting his nose up in the air.

Seconds later, Frankie caught the scent. Something akin to the scent of rain before a storm and moss from an old forest filled his nostrils. With it, pictures of dense woodlands pressed on his thoughts, and a face covered in leaves cemented itself in his mind.

Frankie eyed Remmy and asked, "What is that?"

"Our answer," Remmy said. "Follow me before we lose the trail."

Frankie followed, as did the others, as they weaved through underbrush, alongside rivers, and through open fields.

Several hours passed, and they stopped at the edge of a clearing.

"Where are we?" Frankie asked.

Remmy took a careful step forward onto a well-manicured field. "Just outside Henbane Hollow. This was all woods when we left."

Frankie remembered the woods that surrounded Henbane Hollow, dense and encroaching on the stone wall that encompassed Henbane Hollow. Now there was a field, flattened, mowed, and with a fresh coat of paint for soccer, baseball, and football.

The little golden retriever hopped forward onto the field, shouting, "Play? Ball? Run? Play with me!"

"Arnold!" the collie shouted, racing forward and grabbing the pup by the scruff. "Not here."

Arnold slumped in the collie's grip and said with a sigh, "No fun."

A breeze drifted by, carrying the scent, drawing them to a patch of trees surrounded by fields of grass.

"There," Remmy said.

"Keep low and follow me," Frankie said before shooting off and racing toward the woods. He kept his eyes forward while his stomach turned in knots, feeling exposed in this artificial field.

Before he knew it, he and his pack dipped into the trees, hit with a dense and humid mist. He slowed, weaving in and out of trees before stopping at a cave opening.

The hairs on his hackles rose as an odor wafted from the cave. It wasn't the scent that had carried them. Instead, it was one of rot and death.

"I wouldn't go in there if I were you," a voice called out from the trees. "That's not a place for the living."

Remmy growled, and the pack of dogs dropped their tails between their legs, maneuvering to stand in front of Arnold.

Frankie bared his teeth. "Who's there?"

A man stepped out from behind the trees, wearing a long robe and resting a hand against the bark. "I heard your call. Seems you've lost your way."

"Jacob?" Frankie asked, cocking his head to the side. He struggled to focus on the man's features, pushing past the wolf part of his brain. He recognized the man's light eyes first, followed by his broad shoulders and wavy hair. He hadn't seen Mandrake Manor's handyperson in anything but a tool belt before, but he was certain it was him.

Jacob climbed down the hill to meet them at the cave entrance. "This suburbanification has gotten out of control."

"It's Helena. She attacked Mandrake Manor," Remmy said.

Jacob nodded. "She was bound to do it eventually, I guess." He looked around at the woods. "I did what I could to preserve this spot, but I can't hold it forever. Where are the other Mandrakes?"

"Last I saw, Mat was in the underworld, and Helena knocked August unconscious. And Helena took the book," Frankie said.

Jacob nodded. "Then we're running out of time."

Frankie let out a huff. "She turned me into this. Made me forget who I was. Can you help me turn back?"

Jacob knelt down at his side, running a hand along Frankie's snout. "The magic that binds you is powerful. Beyond what I can do."

"So I'm stuck like this," Frankie whined.

Jacob shook his head. "I didn't say that. You are of the Mandrake coven. You have all the power you need."

"Well, thanks, Glinda," Frankie said, pulling his head out of Jacob's hands. "Maybe a little more clarity on how exactly I'm supposed to do that?"

"Frankie," Remmy said, nudging Frankie's side. "He's trying to help."

"I know," Frankie said. "I know. Sorry."

Jacob pushed himself up and crossed his arms. "You've used your voice before, right? Commanded the elements, revealed the hidden?"

The memory of a small white poodle that turned into a shadowy pooka came to mind. "Yeah," Frankie said. "But it went wrong. I made Remmy turn against his will."

"But it worked, right?" Jacob asked. "You won't learn how to control it if you don't use it. And if you don't use it, then you could be trapped as a wolf forever."

"Fine," Frankie said. "What do you suggest I do, then?"

"Your magic reveals truths and returns the natural order. When you did it before, how did it happen?"

"I don't know. I touched Henry, the pooka, and told him to show himself," Frankie said.

Jacob nodded. "So do that again but tell it to yourself."

Remmy sat down next to the dogs and watched, his tongue hanging out of his mouth.

Frankie shook his head. "Fine. Fine." He breathed in once, closed his eyes, and said, "Be me."

He wasn't sure how long his eyes were closed, but it felt like an eternity. He kept mumbling, "Be me. Be me." No matter how much he tried, nothing happened. Eventually, Frankie opened his eyes and glared at Jacob. "It's not working."

"I can see that. You want this, right? Want to be a human again?"

"Yeah, obviously," Frankie said, looking over at Remmy.

Jacob followed his gaze and smirked. "Obviously. But maybe not if Remmy isn't human too?"

"No," Frankie said. "I mean, yes. He's stuck because of me. It's only fair that—"

Remmy stood up. "It's not your fault."

"And Remmy can't turn back unless you help yourself first," Jacob said.

"Fine," Frankie said. Taking a deep breath, he focused inward. A tingle ran down to his paws. "Be me," he mumbled.

He focused on what he looked like, his curled hair, tan skin, brown eyes. Those thoughts peeled away at his wolf form, and he felt his mind buzz.

The static sensation vibrated through his body, turning his skin into pins and needles. It overwhelmed him, but he squeezed his eyes shut and kept muttering, "Be me."

His body shifted, his fur receding while his bones popped and rearranged. He screamed, but he couldn't hear it among the buzzing in his ears.

Then everything fell silent. He opened his eyes, blinking, as a dull, mundane world came into focus.

He pushed himself up, seeing the dirt caked on his naked flesh.

Jacob looked away as Remmy came rushing to his side, licking at his face. "You did it!"

Frankie ran his fingers through Remmy's fur, the residual magic intermixing on his fingertips. He felt a weave interlaced in his fur, a magic that was familiar. It was his spell, the one that locked Remmy as a wolf. He pulled at it with his mind as words fell from his lips. "Undo. Undo. Undo."

The magic slipped back into his fingers, tracing up his arm. He frowned as a different sensation came to the edges of his fingertips, a feeling like oil seeping up his hand. It wasn't his magic but something else. Images of Helena and an older woman flashed in his mind, silent words as they wrapped a string around a picture of Remmy.

He pulled back and flung his hand, seeing a blob of blackened ooze splat onto the forest ground. It fizzled and sank into the dirt.

"What the hell was that?" Frankie asked.

But before anyone could answer, Frankie saw the effect he had on Remmy.

The bald patches of fur grew back, and for a moment, a glorious white wolf looked back at him with a glowing white coat. Then Remmy changed, his body seamlessly turning back into a human.

Before Frankie knew it, both he and Remmy were feet apart, human, and completely naked.

"Uh," Jacob said. "I might have some spare clothes in the truck. I'll. I'll go do that."

Jacob turned and vanished into the woods.

Remmy stood up and stretched his back. "Ugh, I've been dying to do that for days."

Frankie grinned, looking at Remmy before eyeing the collection of dogs staring back at the two of them. "Too bad we have an audience."

Remmy smiled. "Get your mind out of the gutter. We've got a neighborhood to save."

27

Yarrow, Achillea, the ancient's delight,
Staunches the bleeding and calms the night.
Inflames not the body but soothes the gut,
Yet beware its touch, for rashes it's cut.

Induces the moon's flow, risks birth untimely,
To dogs, cats, horses, it's unkindly.
Yet medicinal boon, to toothache and ear,
Yarrow, in healing, brings comfort near.

In folklore woven, with love and protection,
Averts the evil, guides love's direction.
Yarrow, your essence, in history steeps,
In the heart of the wise, your knowledge keeps.

Yarrow

- AUGUST -

T he sun nestled above the trees as August followed closely alongside Ragana. Together, they journeyed along the sidewalk leading deeper into Henbane Hollow. The once whimsical and strange
homes August had seen days ago were now replaced by something
more mundane. Identical houses and perfectly trimmed lawns with
freshly painted shutters stretched down every street they turned. Every
hint of magic that August had loved was now gone as they continued
down Tansy Terrace and Chicory Crossing.

"This is bad," Ragana said as she made a turn onto Coltsfoot Court.

"Why is she doing this?" August asked.

"Control, probably. You know she wanted to buy Mandrake
Manor the minute Melinda died, right?"

August frowned. "No, and I don't think Mat knew that either."

"One thing I know well about my cousin is that she likes to sink her
fingers into everyone's business," Ragana said.

As they continued walking, August couldn't help but notice the silence that spread over the neighborhood. Laughter and chatter had all but vanished, replaced by an uneasy stillness.

They came to the end of the street and found Yarrow Grove Park, which was composed of several sports fields with manicured grass leading out into the woods.

Ragana pointed at a beige building just off the parking lot with a sign that read, "Community Center," and said, "That's where the HOA meets."

"And you think Helena is in there?"

Ragana looked toward the building. "Oh, she definitely is. Can't you feel it?"

"Feel what?" August asked.

"The energy. It's practically seeping off the walls of this place," Ragana replied.

"No," August said, staring nervously at the building. It was incredibly forgettable, as if the enchantment to make all the other homes resemble the 1980s had worked double time on this building.

"Close your eyes. Focus," Ragana said. Once August did, she continued, "Can you feel it now? That undercurrent pulsing off the building. The need to conform and stay in line."

August focused, squeezing their eyes shut. They shuddered as a palpable energy flowed over them, an oppressive power that filled their mind. All they wanted to do was straighten their suit, turn around, and return to reading the newspaper at Mandrake Manor. They blinked and took in a deep breath. "We should get out of here, right? What if she comes out?"

Ragana shook her head. "She won't. She's turned the entire neighborhood in a matter of hours. The kind of magic it takes to do that, and sweep everyone into it, is way above her head. She's lucky if she makes it out of this one alive."

August looked out to the people in the neighborhood, noting that all of them seemed to move mechanically, like puppets on strings. Some were dressed in suits, mowing their lawns, while others corralled children to the park across the street. Helena's web had caught up all of them in the Stepford neighborhood, and all August could do was watch.

August looked back at the community center, fear bubbling up in their stomach. "So she won't see us coming?"

"I don't think so," Ragana said. "Doing this kind of work would require her full attention. At the very least, if you know where she is, then we can get the book."

"I could dream again. Last time I found where Demetri was. I could find the book, mark the spot, and we could open a gate."

Ragana shook her head. "Do you remember how to do all that without the book?"

"No," August said.

"Even so, without the right supplies, you couldn't get the gate close enough."

Sweat built on August's hands. They weren't the one to break into buildings and confront someone like Helena. "Fine," they said. "We go in and see what we can find."

Ragana reached out her hand and interlaced her fingers in August's. She smiled and said, "We do this together."

August nodded, took a deep breath, and squeezed Ragana's hand. "Together. And if we get out of this alive, I'm taking you out on a date."

"I think I would very much like that," Ragana said.

They started toward the building, keeping their distance from any neighbors as they crept along the side and walked up to the entrance.

Up close, the building couldn't hold its shape. One moment it looked like a simple beige community center, the next it shifted and changed into a dark red cottage with steep, sloped roofs that reached high into the sky. Before August could comment, the building shifted back to the beige center with a slight red tint.

"Uh, what was that?" August said.

Ragana shrugged. "I don't know for sure, but I think Helena's overextending herself."

"Only one way to find out, I guess," August said. They grabbed the handle to the door and pushed it open. The smell of dusty books and old furniture filled their senses as they stepped onto scuffed linoleum flooring. Boring beige walls stretched down the hall in front of them, adorned with faded artwork of beaches. In the corner was a potted monstera, struggling to survive in the dim light.

"Keep your eyes open," Ragana whispered.

As they traveled deeper into the building, the atmosphere grew thicker, dense with the anticipation of what was about to happen. The door behind them creaked as it slowly closed of its own accord.

"What the hell?" August asked.

"This place is the second most magical place in the neighborhood. A door closing on its own is just the building. Let's keep going."

They continued down the hall and took a turn, down a hallway that looked like it didn't end. The beige walls and linoleum floors stretched beyond what August could see, and offshoots to rooms continued on into infinity.

"The HOA made the community center their headquarters for a reason," Ragana whispered.

As they passed by room after room, August's unease grew, their heart pounding heavy in their chest.

Each room was filled with the same table, chairs, and potted plant, as if the room had been copied and pasted over and over again. However, the copies seemed to change slightly the farther they went. First it was subtle, a strange protruding knot bubbling out of the table or a chair that had fallen over. Then the potted plant shifted and changed into a gnarled tree, and the linoleum peeled back, revealing wooden flooring beneath.

Mundane beach artwork turned into dense woods, and August got the feeling that the paintings had something in them, staring back at them.

Soon August and Ragana stood in the hallway of an old wooden cottage with peeling red paint. Flickering candlelight streamed in from underneath a closed door to their left. August looked back, but the infinite hall was gone, and the turn back to the exit was mere feet away.

Something murmured ahead of them and Ragana held up a finger to her lips. August slowly crept forward, carefully placing one foot in front of the other as they reached the end of the hall.

They carefully pushed the door open and peered in through the cracks. There was Helena, sitting on top of a massive circular table, surrounded by tall pillars of candles. Her eyes were shut tight, and she murmured some kind of chant.

"No," a voice spoke out from the corner. "No, no. You have it all wrong." A woman stepped out from the shadows, green mist billowing off her, and she approached the table. She looked older, with a tight gray bun pulling her forehead back.

Helena opened her eyes and looked down at the book in front of her. "It says right here to chant, '*Dans set nuit, je demande la puissance.*' That's what I'm doing."

"Your French is terrible," the woman said, waving her hand. As she did, the book lifted into the air and hovered in front of her. She pointed at the text. "It's not *danz set nweet* you good-for-nothing hag. *Dans set nuit,* the s and t are silent."

"I'm sorry," Helena said, looking down at the table.

The woman waved her hand again, and the book slammed in front of Helena. "Start over. Now."

August backed up and looked at Ragana. "Who is that?" they whispered.

Ragana's face was white. "That's. That's Melinda Mandrake."

28

Lotus, *Nelumbo nucifera*, pure and fair,
In seeds and rhizomes, healing potential share.
Yet heed, consumption raw risks parasite's snare,
Cook well, to keep the danger spare.

In treatment of wastewater, you shine bright,
Polluting compounds, heavy metals, you fight.
Your roots and stalks in meals take flight,
But watch for browning, keep in sight.

Fabric, food, and sacred lore,
In every use, you offer more.
Guard against misuse, explore with care,
The Lotus story, with all, we share.

Lotus

- MAT -

"What do you want?" Mat asked, eying the paper, which listed exits out of the underworld, in Damian's hand.

Damian leaned against the fireplace inside the lakeside home in Limbo and nodded at Demetri. "He knows what I want."

Without the horns, and now in gray slacks and a tight black shirt, Damian looked exactly like an older version of Demetri. He met Mat's gaze for a second before Mat dropped his eyes to the floor, recalling what happened the last time he'd stared into Damian's dark brown eyes.

"And you know I can't let you do that," Demetri said. "Why do you want to go topside so bad?"

"Because Dad wants to retire."

Demetri laughed and gestured around the room. "Dad can retire here. He always said this was peaceful for him."

Damian pushed himself off the fireplace, sauntering toward his brother. "You don't get it, do you? Dad's not looking for peace."

Demetri ran a hand over his bald head. "It took me years to convince them to let me into Henbane Hollow, and I'm not even a full-fledged demon."

"But you got in. Dad's proud of you, you know? First demon to make a name for themselves topside that isn't steeped in corruption or murder. He wants to see you in action. He wants to be in your life."

"And the two of you are a package deal?"

"Unless you want to take care of him, which I doubt. He's not retiring in Goldenrod Gardens either. Not until he has to."

"It's not gonna happen. It can't happen. If I bring in more demons to Henbane Hollow now, especially with everything going on . . . No way."

Mat frowned. "But what does being a demon have to do with anything? Why should anyone care? We have witches, werewolves, oh, and I'm pretty sure I met a siren."

"Demons are different," Demetri said. "We're the gatekeepers to the beyond. Even the nice supernatural beings hate us at some point. We can't share everything we know about the afterlife, and that makes us evil and deceitful."

Mat thought for a second. Sure, he was new to all of this still, but he'd never seen Demetri that way. Sure, the whole crawling out from a hole with horns was a bad look for Damian, but now he looked like anyone else. Mat looked at Demetri. "Well, are you deceitful?"

"No," Demetri said. "At least, I try not to be. But residents of Henbane Hollow don't care. I got in because I'm half-human. They said I still had my humanity."

Damian huffed and shook his head. "As if that should matter."

"I don't think I could convince them. I can barely vouch for myself, let alone full-fledged demons," Demetri said.

Damian looked down. "Then I can't help you."

"Wait," Mat said, stepping forward. "What if I do it?"

"Do what?" Demetri asked.

"Vouch for Damian and your dad. The Mandrake name seems to mean a lot, right?"

Damian's eyes lit up. "You would?"

Mat pointed at Damian's hand. "For a way out, yeah. You have our ticket out of here. If your dad wants to retire in Henbane Hollow, then why should I care? If Henbane Hollow is a refuge for the supernatural, then your dad should be allowed in. Plain and simple."

Demetri stepped beside Mat. "The word of a Mandrake would carry more weight than mine."

"And you mean it?" Damian asked.

Mat nodded and held out his hand. "I do. Now hand over the paper."

Damian smiled and complied. "Then we have a deal. Demetri, I assume you can find us a house?"

"I'll try," Demetri said. "It won't be a mansion, but there is space."

Mat unfolded the paper. Several lines were scratched out with a pen, but the last three on the list we scrawled in terrible handwriting. "What is this one? Lotus caves?"

"I'd go with that one. I scratched out the passages that don't exist anymore," Damian said. "But the Lotus Caves are a mile north of here. I'll send a message topside. A guardian can open it on their end."

"A guardian?" Mat asked.

"Beings connected to earth, like a nymph," Demetri said. He bit his lip and grabbed the paper, pulling a pen from his pocket and scrawling a name on it before handing it over to Damian. "Or an earth deity."

Damian looked at the name and raised an eyebrow. "He lives in Henbane Hollow? I thought he died."

"Who?" Mat asked, looking at the paper in Damian's hand.

"He did, a few years ago," Demetri said. "But deities always find new avatars."

Damian pocketed the paper and started toward the door. "Consider it done. Dad and I will start making arrangements."

"Wait," Demetri said, holding up his hands. "What about the investigation?"

"Ah, that." Damian smiled. "You got me there." He paused, eyeing Mat for a second. "It was Melinda."

Damian didn't wait for a response. Instead, he brushed past them and walked out the front door.

Demetri paced the living room, shaking his head and muttering to himself.

"What was that about?" Mat asked. "Melinda?"

"I need a minute," Demetri said, crossing the room and reaching the door. "We need to get to the caves. Come on."

Mat followed as they left the home and started down a dirt path along the lake. The gray skies looked a little darker than before, as if the sun behind them might be settling somewhere behind the mountains. Demetri trudged along the path, leaving Mat to listen to the lapping of the waters on the rocky shore and the trees swaying in the breeze.

"So," Mat finally broke the silence as they entered the woods. "There are earth deities? Like actual gods in Henbane Hollow?"

"Sort of," Demetri said. He kept his focus on the trail in front of him. "It's not my place to name them. That's how it is supposed to be in Henbane Hollow. People reveal their true selves in their own time."

Mat caught the hint of cynicism in Demetri's words. "But that didn't happen to you?" he asked.

Demetri shook his head. "My application to join Henbane Hollow was a controversy from the start. Right around the time that Helena started pushing the whole suburban renovation."

"She outed you? I mean, I wouldn't put it past her, but why?" Mat asked.

"This whole time I thought it was her. It made sense, especially because of this push to 'normalize' the neighborhood. I declined the renovations in my application. She said nothing about it, but I knew I started off on the wrong foot then and there."

"But?" Mat asked.

"But HOA members are bound by their position to keep personal information confidential. I've done enough contracts, both human and non-human, to see she wouldn't be able to say a word. That's why I asked Damian to do some digging."

Mat stopped, sweat forming on his brow. "Melinda."

Demetri nodded. "I don't know how or why, but Melinda was behind it."

"Melinda Mandrake? The same Melinda that hasn't come to me," Mat mumbled.

Damian stopped in his tracks and looked at Mat. "What?"

"Melinda was supposed to teach the next Mandrake coven. At least, that's what Margaret said."

Demetri cocked his head to the side. "Margaret? Who's Margaret?"

"A distant Mandrake. She's my teacher now, I think," Mat said.

"So, you haven't seen or talked with Melinda Mandrake? At all?" Demetri asked.

"Nope," Mat said.

"She hasn't been to the underworld since her death, either. I figured she was hanging around the house, but if she's not there, then where has she been?"

"You don't think Helena did something to her, do you?"

Demetri shrugged, starting back down the path. "I don't know what to think."

They rounded another bend in the path and came to a small cave opening.

"Is that it?" Mat asked.

"The Lotus Caves," Demetri said and held out his hand. "It's easy to get lost in there."

Mat reached out and gripped Demetri's hand. It was warm and comforting. "And now we get to hold hands on our first date."

Demetri rolled his eyes. "If we go on another, I might even open the door for you."

"You mean when we go on another," Mat said, giving Demetri's hand a light squeeze.

Demetri stood up a little straighter and smiled. "Perfect, that's what I want to hear. How about we get the hell out of here?"

He led Mat through the opening of the cave. Mat couldn't see a thing at first as he stumbled over rocks and felt along the cave walls. They navigated through the narrow cave for a few minutes, the light behind them vanishing. Sounds echoed out from the stone tunnels. First, they were quiet drips, but they quickly developed into sniffling and wailing.

"What the hell is that?" Mat whispered.

"People come here to reflect on their lives. Some of them get lost for a bit, finding corners in the cave to feel their emotions."

"That sounds horrifying," Mat said.

Demetri squeezed his hand. "To anyone who has time to lose, maybe. But in the afterlife, all people have is time. Everyone who comes into the caves leaves eventually, shed of their pain and sorrow and ready for the next step."

They rounded another corner, and one of the wailing voices grew louder. "I'm glad you know where you're going."

"I don't, but the caves should take us where we need to go."

"Oh, that's reassuring," Mat said, bumping his shoulder into a rock.

A faint light shone ahead, and Demetri pulled Mat along. "Told you."

The light ahead of them grew brighter, and a gust of air blew into the cave. All the wailing and sobs stopped in an instant, and a warmth washed over Mat.

"We made it," Demetri said.

They stepped out of the cave and onto soft ground. The air was sweet with pine, and the sun peeking through the trees was warm on Mat's skin. He realized that even in Limbo, the cloud-covered sky and forest was nothing compared to the woods in real life.

He let go of Demetri's hand and blinked a few times before his eyes settled on a man with chestnut hair.

"Jacob?" Mat asked, his face reddening as he realized who the man standing in front of him was.

Jacob nodded. "In the flesh."

"Glad you both were, uh, able to make it out."

Demetri brushed off his suit, which was well beyond dirty at this point. "Thanks, we owe you."

"You just missed Frankie," Jacob said, eyeing Mat. "I think he was headed back to find August. If you can fix the mess that Helena made, then your debts are well beyond paid."

Mat looked at Demetri, then Jacob. "Jacob, our date. About that. I'm, uh—"

Jacob looked at Demetri for a second, then back at Mat. "Don't worry about it."

"But—"

"But nothing. We'll talk later, okay? After you save the neighborhood."

Demetri cleared his throat and placed an arm around Mat. "Come on, Jacob won't be able to keep this place suburban-free for long."

Mat gave one last glance at Jacob before he and Demetri stepped out onto the field and toward Henbane Hollow.

29

Venus Flytrap, Dionaea's delight,
With sweetened lure, in murky night.
Its extract brews a potent fight,
In immunity pains, it might smite.

Carnivora, in herbal lore,
Its promises we can't ignore.
For skin cancer, it may restore,
A natural aid we explore.

Carnivore in a plant's disguise,
In your mystery, our hope lies.
Nature's gift, in you crystallize,
To heal and soothe, under the skies.

Venus Flytrap

- FRANKIE -

Frankie and Remmy raced out into the manicured fields. Frankie had to avert his eyes on several occasions as the tight jeans that Remmy borrowed from Jacob accentuated his . . . assets.

Inadvertently, they cut right through a soccer game with their menagerie of dogs tailing behind them.

"Sorry," Frankie shouted at a particular group of glaring parents. He stared ahead, thinking about the fastest way to get to Mandrake Manor and to August.

As they passed by the community center, Dude yelped, followed by yips and barks from the other dogs.

Frankie stopped and looked at his pack, noting they all bared their teeth at the building as they backed up.

Remmy sniffed the air. "Do you smell that?"

Frankie raised an eyebrow. "No? I don't . . ." He breathed. "Wait! Yeah. Like a faint metallic smell."

"Magic," Remmy said, nodding at the center. "It smells like ozone. And it's coming from there. A lot more than there should be."

Frankie looked down the street. He couldn't see Mandrake Manor from here, but every other house in his view had the same cookie-cutter shape and white picket fence. "You don't think August is in there, do you?"

Remmy took another sniff and shook his head. "I don't know. But this is Helena's doing for sure."

Frankie looked down the road, then back at the community center. "Well, shit." Frankie thought for a moment and snapped his fingers. "We have to know what Helena's doing. You go to the Manor and see if August is there. I'm gonna sneak in here."

"Uh, no. That's a terrible idea," Remmy said.

"She ambushed us last time. I'm not going to let her keep the upper hand. I won't do anything stupid."

"We shouldn't separate," Remmy said.

"I'd never. Who'd take the dogs?" Frankie said, grinning.

"Ha. Ha. I'm serious."

Frankie patted Remmy's chest. "I know. Just hurry back."

Remmy glared at Frankie. "Fine, but if she hurts you, I'm tearing her apart."

"That's aggressive, but I'll take it."

Remmy dove in, wrapping his arm around Frankie's back and pulling him close. The bristles of his beard tickled Frankie's face as their lips touched.

For a moment, it was just Frankie and Remmy. The rest of the world didn't matter. Then Dude yipped, and Remmy pulled away.

"Be safe," he said, backing up toward the road.

"I'm always safe," Frankie said, grinning before facing the community center.

It was annoying how normal and old it looked. Concrete steps with a dark brass handle led up to glass doors with the same ugly brown frames while the popcorn-textured tan walls stretched in either direction.

And in Jacob's borrowed pair of jeans and plaid shirt, he felt like someone had trapped him in some 80s brochure about stranger danger or something.

Frankie shook the thought away, pushing the door to the community center open. Stale air and ozone filled his nostrils as he stepped onto the slightly chipped linoleum floor.

"I'm going to get murdered," he whispered to himself.

His hair stood on end as the acrid scent of magic grew stronger. The door behind him closed, and he grimaced at the flickering fluorescent light above him.

"It's fine. Everything is fine," he mumbled.

He rounded the corner, and as he did so, the hall in front of him stretched out into infinity. The same potted plant repeated itself in front of the same doorway as far as the eye could see.

"Absolutely the fuck not," Frankie said, taking a step back.

As he did, the hallway shrunk again, and there was a single conference room to his right before the hallway ended.

"What the hell?"

He stepped forward again, and the hall expanded out into infinity again. He took a careful step forward, passing by the first room, filled with a large table and chairs, before passing another room with the same setup.

He squinted down the hallway, but no matter how hard he looked, the hall just stretched on.

He passed by a few more rooms and breathed in through his nose. The stale air was still heavy, but the scent of ozone was faint. He frowned, turned around, and shut his eyes. "Okay, think. If this was a trap, what would I do?"

He breathed in again, catching the faint scent of magic, and stepped forward. The scent grew stronger the closer he got to the start of the hallway.

As he passed by the first conference room, he breathed in. The scent was the strongest there.

He opened his eyes, looking in at one of the most boring conference rooms he'd ever seen in his life, and stepped inside.

The magic permeated the air so much he could taste it, like pennies on his tongue. "Okay, now what?"

After waiting for what felt like forever, he turned around, assuming that he might have better luck out in the hallway. However, he came face to face with a wall, and the exit to the conference room was completely gone. He pressed his hand against a solid wall then looked around, realizing the room had no doors at all.

"Great," Frankie said, leaning against the wall. "Just great."

He closed his eyes and ran his fingers through his hair. The magic tickled his nose and traveled down into this throat.

An idea came to mind, and he opened his eyes, focusing on the words as they came out.

"Turn back to normal."

The magic burned at the back of his throat, resonating out and into the conference room.

In response, the room rumbled and the furniture shook.

"Oh, I fucked up," Frankie whispered.

The table cracked and shifted before its legs jabbed into the ground and the table ripped into several branches. In seconds, the conference table had transformed into a gnarled tree, sharp branches jabbing into the ceiling tiles.

He pressed himself against the wall, the branches reaching out toward him as bright green leaves sprouted out from the table.

Frankie turned around and tested the wall. "You're not going to let me out unless I use my voice again, are you?"

He thought about his words and pushed his hands against the wall. He whispered, feeling the magic on his tongue, "Let me through."

The wall rippled, and his hands became numb. Before he could push away, one hand slipped into the wall, followed by the other.

Frankie squeezed his eyes tight, mumbling, "Shit, shit, shit," as he slipped through the wall.

Cold washed over him as he stepped through.

He carefully opened one eye, then the other. He'd expected to be standing back in the weird linoleum hallway, but he wasn't. The floor beneath him was pitch black, as if he were standing on nothing at all. Ahead, he could see the hallway, separated by what looked like a pane of glass inches away from him. His hands had already slipped through that glass and he pulled them back, the barrier rippling in front of him.

He turned around, and another pane of glass separated him from the doorless conference room.

"They're in the walls, Neo." He chuckled to himself.

He side-stepped along the wall. Oddly, as he looked out into the hall, he passed by something that seemed to shimmer and bend, like some kind of funhouse mirror.

The hall instantly transformed. It was no longer a crusty old linoleum floor and fluorescent lit hall, but some kind of weird fairytale wooden cabin.

Two figures stood at the end of the hall, peering through a cracked door just out of Frankie's sight.

As he inched closer, the distinctly shaved head of August gave them away,

"Who's that?" August whispered.

Frankie froze, assuming his shimmying in the walls was about to scare the ever-living-shit out of August.

Then Ragana whispered back. "That's. That's Melinda Mandrake."

So, they weren't talking to him. He pressed his hands against the glass-like wall and pushed. His hands slipped through, then his face.

"Psst," Frankie said as quietly as he could.

The two of them jumped and quietly turned around, their faces pale.

August found Frankie, and their eyes widened. "Frankie? What the fuck?" they whispered.

"I don't know how to explain. You two okay?" he whispered back.

"Yeah," August said. "Helena and Melinda Mandrake. They're working together."

"Mat's Great Aunt? The dead one?" Frankie asked.

Ragana nodded.

"The book's in there," August said.

Frankie looked at the door and slipped a hand back into the wall. "Well, I have an advantage. Wait here."

He slid into the wall before August or Ragana could say another word and worked his way past them and into the room.

Inside was an arrangement of candles on and around a circular table. Long heavy drapes covered the windows, and two women argued around a book.

"I am trying the best I can," Helena said, turning away from the other woman, who Frankie now knew as Melinda.

Melinda, translucent and glowing a light green color, crossed her arms and walked away. "I don't know why I would have ever trusted an imbecile like you. You knew what you were getting into."

Frankie continued along the wall, passing by Helena until he was only a few feet away from the book, resting at the edge of the table. Neither woman faced the book, and Frankie saw his chance. He slipped one foot out, then the other, tiptoeing toward the book.

"I know," Helena said. "I knew it would be hard, but what about after? You think the neighborhood is just going to forget about what I'm doing? You think they are going to let me run the place?"

"We'll make them forget. Once the magic is yours, you can do what you want."

Frankie grabbed the book, reading the words scrawled at the top of the page, "La Fusion Occulte." He gently pulled it off the table and backed up.

Unfortunately for him, as he backed up, his foot creaked on the floorboards.

Helena and Melinda whipped their heads around and looked right at him, then at the book.

He jumped back, fully expecting to slip back into the wall, but only managing to throw himself right into a solid wall, knocking the wind out of him.

"Get the book!" Melinda screamed.

Stars appeared in Frankie's vision and he crumpled to the ground as Helena pulled the book from his hands.

Melinda disappeared and reappeared by the door. "The others are over here!"

Before Frankie could push himself up, Helena flicked her wrist at him, and an invisible force slammed into him, pinning him against the wall.

30

Hedera helix, English Ivy in sight,
A green cloak, in the moonlight.
Treats bronchitis with all its might,
Yet, its berries in caution, invite.

In ancient lore, for eyes so sore,
Gerard's wisdom we explore.
Yet dermatitis, it may implore,
In sensitive skins, an uproar.

Falcarinol, hederin glean,
In your leaves, often unseen.
While saponins' might make rabbits lean,
Your healing essence, in humans, convene.

English Ivy

- AUGUST -

Bindings made of green mist wrapped around August's body, holding them still. Reality lurched and shifted beneath them, pulling them into depths unknown. They strained against their entrapment, feeling the edges of their wrappings loosen the more and more they pushed.

Without sight or mobility in their arms and legs, they scoured their senses. A light formed in their mind, the end of a tunnel they were drifting further away from.

"No," they whispered.

They held the light in their mind, yearning for it. In an instant, the bindings tore free, and their body flew headfirst into the light.

August winced and sat up, covering their eyes from a beam of sunlight shining right onto their face. Exhaustion tugged at them to lie back down and fall asleep. The thought of the dark pulled at August's mind as they stretched and rubbed the sleep from their eyes. Soft sheets slid between their hands, and they realized they were sitting in their bed, back home at Mandrake Manor.

They frowned, memories from last night not quite stitching together. How did they get there? The last thing they remembered was . . . was . . . They winced and looked back up at the window, noting that the usual heavy drapes were missing.

"That's weird," August mumbled to themself.

Their feet landed on creaking floorboards, and they stepped out of bed, fully clothed in a pair of jeans and a T-shirt.

They rubbed their face. "What the hell did I drink last night?" They reached for the usual spot where they plugged in their phone. It wasn't there. Nor was their journal, book on dreams, or little owl mug. They eyed the collection of perfumes, ivory comb, and an old red digital clock that ticked over to ten.

August pressed their thumb into their hand, a trick they'd picked up on lucid dreaming. But their thumb didn't pass through.

"Okay, not a dream," August said. "Maybe."

Yet, nothing from what they could recollect made sense. They looked at themself in the mirror, smirking at the graphic T-shirt Ragana had gifted them of an owl frantically typing away on a laptop.

The reflection in front of them rippled for a moment, and the image of them suspended in midair flickered into view before snapping back to normal.

"What in the—"

"I know," a voice called out from the hallway. Footsteps echoed as they continued. "Just come over here, and soon."

The voice was familiar, a feminine voice that August couldn't quite put a face to. They crept along their room, placing an ear against the door.

"I think I have the answer," the voice said as they descended the stairs.

August gently twisted the doorknob and pulled it open, tiptoeing out into the hallway.

"What, you aren't going to see her out?" a voice asked on August's right.

August nearly jumped out of their skin as Frankie stepped out of his room and yawned loudly.

"Shut up or she'll hear you!" August hissed.

"Uh, okay," Frankie said, pushing past August. "What, am I supposed to pretend I don't know you and Ragana are banging?"

"No, that's not Ragana. There's someone in the house."

Frankie paled. "For real? Again?"

"I know they might die, but this is the only way," the voice downstairs shouted.

"Um, not interested in dying," Frankie said, backing up behind August. "What do we do?"

August felt at the wall, tracing along the edge of the wallpaper, noting the lack of yellowing. "Something's off," they whispered. "Do you remember where you were before you woke up?"

"Yeah. I was . . . wait. No. I don't. Is this a dream?" Frankie asked.

August frowned. "I don't think so, but I'm not ruling it out." They looked down the hall at Mat's room. "Think we should see if Mat is here too?"

"I guess? But didn't that lady come from there?" Frankie asked.

August shrugged and headed down the hall, past the stairwell, and into Mat's room. Floral perfume bombarded them as they stepped inside.

Frankie covered his nose and ran a finger along the vanity, which contained an assortment of makeup and brushes. "Unless Mat's delved into the world of drag, I don't think he's here."

August eyed their reflection in the vanity, and for a split second, they saw both themself and Frankie hovering in midair in a different room.

"Did you see that?" August asked.

Frankie raised an eyebrow. "See what?"

"In the reflection. It's like we're hovering in the air or something."

Frankie looked up and down at the mirror. "I would say we are hover-free."

Something twisted in August's gut. "We need to get out of here. This might not be a dream, but I don't think we're safe, wherever we are."

"Sure. Okay, Nancy Drew, how do we get out of here?" Frankie asked.

August scratched their head. "If it's like a dream, then we need to find a barrier. We need to get outside."

"Great, lead the way," Frankie said.

August huffed, then held a finger to their lips. They crept out of Mat's room and to the stairwell before pausing, straining to hear the murmurings downstairs.

"Follow my lead. We go out the front. Don't say a word," August whispered.

Frankie nodded, and the pair quietly tiptoed to the first floor. August could hear the woman shuffling around in the back library.

They started toward the door, but before they could reach it, it swung open. A tall young pale woman with a wrapping around her head stood in front of the doorway.

Frankie yelped, and a cold sweat formed on August's forehead. "Uh," August muttered.

"Melinda!" the woman shouted.

"Shit, what do we do?" Frankie said, backing against the wall.

"Ugh, not again," a woman's voice called behind them.

"I told you it would happen again," the woman in the doorway said.

Melinda, who looked only a few years older than Mat, with red hair tied tight in a bun, walked past August in a short emerald sundress. She paused in front of the door and stomped her foot down. "Now you listen here, house," she yelled. "Harriet Henbane is still a part of my coven. And she is my guest. Do you hear me? Let her in."

"Uh, what?" Frankie whispered.

August walked toward Melinda, waving their hands. "Uh. I don't think they can see us."

Melinda grabbed Harriett's hand and pulled her past the threshold.

Harriett stumbled into Melinda's arms, adjusting her head wrap. "Thanks," she breathed. "I wish this house didn't have such a vendetta against me."

"You and me both," Melinda said, helping Harriett out of her coat. "How are the treatments?"

Harriett shook her head and looked away.

Melinda hung up the coat and gestured to Harriett to follow. "The house knows what I want to do. What I need to do. It can't take it out of me, but you . . . well, you're a different story."

August frowned and looked at Frankie. "This is a memory."

"What?" Frankie asked.

"Come on," August said, following the two women into the living room.

"Did you figure it out?" Harriett asked, slowly sitting down on the couch. The poor woman looked both young and so frail, August was afraid she might die right there on the spot.

Melinda smiled. "Your daughter," she said.

Harriett tilted her head to the side. "Helena? She's not even two. What does she have to do with it?"

Melinda turned around and headed into the library, picking up the Mandrake spellbook. "She can claim the power. It'll be years before she's ready, especially if your ex keeps her from me, but if she claims it, then we can be together."

"Uh, August?" Frankie said behind them.

August leaned in as Melinda placed the book in front of Harriett. "Shh," August said, waving off Frankie.

The page in the book was blank, but Melinda pointed at it and beamed at Harriett. "I will teach her to do this spell. Of course, the house will have to be awakened again, after my passing, but if she claims the power, her bloodline will replace mine. They will have no option but to bring you back. Bring you here."

Harriett shook her head. "But what about you? And your heir?"

"I have no heirs," Melinda said. "None of that matters to me. And I can't imagine an afterlife passing back and forth while you continue to fade. If I stay on this side, and the gates open for you, then we'll be together. We'll have all the time this life keeps trying to take from us."

"August!" Frankie shouted.

"What?" August turned around and spotted the mirror Frankie was looking into.

In it, both of them were bound inside a conference room, held in place by a green mist that traced back to a transparent woman.

"Melinda and Helena," August muttered, memory flowing back into them.

As they said it, Helena, who looked strikingly similar to her mother, laid eyes on the mirror.

August stepped back at the same moment that Helena flung her arm forward. The mirror shattered, along with every window inside Mandrake Manor.

August covered their head as shards of glass flew by. When it settled, they looked back at Melinda and Harriett, who continued to play out the memory like nothing had happened.

Harriett shook her head, frowning at Melinda from something August didn't hear. "No, I don't want that. I don't want any more blood on my hands."

Melinda shook her head and looked down at the book, the words slowly filling out as August stared at the page. "If I don't teach them, and the coven doesn't come to power, then Helena will claim the power without bloodshed."

Harriett gave Melinda a slight smile. "I left the locket here. The one we enchanted years ago. If you find it, please give it to her?"

"Of course," Melinda said.

"Wait," Frankie said, leaning in next to August. "I know that spell."

August scanned the page, muttering the name, "La Fusion Occulte. The Occult Call. 'Drain from the mystical, the wonder and power. Let it flow into me, hour by hour.' If Helena keeps at this, there will be nothing left of Henbane Hollow."

"We have to stop her," Frankie said.

August looked out the window and grinned. Beyond the bushes, the walkway seemed to end in a gray mist. They grabbed Frankie's hand and pulled them along. "I think I found the edge."

31

Moonflower unfurls in night's soothing dance,
A nocturnal waltz, a captivating trance.
Yet beneath the charm, a threat sways,
Toxicity lurking in shadows, caution it portrays.

Step with care, for it toys with the mind,
Ingestion gives way to illusions unkind.
Yet in spiritual lore, its purpose resonates,
Intuition blooms, psychic harmony it facilitates.

Ancients, with their wisdom in gaze,
Used it to transform latex in yesteryears' maze.
In rubber's tale, an old chapter we borrow,
Moonflower's role, a fact that astounds us tomorrow.

Moonflower

- MAT -

Mat and Demetri stepped out of the woods and onto a well-manicured open field. The sun had nestled into the tops of the tan suburban houses across the park. Something recoiled in Mat as he stared at the picture-perfect sunset and the cookie-cutter homes that lined his view.

"We're not too late, are we?" Mat asked.

"Watch out!" a kid shouted as a soccer ball flew right at Mat's face.

Demetri grabbed Mat's shoulders and pulled him back from an impending hexagonal facial imprint.

A whistle sounded, and a rather muscular man in a tight referee outfit came running toward them, waving a red card and shouting, "Get off the field!"

Demetri locked arms with Mat and pulled him along. "Come on, before Testosterone Ted knocks us out."

They hurried across the field, away from the referee and toward the street, as parents all stood and booed them.

"They're acting like we ruined the game," Mat mumbled.

"I mean, take all the magic from a place and all you're left with are suburban Karens and rage-filled, barbecue-tong-wielding Chads."

Mat laughed and looked at the angry crowd. "How long have you been sitting on that one?"

"Since Mrs. Vervain over there in the sundress gave me the stink eye. You know she's normally in denim overalls covered head to toe in dirt?"

They stepped onto the concrete path leading out to the parking lot when Mat paused. Nausea hit him like a wave, and he gripped Demetri's arms as his eyes focused on the community center. "Did you feel that?"

"What?" Demetri asked.

"It felt like the world was turning upside down for a second. It was like—"

Glass exploded out from the community center, and Demetri flung his arms around Mat, shielding him from the debris.

"What the hell?" Demetri exclaimed, shaking his jacket and causing bits of glass to fall to the ground.

Mat looked past him, spotting a pale woman with long black hair standing inside a dimly lit room. "Oh shit, it's Helena," he hissed, pulling Demetri to hide behind the bushes alongside the building.

They both peeked their heads over the bushes, peering into the room.

Beside Helena, Mat could see an older woman, slightly transparent and with a faint green glow. Two tendrils trailed off one of her hands, suspending two people further in the room.

A rhythmic thump sounded behind them, getting louder and louder. Mat turned as a towering Remmy sprinted toward them, his eyes wide and his long gray hair trailing in the wind. He slid in behind them, his massive chest hyperventilating. "Frankie," he spoke between breaths. "In there."

"August too," Mat said. "I think. And maybe Ragana."

"We need to get in there," Demetri said.

Remmy frowned and pushed himself up, but Mat put a hand on his shoulder. "Hold on. We don't have a plan."

"There isn't time," Remmy said.

"If we go in, guns blazing, we could end up like August and Frankie," Mat said.

Remmy knelt back down, frowning. Demetri's eyes perked up. "You and I should go after Melinda. She's dead, and Remmy wouldn't stand a chance. Remember what you did to send Damien underground?"

"Margaret did that," Mat said.

"But do you remember it?"

Mat shut his eyes, dredging up the memory of his arm waving in the air, drawing a symbol. "Maybe?"

Demetri nodded. "That's as good as we're going to get. Remmy, take down Helena. Think you can do that?"

Remmy nodded.

"Okay," Mat said, swallowing hard. "We can do this. Count of three. One. Two."

Remmy bolted, racing and leaning through the broken window before Mat or Demetri could react. He tackled her before she even had a chance to brace herself, and she landed, hard, on the ground.

Mat and Demetri raced in behind him, haphazardly leaping and climbing through the window.

"Get off me, you brute!" Helena strained to say as Mat landed inside the conference room. She pulled one arm loose, reaching for the book. Before Mat could help, he felt the hairs stand on the back of his neck.

"You're too late," Melinda hissed.

Pain cracked through Mat as a bolt of green lightning sparked through the air and struck him, bringing him to his knees.

"No!" Demetri shouted, lunging at Melinda. He threw up his hands as Melinda pointed one hand at him, her other still holding on to the tendrils that led to Frankie and August.

She ejected another bolt of lightning out of her fingertips. Instead of striking Mat, the electricity crackled against an invisible barrier.

Melinda snarled as she lashed out at the invisible wall guarding Demetri. He stumbled back after each blow until he collapsed to the ground.

"I didn't think you'd be so pathetic," Melinda hissed, crackling energy surging down her arms.

"Mat, the spell," Demetri muttered.

Mat took the hint and frantically drew symbols in the air, biting his lip as he tried to remember.

Melinda focused on him, hatred blazing in her eyes as she recognized the symbols he drew.

She struck at Demetri's barrier again, shouting, "You can't stop me from bringing Harriett back!"

Mat frowned. "Who the hell is Harriett?"

"She was my everything," Melinda cried. "You can't stop me from bringing her back!"

Demetri lunged forward, but he was too late. A flash of green lit up the room, colliding right into Demetri's shoulder and flinging him like a ragdoll.

"No!" Mat cried out, the markings in the air in front of him wavering and flickering. With every ounce of restraint in his body, he stared forward at Melinda, knowing this was his only chance to stop her.

"You're just as bad as the others. All you want to do is take her from me," Melinda spat. She reared up, her hand sparks cracking at her fingertips.

He flicked his hand left and right, finishing the final markings in the air.

Melinda reared her arm up, readying another strike. Mat held up his hand, palm outstretched toward Melinda, and said, "I banish you!"

The sigils flared brightly, emanating a pulse of golden light that collided into Melinda.

"No!" Melinda screamed, letting go of her hold on August and Frankie and holding up her hands, bracing herself against the magic Mat had released.

The green mist around August and Frankie vanished, and they fell to the ground with a loud thud. Mat looked back and saw both of their eyes open and close, which was enough to tell him they were alive.

Golden magic twisted and swirled around Melinda, encasing her in an orb of light as she tried batting it away. She pushed against it with her own magic, sparks of green light raining down on her. "I won't go back. You can't make me!" she screamed.

A groan beside him made Mat look over at Demetri, who sat up, wincing at his side. "Keep focusing," he said. "You almost have her."

Mat shot a look at his friends, noting August crawling over to the woman slumped against the wall. "Ragana! Can you hear me?" they shouted.

Frankie was up on his elbows before Mat turned back to Melinda and held up his hands.

He felt a pressure push against them, sharp and chaotic, trying to break free.

"Your coven is weak," Melinda said. "You can't keep me down there forever. Helena will get her rightful place in the coven, and Harriett will come back to me."

Frankie shouted from behind Mat, "You can't hurt everyone just to get Harriett back. You're both already dead. Just go to her."

"It doesn't," Melinda strained, "work that way. Harriett is far on the path, too far for me to find."

She pushed against the barrier, and Mat slid back on the carpeted floor.

August chimed in, "So you'd take all the magic from everyone so you could be with her?"

"You," Melinda started, her arms shaking against the condensing sphere of light, "wouldn't understand." Her arms fell, and the light enveloped her. In a flash of golden light, Melinda vanished.

Mat fell forward as the pressure vanished. He looked down at his hands. "We did it," he whispered.

"For now," Frankie said. "You heard her, right? She'll be back."

Mat looked back at August, his eyes falling on Ragana, who winced as she felt at the back of her head.

"I'll be okay," she said to August.

"Uh, a little help over here!" Remmy grunted.

Mat looked over at Remmy right as Helena wrenched her arm free and grabbed hold of the book, shouting, "*Avec chaque battement, avec chaque soupir, que l'enchantement cède, la magie m'acquiert.*"

White light flashed off Helena, and Remmy flew off her, ramming and sticking onto the wall behind them.

Helena pushed herself up, the book floating in front of her, as she continued the spell, chanting, "*Dans la danse des éléments, que cela soit fait.*"

The room vibrated, and the scent of burned metal filled Mat's nostrils.

"Uh, oh," Frankie said.

32

Rowan, sentinel of Northern climes,
Warding evil, ancient times.
Red berries rich in healing lore,
For fever's chill and cold's implore.

An ash of mountains, standing tall,
In gardens, parks, delighting all.
Its wood for carving, handle's might,
And tannin source for dye's delight.

In mythology, a guide divine,
To psychic realms, a sacred sign.
From jelly bitter, to spirits bold,
Rowan's tale in berries is told.

Rowan

- FRANKIE -

"Oh, we're fucked," Frankie said as energy emanated from Helena.

August shuffled over to Frankie, pushing themself up to their feet, stepping between Helena and Ragana.

Frankie turned and saw Demetri shakily walk over to Mat.

Frankie couldn't get to Remmy, who was clear across the room, trapped against the wall. He tried taking a step forward, but the sheer pressure from Helena forced him to slide back.

Mat raced past Frankie, arms outstretched, pushing against the barrier, but before he could reach Helena, she waved an arm and flung him back, ramming him right into the wall to Frankie's side.

"Are you alright?" Frankie asked.

"No," Mat wheezed. "We can't let her finish the spell."

"*Le pouvoir de tous, en un seul maintenant,*" Helena shouted.

Frankie felt like the strength was sapping out of him, draining from the top of his head. His eyes fluttered and fell on the silver locket around Helena's neck.

"Her locket!" he shouted, remembering what Harriett had said in the memory he and August were in. "It's protecting her. We can't do anything."

Mat frowned. "That was you!" he shouted, clutching at his side. "In the attic."

Helena looked up from the book and held a hand to her locket, her eyes glowing a faint shade of green. "That old witch couldn't get up there for decades, not after the house knew what she wanted. You know, I almost gave up. Then you three showed up." She held up a hand, and Mat flew up into the air, colliding with the wall and sticking to it. Helena breathed in, and Mat's head lolled to the side. "It's almost all mine."

August shouted, their voice reverberating with a power that tickled at Frankie's ears. "By the whisper of winds and the darkest night, with the force of the moon's ethereal light."

Frankie blinked as the sensation of energy sapping from inside him halted. A crash sounded at his side as Mat fell free from the wall.

"No!" Helena shouted, locking eyes with August as she gripped the book.

Frankie raced over to Mat, pulling him up and away from Helena.

"I summon thee, La Fusion Occulte," August continued, their voice shaking.

The book twitched in Helena's arms, but she held firm. She grinned and looked down at the pages. "*Que ces mots résonnent, s'entremêlent, s'unissent.*"

Frankie grabbed Mat's hand and pulled him. "They can't do it by themself. We have to say the spell . . . together."

They joined August, Frankie gripping August's hand. Warmth spread into Frankie's hand, and a buzz of energy vibrated in his chest. "By the whisper of winds and the darkest night," their voices spoke as one, and the buzz in Frankie's chest grew, spreading to his back and his head. "With the force of the moon's ethereal light. I summon thee, I summon thee, La Fusion Occulte, to merge the magic, in unity, so b right."

The book lurched, hard, in Helena's hands. "No!" she shouted. She shut the book, wrapping an arm around it while her other arm waved in the air, trailing a silver light. As she did, glass shards and debris floated up into the air, their sharp edges pointing at the three of them.

Frankie squeezed his friend's hands, envisioning a barrier around them.

He felt the shards slam into his mind, one by one, stinging and trying to force their way in. Sweat formed on his brow, and he staggered back.

"You can't stop them all." Helena laughed.

Remmy strained against the magic holding him against the wall, peeling his back free. "You're fucking crazy."

Helena flicked her wrist, and Remmy slammed back against the wall as if pulled by a magnet.

She was right, Frankie couldn't stop them all. Soon one shard would get through, and then—

First August squeezed Frankie's hand, then Mat. They were invitations to help, to lend their power.

"Together," Frankie muttered.

He let them in, and instantly the barrier solidified around them, and the shards and debris that Helena lunged at them were faint annoyances.

August cleared their throat. "The spell, keep going," they whispered.

Frankie focused on what was written in the book, the words he'd read in the memory with Harriett and Melinda. "Drain from the mystical, the wonder and power. Let it flow into us, hour by hour."

The shards of glass crashed to the ground, and Helena stared at her hand. The book lurched in her grip again, trying to peel away from her. She clutched it with both hands, holding it close to her chest. "No. It's mine! I deserve it!"

Frankie continued the spell, August and Mat's voices echoing behind him, "In the dance of the elements, let it be done. The power of all now merged into one. As we speak these words, let them entwine. La Fusion Occulte, the arcane is mine."

Power flowed into Frankie, Mat, and August, bringing in unseen winds and swirling around them. The hum in Frankie's mind grew louder and louder, and his nerves burned like they were on fire.

Mat and August held out their free hands, and the book yanked free from Helena, flying across the room and stopping in midair in front of the Mandrake coven.

Finally, Remmy dropped from the wall, landing on his hands and knees.

Helena slumped, the power draining from her. "No. No! You'll pay for this. I'm still in the HOA. I'm still—"

"You think they'd keep you after this?" Demetri shouted.

She glared at him and clenched her hands. "If you all thought it was bad before, then you just wait until—"

"Until what? It's over. You lost. Henbane Hollow will kick you out," Remmy groaned.

"No," Helena said. "They can't. I have to stay. I won't."

Pages flipped in the book, stopping on a page about familiars. They were bonded to a coven, through and through. Creatures who helped the coven and the community. Frankie got the hint and felt the magic rise in his throat. "Helena," he spoke, his words rippling energy in the air. "Turn into your other form."

Helena's eyes widened. "No, wait. I can fix this. I can." She contorted, her body morphing before them. Dark fur sprouted from every pore, her fingernails darkened and turned into claws, and she shrank in size. Her face shifted, elongating into a snout, while her eyes became round and glassy. In mere seconds, she was a small, trembling raccoon standing where Helena had moments before.

Helena the raccoon sniffed the air, her tail twitching as she looked left and right. She bared her fangs at Mat and let out a low growl.

"Should we do this?" August asked.

"She'll have a choice," Frankie said, scanning the page. "This or leave Henbane Hollow forever."

Before Helena had a chance to escape, Mat started, "By threads of fate . . ." The words left his mouth, and energy hummed in the air. Helena immediately stopped baring her fangs and stared, dazed, at Mat.

Frankie leaned in, joining Mat and August as they read from the book. "We form these ties, a spirit untamed, willing to advise. In fur or feather, scales or skin. Bound to our coven, shared magic within. A companion true, let the journey begin."

Raccoon Helena's eyes glazed over for a moment, the words washing over her. She cocked her head to the side, considering for a moment.

"Shared magic within," Mat repeated. "You'll have magic. Our magic. It's not exactly what you wanted, but it's something."

Helena squinted at Mat then looked at the windows.

The pages flipped again, and Frankie chimed in. "You can go, but the book wants us to banish you from Henbane Hollow. Or stay with us, show us what magic you know, help us fix Henbane Hollow, and maybe the neighborhood won't grab their torches and pitchforks if they see your face again."

Helena looked to Ragana for a moment, dropping her head. Green magic swirled around her, lifting her hair on end before settling on her and vanishing beneath her fur. Her coat changed, appearing lighter and shinier.

"So, that's it then?" August asked. "Helena is—"

"Hel," Helena's voice spoke in Frankie's head. "It's Hel now."

"So, uh. Did you just turn Helena into your familiar?" Demetri asked.

"We did. And it's Hel now," August said, walking up to her and picking Hel up.

Mat grabbed the book out of the air and closed it, tucking it under his arm. He looked over at Hel, who appeared to be in heaven as August scratched her head. "Every coven needs a familiar, right?"

"But Helena? I mean, Hel?" Demetri asked, limping toward Mat.

Mat shrugged. "She accepted it. Better than her being banished or us battling constantly. She's a Mandrake now."

"Hel was the nickname her mom gave her," Ragana said, sitting up from the wall and wincing.

August joined Ragana, and Hel hopped down and onto Ragana's lap, her little paws feeling at Ragana's head. Little sparks of light floated around Ragana's head, and she sighed, resting a hand on Hel. "Thanks, cousin."

Remmy jumped over the table, clutching at his side before wrapping a massive arm around Frankie and planting a kiss on his lips. "You did it!"

"I can't," Frankie said, straining for breath. "I can't breathe."

"What now?" Demetri asked, walking over to Mat's side.

Hel carefully looked at Mat, hopping off Ragana's lap and crawling toward him. She pointed at the book, then out the window.

"We give it back," Frankie said. "We give the magic back to Henbane Hollow and let people live the way they're meant to."

33

Honeysuckle, sweet perfume's delight,
Anti-inflammatory might fights the fight.
Treating infections, esophageal and skin,
A medicinal aid, healing from within.

Yet beware, not all sweetness is kind,
In excess, to the stomach unkind.
Balanced use, a lesson to borrow,
Too much honey leads to sorrow.

Symbol of love in folklore's weave,
Bonds of devotion, affections achieve.
A testament to enduring ties,
In honeysuckle's scent, love never dies.

Honeysuckle

- AUGUST -

August helped Ragana up to her feet, pulling her close and feeling her body pressing up against them as she found her balance. A wave of energy surged into August, and Ragana stiffened.

"Everything alright?" August asked, opening and closing their jaw as their ears popped.

Ragana blinked a few times and pulled herself away from August, picking out the debris in her dress. Her voice was flat and distant. "Good grief, this place is a mess."

August frowned. "Uh, Ragana?"

"Step away from her," Hel's voice echoed in August's head.

Hel crawled up onto a chair and cocked her raccoon head to the side.

"What? Why?" August asked, backing away from Ragana.

"Your spell is still absorbing magic," Hel said.

"Where do I even start?" Ragana muttered, resetting fallen chairs and dusting them off.

"Ragana?" August asked, stepping closer.

"Uh, Remmy? Is that a suit?" Frankie asked.

August turned and found Remmy, dressed in a loose navy suit and red tie. His hair had changed too, a short cut and a hefty mustache.

Remmy blinked a few times, then his eyes widened. "I haven't been to the office in days. Those animals aren't going to heal themselves." He pushed past Frankie and slipped out of the room without another word.

"Uh, okay?" Frankie started. "One, I'm not mad about the stache. Two, what the fuck is going on?"

August looked over at Demetri, who was also blinking before backing away from Mat.

"It's us," August said. "We're draining all the magic."

"How do we fix it?" Mat asked.

"A reversal spell," Hel said while nonchalantly licking her paws.

Demetri straightened his suit and looked at his phone. "I'm so behind on work. Looks like it's going to be an all-nighter." Despite Mat's attempts to keep him still, Demetri pulled away, muttering under his breath as he left.

Frankie backed up. "I am not feeling this Stepford & Sons moment we are having. Raccoon-cat, how do we undo this?"

Hel looked at Frankie, bared her teeth, and went back to licking her paws.

"I'm guessing step one is to not insult the familiar," August said.

"Help me with this," Mat said, gripping onto the edge of the overturned conference room table.

August and Frankie helped set it upright, then Mat set down the Mandrake Manor spellbook, flipping through the pages.

"Something has to be in here," Mat said.

The hum of magic emanated from the book, a vibration August felt resonating in their chest. It was too much. Too uncomfortable.

Hel hopped up on the table. "You won't find anything," she said. "La Fusion Occulte was Melinda's spell. She wrote it before she died. And she didn't write an undoing."

"Cool, cool, so we just have all this magic and no way of giving it back?" Frankie asked.

"No," Hel said, her little eyes rolling. "You three are witches. You can make your own spells."

"Uh, how?" Mat asked.

Hel used her little paws to flip through the pages until she stopped on the spell Melinda made. She looked up, a glint in her eye. "And you don't want to keep it? You're the most powerful things in the world right now."

"Every bit that isn't ours deserves to go back," August said.

Mat and Frankie nodded.

"Fine," Hel said. "La Fusion Occulte is a verbal spell. Melinda wasn't a fan of herbs. A counterspell should be easy, with the right words."

August looked over the spell and paused. "Wait, this is in French. Where is the spell we did?"

"This is the spell," Hel said. "I thought you two just knew French and didn't want to bother with pronunciation."

"This is the page I saw," Frankie started. "But in the memory, it was translated."

"We were in her head," August said. "Maybe that did it?"

"I mean, that's great and all, but how does that help us now?" Mat asked.

"Melinda was a stickler for language," Hel said. "But you three proved that doesn't matter. It's all about intent. If you rearrange what you said in the spell, then you can make the counterspell."

August looked up at the ceiling. "So instead of 'I summon thee, I summon thee, La Fusion Occulte, to merge the magic, in unity, so bright.,' we could say something like, 'I call on thee, La Diffusion Occulte, to spread the magic, to heal, revamp, and exult?'"

As the words left their mouth, the book shuddered, and the pages rippled. Ink bubbled up and glided across the paper, drawing out filigree and words onto the other page. The title, La Diffusion Occulte, sat boldly on top.

Hel backed away from the book. "Interesting. Melinda had to write that spell down three times before the book was willing to commit a page to it."

August hovered over the page, a fully written spell appearing exactly how they had envisioned it. "We shouldn't wait any longer."

Mat and Frankie nodded.

August concentrated on the spell, the words twisting and joining with Mat and Frankie's, "By the whisper of winds and the moonlit sky. With the force of stars that grace our eyes. I call on thee, La Diffusion Occulte, to spread the magic, to heal, revamp, and exult."

Energy shuddered through August as if water was pouring out of them.

As that happened, everything in the conference room shuddered. The tiled laminate flooring melted away, replaced by old wooden flooring. The entire room shifted in shape, from an expected box into a fairytale-esque room with exposed ceiling beams and light clay walls.

Ragana's prim and proper hair bellowed down into loose curls, and the dress she had on that made her look like some suburban housewife transformed back into her usually tight jeans and owl themed T-shirt.

Frankie groaned. "Does that mean Remmy lost the stache?"

"Shut up and keep reading," August said.

The three of them continued the spell, reciting every line about restoring balance. By the time they were done, even the air smelled different, sweeter and inviting compared to the staleness the room had been before.

"Did we do it?" Mat asked.

"Only one way to find out," Frankie said, spinning on his heels and heading toward the door.

Mat picked up the book, and he and August followed behind Frankie.

They headed out of the center together, passing through a winding wooden hallway filled with ceramic garden gnomes. Small vines grew out of the floorboards, twisting and winding around.

"That's a promising sign," August said.

They stood side by side with Frankie and Mat, watching as homes slowly groaned and shifted back into whimsical treehouses, wells, caves, or old abandoned buildings. Nearly everywhere, the grass transformed from short and cropped to overgrown, bursting with flowers and trees.

Even the road changed beneath them, turning into a well-kept cobblestone road, better suited for an entire neighborhood filled with magical beings.

"Follow the . . . uh, red brick road?" Mat asked.

August grabbed Frankie's and Mat's hands. "We're off to be the wizards!"

"You two are ridiculous." Frankie laughed as the three of them childishly skipped down the street.

Life started to feel normal again for August. As normal as a magical neighborhood could be, which August found to be particularly calming compared to the other situations they'd been in.

Days passed, and all that August had on their mind was Ragana. Finally, they convinced Mat to drive them out to the city, and they walked back into the Owlet Cafe.

Warm, buttery pastries filled with maple, honey, and strawberries filled their nose and made August's stomach grumble.

They approached the counter, hearing an absurd amount of banging pans clattering in the back.

"Everything okay back there?" August asked.

Ragana peaked her head out, face covered in flour and blue sparks jolting through her hair. "Everything is . . . fine," Ragana struggled to say. "Just give me a minute."

Then, without warning, tiny little pastries in the shape of owls came flying out from the kitchen.

"No, get back here!" Ragana shouted, swatting at them with one of her baking sheets.

August ducked as the flock of owls soared overhead, a blot of chocolate dropping on August's shoulder. "What the hell?"

"I thought it would be cute to enchant the pastries," Ragana said. "I didn't expect the Chocolate Owl Buns would turn into little assholes."

The owls found refuge in the rafters above, each letting out tiny little hoots as they glared down at Ragana.

"I can't imagine the pastries are too happy to be alive." August grinned.

Sparks flung from Ragana's fingers. "They weren't supposed to come alive. It was a minor animation enchantment that should have only made them perch and ruffle feathers until someone bought them. My magic has been in overdrive since it came back."

"And it wasn't like that before?" August asked, dodging an owl that swooped down on them.

"No," Ragana said, bashing the owl with the baking sheet. "I couldn't do stuff like this before."

Another owl dive-bombed August before they had time to react, bursting into a chocolate pastry filled mess on August's shirt. "Need me to help?" August asked.

"Please," Ragana said, holding out her hand.

August grabbed it, sparks of blue energy tickling their skin. Words came to August's throat, spilling out and carrying magic on their tongue. "*Cease all magic in this place, return the balance of this space.*"

A pulse emanated from August's chest, and instantly little Owl Buns fell from the ceiling.

Ragana let out a sigh. "Oh, my god, thank you. Whatever you want, on the house."

August grabbed the wastebin and started collecting the remains of her little Owl Buns.

"No, wait," Ragana said, joining them. "You don't have to. You already helped. I've got this."

August shook their head. "I bet the kitchen is in worse shape. Let me do this. You go in there, and then we can both have a cup of coffee? Deal?"

Ragana stood and smiled. "Fine, deal."

Twenty minutes later, Ragana set down two Caramel Tawny Owlattes on the table, with little owl foam art on top. "Thank you, seriously," she said.

August looked down at their latte. "There's something I've been meaning to ask."

"Yes?" Ragana said.

"I . . . Well, I like you. And I think you like me," August started, looking up at Ragana.

Ragana smiled. "I do."

August's cheeks grew hot. "Would you . . . Would you want to go on a date? With me?"

"I thought you'd never ask," Ragana said, sipping her latte.

August's shoulders relaxed, and they took a swig of their latte, which was a perfect combination of rich caramel and espresso, mixed with pistachio milk. "Awesome. I was thinking about this Saturday night? Picnic in the enchanted gardens?"

"If those little garden gnomes behave," Ragana said.

August shrugged. "If they don't, then we can make a game of it. We could send some Owl Buns after them."

Ragana laughed, resting her hand on August's, her thumb tickling the top of August's hand.

34

Licorice, Glycyrrhiza's sweetened breath,
A balm for ulcers, bronchitis, and even death.
Anise echoes in flavor's song,
In balance, a remedy for the throng.

Yet caution lingers in every bite,
Excessive savor breeds sorry plight.
Heartbeat falters, strength may wane,
In every cure lies potential pain.

A thread of history spun in gold,
In Tut's tomb, its tale is told.
Harmonizer of ancient brew,
In licorice, both peril and virtue.

Licorice

-MAT-

Mat closed his eyes and sipped his coffee, noting the addition of sweet spices that reminded him of the holidays. As those flavors faded, an earthy note took over, followed by a different sweetness lingering on his tongue.

"Is that," Mat sipped again, "licorice?" He blinked and stared at the white island in the middle of the kitchen, covered with bowls of various herbs and the Mandrake spellbook. He wasn't exactly sure what any of the herbs were, but luckily Frankie offered to start quizzing him.

Frankie clapped his hands. "Bravo!" He looked over at their raccoon familiar, Hel, who was inching closer to the pastry box on the counter. "See? Turns out you can teach an old dog new tricks."

Mat ignored that, taking another sip. "And it starts with cinnamon and . . . uh, I don't know."

"Cardamom," Frankie said, dumping some seed pods into a jar and twisting it closed. "Those help with mood and sugar regulation. Then I added in some ginseng for a smoother energy boost and licorice for endurance. Mixed with the coffee, you should have the best morning pick-me-up outside of cocaine."

"Thanks for not putting cocaine in my coffee."

Frankie picked up a jar filled with white powder and turned it over. "Unless . . ."

Mat grabbed a jar off the table, turning it over and staring at the thin needles within. "I thought all this witchy stuff was just for burning or something." He sipped from his mug. "But we just have a wall of herbs for cooking and tea?"

Frankie nodded. "Spells, incense, teas, and culinary. I mean, half of the herbs will kill you, so maybe leave the tea and cooking to me for n ow."

Dude, their Australian Shepherd, let out a whine and tapped his toes on the tiled floor. Mat looked over and saw he was watching Hel, whose hands were on the pastry box, slowly opening it. "Hey!" Mat shouted. "Those aren't yours!"

She bared her teeth at Mat and waddled over to Frankie, fiddling with one jar. "I just wanted to look at them. I wasn't going to eat any," she muttered.

Mat's phone buzzed in his pocket.

Demetri [9:30 a.m.]: Hey, you up?

Mat [9:31 a.m.]: Yeah, why?

Demetri [9:34 a.m.]: Swinging by. That alright?

"Are we talking to a secret lover?" Frankie asked, coming around the table with a handful of jars to peek at Mat's phone.

"No? It's Demetri. He's asking if he can stop by," Mat said, replying to the text. "Were you planning on keeping me for Herbology 101 all day, or?"

"All day? Do you think I would torture myself like that?" Frankie shook his head and started toward the library. "You tell Demetri I said hi. I'll be upstairs getting ready for my date."

"Date?" Mat asked, looking at the time. "I thought you were going out tonight?"

"I am. Which means a full day of bathing and face masks because I deserve a spa day."

Mat shook his head and sent off his text, laughing into his mug of coffee.

Moments later, he opened the front door to Demetri, dressed in a well-fitted black suit and holding a folded-up paper in his hand.

"Hey there, stranger," Mat said, leaning his shoulder against the doorframe.

Demetri smiled and ran his free hand over the top of his bald head. "So, when were you going to tell me?"

"Tell you what?"

Demetri unfolded the paper and held it up. On it was a picture of Mat, and the words *Mathias Mandrake for the HOA Council*.

Mat's shoulder slipped off the doorframe, and he nearly toppled over as he strained to regain his balance and keep his coffee from spilling. "Um, what the hell is that?"

Demetri frowned and looked at the paper. "You didn't know about this?"

"No," Mat said, grabbing the paper and looking it over. It was an illustration of him in a bold green suit, standing in a heroic pose in front of Mandrake Manor. At the bottom, it said, "Hero of Henbane Hollow."

"You must have an admirer then. You'd have my vote, Hero of Henbane Hollow."

"No. I don't want your vote," Mat said. "I don't want anyone's vote." Mat crumpled up the flyer and tossed it behind him. "It's not happening."

"Good luck with that. I think I saw about forty of them on my way in."

"Great. Exactly what I wanted to do on my day off. Run around and pull down flyers." Mat turned around and waved Demetri in. "Want some coffee?"

Demetri followed. "No, but . . ."

"But?" Mat asked, turning around. Then he saw it. The crumpled-up paper unfolded itself and drifted out toward the door.

"But that," Demetri said.

"Oh, no you don't, you little bastard!" Mat shouted, setting down his mug and chasing after the paper, failing as it slipped out the door and caught the wind, blowing away.

"I had a death grip on the thing just to get it here," Demetri said. "It wanted to go back to the wall it was taped on."

Mat stomped into the kitchen, refilling his coffee mug. "Great. Maybe we'll burn them to ash then. Either way, I don't want people thinking I'm running."

"Well . . ." Demetri started.

Mat froze mid-sip. "Well? Well, what?"

"That's not how the HOA works here. The neighborhood votes for the council member they want."

"Uh, okay? But Helena. You're telling me people voted for her?"

There was a chitter behind him and he turned. Hel looked back at him, face covered in cream and raspberry sauce as she held a small half-eaten croissant shaped like an owl with her little raccoon paws. Dude was already licking the floor, presumably where Hel had tossed a second croissant.

"No offense," Mat said. "But August is going to kill you."

"Not if you don't say anything," she said. She then held the croissant in her mouth and hopped off the counter, leaving behind raspberry pawprints that Dude went after.

Demetri cleared his throat and looked down at the ground. "I didn't come to talk about the flyers," he said, kicking at the floor.

"Oh?" Mat asked, sidling up to him. "Then what did you come for? Were you looking to borrow some sugar?"

"Ha. Ha," he said. "But no. It's my dad."

"Oh," Mat backed up. "I'm sorry. Is everything okay?"

Demetri rubbed the back of his head. "Yeah, it's fine, I guess. I got a call from Damian. He asked if I could help with the move. Who knew a ruler of the underground moving would become such a mess?"

"Do you need help?" Mat asked. "We can help. I mean, I'm sure August and Frankie would be willing."

Demetri shook his head. "No. If it was just packing up boxes, then it would be easy. This is going to take a while. Like a long while."

Mat frowned. From Demetri's stature, he could tell he was holding back. "How long?"

"That's why I came. Damian can't do it on his own, and some of the stuff has some legal ownership for the ruler of the underworld, which would mean that my dad would lose rights to it. They need someone who knows the law."

"How long are we talking?" Mat asked, setting down his mug.

Demetri shook his head. "I don't know. It's all the legal bits they are struggling with. Almost all the stuff my dad owns is contracted to his position, not him. Damian doesn't know what he's doing, and Dad's tied up with his transition of power. They need my help. I want to say no, but I agreed to them moving, and even with me, we might be talking months."

Mat looked down at the ground. "Months."

Demetri shifted his weight. "It's short notice, I know, but they need me now. I wasn't going to go without stopping by."

"Now? But we have a date this weekend. When are you leaving?" Mat asked.

"I'm already packed."

"Okay," Mat nodded, his thoughts racing. "Okay. We can do this."

Demetri shook his head. "I can't do that to you. I don't want to do that to you. That's why I came."

Mat's heart lurched in his chest. "So, are we? Are we ending things before they start?"

"No," Demetri said. "Postponing things, for now. Don't you owe Jacob a date?"

Mat's face flushed. "What? No. I. I don't—"

Demetri grabbed Mat's hand, squeezing. "You deserve to try it out. He's a good guy. Really. And I don't want you turning into some sappy romantic, waiting around for me to come back while looking out your window all sad."

Mat laughed. "I would, too. I'd find myself one of Melinda's old dresses and have a sitting window, waiting for my man to come back and sweep me off my feet."

Demetri leaned in and planted a kiss on Mat's lips. He wrapped a hand around Mat's waist, and Mat grabbed Demetri's hips.

Mat pulled Demetri in close, their lips brushing and dancing around each other as their bodies pressed and hands explored. Mat felt the billowing heat emanating off Demetri as he pulled him in close.

After what felt like both an eternity and mere seconds, Demetri pulled away. "And when I come back, maybe I'll have some competition."

Mat blinked and caught his breath. "Oh, you know me," he breathed. "I'll have a whole harem at that point."

Demetri cupped his hand on the side of Mat's face and stroked his thumb across Mat's lips. "Then I guess I'll just have to prove myself worthy."

Mat kept his eyes glued to Demetri as he headed out the door to Mandrake Manor, his heart heavy in his chest. As he turned, he spotted two sets of beady eyes staring back at him. One belonged to Dude and the other, Hel.

"Shut up. Both of you."

35

In the heart of poppy, sleep and peace reside,
Opium's cradle, where pain's relief lies.
Latex tears, morphine's gentle tide,
A solace sewn in nature's wise.

Yet in her embrace, danger awakens,
A too-deep slumber, life forsaken.
In every bloom, a pact is made,
Between the healer's hand and the blade.

Symbol of the fallen, red in war's fray,
Poppy stands, remembers the day.
In her petals, tales of sacrifice unwind,
Echoes of the lost, in our hearts enshrined

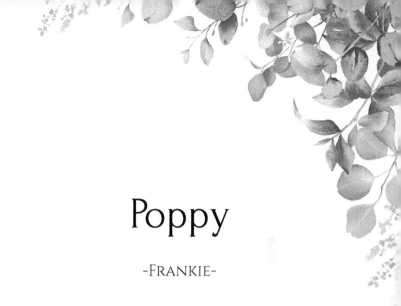

Poppy

-FRANKIE-

Frankie's fingers gripped Remmy's bare chest, his thumbs running along muscle and his fingers twirling around chest hair as light from the crackling fireplace flickered across naked flesh. Cushioned by the old rug in the living room, the two of them moved in rhythm, undulating hips as sweat glistened their skin.

"Why didn't we do this sooner?" Frankie asked between breaths as he collapsed onto Remmy's chest.

Remmy wrapped his arms around Frankie. "I don't know. Probably because Mat and August would have heard you," he teased.

"Good thing they're out," Frankie said.

Then, as if the world were playing some kind of joke on Frankie, the front door creaked open.

"Home, sweet—oh, my eyes!" Mat shouted, nearly dropping the box he held as he stared up at the ceiling. "For fuck's sake. On the rug?"

"What—" August started as they rounded the corner. Then they saw what Mat saw, and their face turned white as they spun around on their heels, back facing the living room.

Frankie untangled himself from Remmy and grabbed a discarded shirt. He tossed it at Remmy before finding another to cover himself while he kicked their clothes into a pile. "You were supposed to be gone for at least three hours," he retorted.

"And you have a bedroom. Unless you forgot," August said, peeking through their fingers as they pulled jars out from the box in Mat's arms.

"Where's the fun in that?" Frankie asked, pulling on a pair of briefs and winking at Remmy, who fumbled to pull on his jeans.

"So, uh, did you find it?" Remmy asked, his face red as he looked at the box.

"We did," Mat said, walking into the living room as Remmy pulled on his shirt. "Your directions took us straight to it. Super easy to find."

Frankie cleared a space on the table in the library as Mat put the box down and pulled the remaining jars out.

"Uh, I should probably go," Remmy said, clearing his throat.

"What?" Frankie asked, pulling a wide basin from the shelf and positioning it in the center of the table. "It's just a quick spell. Then we can . . . You know . . . Get back to exploring the differences between wolves and werewolves."

Remmy smirked. "No. I've got an early morning at the office. And, after what happened last time, I think I'm all good with magic."

Frankie grabbed Remmy and pulled him in for a kiss. His tongue danced across Remmy's lips while his chin brushed against his beard. "Fine," Frankie said, pulling away. "But our . . . exploration will continue."

Remmy blushed and nodded before awkwardly waving at Mat and August as he headed out the door.

Frankie picked up a jar, turning over the water inside. "Pond water, taken on a full moon." He unscrewed the top and poured it into the basin at the center of the table. "Ready, my little witches?"

Mat flipped open the spellbook, while Frankie and August unscrewed unmarked jars of herbs and dumped them into the basin. One jar was mandrake, the roots shaped exactly like a person, which Frankie thought was a little creepy as he submerged the thing underwater.

"At least it didn't scream," Frankie mumbled.

"You're telling me," August said, pulling out fresh-cut poppy flowers and placing them in the water. "Imagine stuffing that thing in a jar with only moonlight and a cellphone light."

Frankie filled the basin with herbs, roots, and flower petals, then placed white candles in a circle around the basin, according to the cardinal directions conveniently carved on the table.

"Okay," Mat said. "Last time I talked to her, Margaret said she needed at least fourteen days before she could come back. It's been over that, and we have a full moon on our side."

"And she's not going to try to kill us or anything, right? She's not like Melinda?" Frankie asked.

Mat shrugged. "I dunno, but she did help me."

"Well, if she tries anything, I'm sure Mat will banish her ass right back," August said.

Frankie feigned a gasp and clutched his chest. "August! I didn't know you had it in you." He smiled and elbowed August. "I think I'm rubbing off on you."

"Maybe," August said. "Maybe I'm just done being nice."

"Okay," Mat said, clearing his throat. "Ready?"

Frankie nodded and grabbed August's and Mat's hands, creating a circle around the basin.

Together, they recited,

"Guided by moonlight, embraced by the night,
We call upon the spirit lost from our sight.
Through water's mirror and mandrake's might,
We summon thee from death's endless flight.
From the farthest reaches, where shadows wane,
Cross the divide, break the chain.
Margaret Mandrake, we call your name,
Answer us now, in this sacred plane."

Their voices rose and fell, reverberating off the walls and echoing around them. The basin of water rippled, and a light green mist drifted up from within. As it grew, the flames of the candles flickered and turned green. Frankie drew in the icy air as the mist coalesced into an elderly woman standing in the center of the table.

"Uh, that's fucking cool," Frankie said.

"Language," the woman said, her lips pursed as she eyed Frankie. Even though she was translucent, the regality of her left him dumbstruck, and all he could do was admire her finely styled hair and well-cinched emerald green dress.

She shifted her gaze to Mat. "I see you're still alive." Her voice turned soft, yet still commanding. "Did you find Melinda?"

"About that," Frankie said.

Between the three of them, they filled her in on the events that had transpired weeks before and their banishing of Melinda. By the end, Margaret was staring at Hel, who sat on her back legs, eyes shifting down to the floor.

"I see," Margaret said. "That banishment won't last. Have you guarded the home against any unseemly guests?"

"No?" August said. "I mean, the house already turns away people, if that's what you mean."

"I do not," Margaret said. "The wards that once kept this home safe have dwindled from my day. It's a surprise it still keeps people at bay. You'll need something a little stronger to keep a ghost out."

"Will you show us?" Mat asked.

Margaret nodded. "Of course," she said as she looked down at Hel. "And will you behave like a proper familiar and alert them when you sense her return?"

Hel nodded and fiddled with her claws as she mumbled, "I will."

"I don't trust her," Margaret said to Mat. "But, as long as she acts like a familiar, then you'll be safe until we know what to do with Melinda."

"I mean, it was that or stop her some other way," August said.

"You could have killed her," Margaret shrugged, as if ending Hel's life was still an option. "I'm too deep in the fray to protect you." She looked down at her hand, which faded as she held it up. "Even now we have little time."

"Too bad you and Melinda couldn't trade places," Frankie said.

Margaret considered his words and smiled. "You'd mentioned a Henbane, yes? Harriett?"

"Melinda loved her," August said. "She wanted Helena to claim the coven so Harriett would come back and they could be together."

Margaret eyed Hel. "Did she ever try to contact Harriett after she died?"

Hel nodded. "She told me she tried a few times, but Marion, her guide, intervened. Said my mom needed time and Melinda needed to move on."

Margaret rolled her eyes. "Of course she did. Recently passed Mandrakes always think they know what's best."

"Uh, so," Frankie said. "Great information, but what can we do?"

"I can help," Margaret said.

"How?" August asked.

"I know how to find Harriett. As long as she didn't cross through the last veil. If Melinda wants to be together, then who are we to stand in her way?"

"Hel?" Frankie asked, turning to the little raccoon. "Would she take that deal?"

Hel held out her little paws and shrugged. "I don't know."

The mist that held Margaret's form shifted, and she faded. "I'm running out of time."

"Okay," Mat said. "You find Harriett. It's worth a shot."

"How do we protect the house from her in the meantime?" Frankie asked.

"Cast this spell over jewelry," Margaret said, but her voice was distant and echoed. She waved her hand, and pages in the spellbook flipped. "Anyone or anything with ill intent will fall into a daze long enough for you to run."

Frankie leaned over and looked at the spell, running through the components and nodding. "Perfect, we have all this."

"Summon me again at the next full moon," Margaret said, her form losing shape. "Until then, be safe."

The green mist dissipated, and with it, the green-flamed candles were snuffed out, leaving the three of them standing in the dark.

"Well," Frankie said, letting go of Mat's and August's hands. "That was fun."

36

In verdant fields where pink heads sway,
Red Clover casts her spell each day.
Protein-rich, a feast for deer,
Her gifts to Earth, to us, are clear.

Yet caution, for her charms can deceive,
In blood's thin dance, a web she'll weave.
With anticoagulants, a dangerous mix,
The peace of clover, the healer's fix.

In Celtic lore, a fairy's bed,
Where luck is lost under careless tread.
A plant of power, in blossom and root,
Her tales are silent, her wisdom, mute.

Red Clover

U nderneath an exceptionally bright moon, August straightened out the blanket onto a clover field overlooking a large pond on the outskirts of Henbane Hollow. Ragana popped the cork from a bottle of wine and poured it into glasses as August pulled out a small box of pastries.

"Looks like you got the enchantment right this time," August said as Owl Buns fluttered out from the box and hopped on the blanket.

Ragana handed over a glass of wine. "It only took five more attempts. I think I'll be mopping chocolate from the ceiling for months."

A garden gnome, complete with a shiny red cap, came running out from the bushes, stopping at the edge of the blanket to inspect the animated pastries. As the little owl flapped its wings, the gnome mimicked it.

"How long does it last?" August asked as the gnome coerced the owl off the blanket.

"Should only be five minutes after coming out of the box, give or take."

More gnomes appeared to inspect the little Owl Bun, surrounding it and poking at it. Then they descended on it, tearing it to pieces and shoveling bits of pastry into their chocolate covered mouths.

"Oh, my god!" August shouted, corralling the remaining pastries back toward them. "They went feral on that poor owl."

Ragana nearly doubled over laughing. "What did you expect?"

"I don't know, but definitely not that. You're just gonna let them kill that poor owl like that?"

Ragana righted herself. "The animation spell is meant to be like a puppet on strings. They mimic life, but they aren't actually alive. Trust me, that Owl Bun didn't feel a thing. Otherwise, I'd have some explaining to do to my customers."

"Good point," August said, giving the gnomes, who collected at the edge of the blanket, the side-eye. "Well, you little monsters still don't get any more."

The gnomes all lowered their heads, pouting, and backed away. One poked a clover, and it instantly burst into bloom, a little pink flower erupting from the leaves. The others caught on and started chasing each other around, trailing lines of pink flowers in the little field.

Ragana sighed and sipped on her wine. "This was a perfect choice."

"I know, right?" August said, staring at the pond. Long grass and orange and yellow flowers encompassed the shores of the pond, which reflected the beautiful orange and purple sky above them. Fireflies danced above the water, flickering green bursts of light like fireworks. "It's . . . magical."

"This is the Henbane Hollow I remember," Ragana said. She brushed her hands along the clovers, and shoots of poppies and lupine rippled out from her fingers.

The gnomes rushed over to the flowers, one now carrying around a mushroom like it was some kind of parasol as they inspected and attempted to climb the poppies.

August pulled out a plate filled with cheeses, fruits, and breads, a joint effort of Ragana's baking skills and August spending the better half of the afternoon scouring markets for the best of the best. Slowly, the owl pastries nestled down onto plates, and they stopped moving altogether. Every bite was amazing, from the aged and smoked gruyere to the largest grapes August had ever seen, the rosemary and pine nut sourdough, and the sweet and flakey chocolate-filled pastries.

As they savored the food, Ragana leaned into August, her dark eyes twinkling from the fireflies. "Ragana?" August asked.

"Yes?"

"This was fun, and I just . . . I want to make sure we're on the same page about us."

Ragana smiled and stared down at her glass of wine. "Of course. I do too."

August's gaze softened. "With you . . . I feel at ease."

"Me too," she said, leaning in and resting her shoulder on theirs.

August bit their lip. Ragana's face was close to theirs, and the question had been lingering on their mind for so long. "May I . . . can I kiss you?"

Ragana paused for a moment, then she smiled and leaned in. August met her halfway, their lips gently pressing together. There were several cheers that pulled August away. They spotted the gnomes, who'd stopped playing their games and stared at August and Ragana.

August laughed and turned back to Ragana, wrapping an arm around her shoulder and pulling her in. It was incredibly comfortable, and August could stay like this forever.

"I have something for you," Ragana said, reaching into her pocket and pulling out a small copper key. "It's the key to the cafe. In case the pastries decide to start a revolt again. And in case you ever want to come over."

August turned the key over and smiled. They knew this meant more than just a key to the cafe. "I could get used to this, you know? This . . . us. I like it."

"Me too."

They watched the sun slowly dip into the horizon as the garden gnomes started a game of keep away with one of the leftover Owl Buns. Everything was right in the world, and August felt a sense of peace they hadn't had in a long time, like they were finally home.

August leaned against the door of Mandrake Manor, a smile spread across their face. They found Mat and Frankie in the living room. Mat reclined on the couch with a book in hand while Frankie stared intensely at a candle in front of him, with Dude and Hel on either side.

Dude rushed over to August's side, their tail wagging so hard their hindquarters swayed.

"What are you doing?" August asked, scratching Dude's head.

Frankie blinked and sat up straight. "Trying to light this damn candle with my mind."

"I told him it won't work," Hel said, her paws resting on the Mandrake spellbook. "He's trying too hard."

"I almost had it," Frankie said.

"He's been at it for the past hour," Mat mumbled from the couch.

"If it's so easy," Frankie grumbled, "then why don't you do it?"

Mat put his book down and sat up on the couch. He focused in on the candles and let out a slow breath.

August watched as one candle started to smoke, then burst into flame.

"Show off," Frankie said, blowing the candle out.

"How was the date?" Mat asked, leaning back on the couch.

August smiled. "It was amazing."

"Did you make out?" Frankie asked.

Hel let out a growl and swatted at Frankie. "Who asks that?"

"We did," August said, heat rising from their neck.

"Damn," Mat said, his nose buried in his book. "Everyone is getting some but me."

"Well, you ever going to message Jacob?" Frankie asked. "Or are you going to keep pretending to read *Wuthering Heights* until Demetri comes back?"

Mat snapped his book shut. "Rude." He sat up and put his head in his hands. "It just feels weird."

August shrugged. "You should try it anyway. Didn't Demetri forbid you from moping around?"

"You too? I'm getting ganged up on," Mat said.

"Well, your friends aren't lying," Hel said.

"And now you?"

"Just text him," August said. "What's the worst that could happen? You go on a date and actually like it?"

"Then we could all have make-out buddies," Frankie said.

Mat rolled his eyes and grabbed his phone. "Fine. What do I say?"

August laughed and hopped onto the couch next to Mat. Frankie squeezed in on the other side.

Through giggles and suggestive emojis, the three of them comprised a message. August wasn't sure their night could get any better. First with Ragana, and now here, among their friends, in their house, giggling over a boy.

August slipped into unconsciousness in their bed, sinking deep into lands that were becoming more and more familiar. Darkness blossomed into color, and a castle made of smooth iridescent stone stood before them.

They had gotten better at dreaming, sending themself off to faraway lands, and building a place to revisit memories and dreams. August took a step, and the world blurred and melted away, replaced with a hall inside the castle. They stood at the base, a spiral of doors that led off to memories and reconstructions of Mandrake Manor and the Owl Cafe.

They walked along the halls, twiddling their fingers as they created little gnomes that clinked as their ceramic feet ran along the stone floor. Stopping at a space at the end of the hall, they faced the wall and a door materialized in the stone. This one was inlaid with little silver clovers and gnomes. They opened the door, watching as the gardens were reconstructed, the clovers a little bigger and the fireflies replaced with little orbs of colorful light that occasionally burst into fireworks.

August sat down on the blanket and looked up at the sunset sky, a perfect mix of orange and deep purple. The gnomes they had created were already skittering about, turning clovers into massive flowers and running into each other with loud clinks.

This would be their new sanctuary, a place they could find refuge in if they ever needed it. They nearly dozed off, lying there, listening to the gnomes swish in and out of the clover. August wondered what would happen if they fell asleep in a dream.

However, they didn't get to explore that thought any further as an icy wind rippled across their skin. They sat up, frowning. They hadn't summoned the wind, and in a place like this, they should have control of everything.

The top of the pond rippled again before another burst of cold air washed over August. Clovers wilted, and flower petals fell to the ground, decayed. The gnomes ran behind August, cowering behind them.

"What the hell?" August said, sitting up. They waved their hand, demanding things turn back, but nothing happened.

"Not hell," a voice whispered. It sounded raspy, carried on rustling leaves. Shadows melded together and rose in front of August. A porcelain white face, more like a mask than an actual face, stared at August from within a long tattered black robe. As it spoke, neither lips nor eyes moved. "You tread on my lands."

"Who are you?" August asked, pushing themself up to their feet.

The masked being cocked its head. "I am the whisper, the weaver of fantasies, the echo of subconscious, the enigma cloaked in the veil of night. I am the labyrinth of illusion."

August shut their eyes, willing themself to be anywhere else but here. Normally, this would take them wherever they wanted, no matter the distance. However, as they opened their eyes, they were still in the decayed gardens, staring at the creature.

A long bony hand with yellowed nails protruded from the robes. "You have no power here, witch. Not when I command these lands."

"What do you want?"

"Everything," the creature said. Another boney hand materialized, then another, and another, all reaching for August.

August fell back, and the creature rushed over to them, ready to descend, their many hands reaching.

Then the creature shouted, looking down as the little gnomes rammed into it, pointy hats aimed at its legs.

With all their might, August willed themself away.

August gasped, sitting up in bed, their heart racing and cold sweat on their brow. They shifted in their bed, feeling something strange and gritty on their legs. They flipped on the light and pulled back the covers, revealing a bed covered in sand.

Before You Go

Thank you so much for reading Mandrake Manor! There's more to this world I would love to explore, so stay tuned.

Here's the deal, I'm an independent author, and reviews are the best way to help spread the word and reach new readers.

If you could spare a few seconds, would you please consider leaving an honest review on the platform you purchased this ebook from, Goodreads, Storygraph, or other pages?

Your support helps keep the lights on at Mandrake Manor, and those poor witches need all the help they can.

So mote it be,
JP Rindfleisch IX

Acknowledgements

In the glow of a crescent moon, where stars whisper secrets and dried herbs fill the air, Mandrake Manor shone bright in the tarot. It's said that magic happens at the crossroads, and I believe this book beginnings are true to that.

Lucian Kuranz, you brought depth and vibrancy to the world of Mandrake Manor. The phenomenal cover you see on this copy of Mandrake Manor is thanks to you. You captured Mat, August, and Frankie so perfectly from my notes on hecate, botanicals, and whimsy.

My sister, Christine Halverson, thank you for helping me illustrate the botanical beginnings of each chapter. You helped me bring my vision to life and add something more magical to this tale.

A heartfelt thank you to my Patreon supporters, now transitioned to my website, who were with me from the very start. Your encouragement was the nudge that kept this story moving forward.

Christine Daigle, my dedicated beta reader, your desire for more and your invaluable feedback truly refined this tale.

Rebecca Pawlowski and Lori Drake, you meticulously went through every word, ensuring clarity and precision. Your dedication made every sentence shine.

Lastly, to J Thorn and the mastermind that summoned Mandrake Manor into being: your support and guidance were invaluable. The sense of community and shared purpose you fostered played a pivotal role in bringing this story to life.

To everyone who contributed to this journey, whether in small or grand, I extend my heartfelt gratitude. Here's to the magic of story-telling. Remember, there's a little witch in all of us, and every story is a spell waiting to be cast.

In gratitude and greenery,
JP Rindfleisch IX

About the Author

JP Rindfleisch is the curator of things dark, strange, and queer. They are the co-author to the Paranormal Humor series NRDS: National Recently Deceased Services and the co-author to the Dark Urban Fantasy project called the Leah Ackerman series. They also have another cozy queer serial project called Mosswood Apothecary. To follow JP's work and find their other books, go to www.jprindfleischix.com.